A PRAYER OF VENGEANCE

A PRAYER OF VENGEANCE

by
John Stafford

CARBON 10

PUBLISHING™

A Prayer of Vengeance
A Call of Vengeance Series – Book 1

www.prayerofvengeance.com
www.callofvengeance.com

Published by Carbon 10 Books
Call of Vengeance Series
2555 Miamisburg-Centerville Rd.
Dayton, OH 45459

Author contact: john@callofvengeance.com

EDITIONS
Paperback ISBN: 978-1-9451591-1-4
E-Book ISBN: 978-1-9451591-3-8

Library of Congress Control Number: 2018935648

Version: C10.01.01

International English Language Edition

Contents

Two forces vie for the soul of the world: Darkness and Light.

It is never easy to write the truth of the Darkness, for it is cruel and attacks both body and spirit, bestowing insufferable pain. To gaze into the heart of Darkness is to feel its horror even when we stand at a distance.

But looking into Darkness is a sharp reminder that there is a prevailing Light, offering hope and deliverance from this evil.

When Darkness gathers its forces … when Darkness performs its evil unchecked … our only recourse is to call on the Light in absolute dependence and trust.

For the Light of Heaven has offered the Prayer of Vengeance to a chosen few.

Chapter One

MARY WRIGHT

Mary Wright lived with Aunt Clare ever since Mary's parents died in a car crash when Mary was ten years old. Aunt Clare was her mother's sister and Mary's only living relative.

Her aunt was short, overweight, a heavy drinker and had been divorced for twenty years. Simply put, she was a drunk. She'd never remarried but it wasn't from a lack of trying. Every night, six days a week she was at the Road Runner Lounge trying to hook up with whoever would have her. Her romances never left the parking lot and remained in the back seat of her date of the night.

When first contacted about the death of Mary's parents, Clare had no interest in taking in her sister's kid. She hadn't seen the child in three years. Clare took a long drag on her Camel cigarette sending a small smoke ring into the air, as she sat in the booth at the bar talking to the social worker. "Hell, I couldn't pick her out of a crowd if my life depended on it," Aunt Clare said when the social worker asked her to take care of Mary.

"Your sister set up a trust fund and put you in charge of Mary and the money," the social worker told her.

With dollar signs in her eyes, Mary's aunt became the caring and loving person the social worker was looking for. She was more than happy to take in Mary, especially since by doing so, Aunt Clare had full access to the trust fund money, to do with as she pleased. The day Mary moved in, her aunt quit her job at the Beaver View Bowling Alley and the spending began.

From the first day at Aunt Clare's house, Mary was basically raising herself. Her aunt cared nothing about her niece's wants or needs. She told her friends at the Road Runner Lounge that caring for Mary was like having a cat that could talk. All Clare had to do was put food in the fridge and her job was done. I don't even need a damn litter box, Clare said with a laugh.

If Mary asked for money for clothes or spending cash the answer was always the same, "Do you think my money grows on trees? Go get a job."

When Mary turned sixteen, she did just that.

She took a job in the deli department at Lofino's, the local grocery store. It gave her the money she needed for clothes and some spending cash. It also made up somewhat for the social life she didn't have. She loved talking to everyone who came to the store, and everyone loved Mary's easy-going personality.

It was May of 1974 and Mary was finishing her junior year.

Working at the deli counter on a Friday night, she met three older boys who seemed to fancy her and flirt with her. Over the next several weeks, they came to the deli almost daily to get items for their lunches or dinner. The boys made it a point to tell her how her hair looked nice, that they loved her smile and liked her figure. The flirting and compliments were endless.

Mary had no idea or experience on how to handle this newfound attention. Every time the boys came in, they would only let Mary wait on them.

"Thank you, but we will wait for Mary to help us," the boy called Mikey would say, to whoever offered to help them as they waited.

Somehow, they always knew when she would be working.

This was all so new and exciting to Mary.

Having one boy pay attention to her, let alone three older boys who worked construction, was overwhelming. Their muscles and tan bodies didn't go unnoticed by Mary, as she so wanted and needed a boyfriend.

It wasn't from the lack of trying with the boys at Beavercreek High School. Mary tried but had never had a date with a boy. She even went so far as to ask the boys she liked out to get a burger or see a movie, but none had taken her up on her offers.

The problem was, Mary had the body that every boy dreamed to touch but she had a face no one wanted to kiss. A nose way too large for her face and teeth that were just a jumbled mess. The acne only added to the problem.

The boys called her Mary10-4, body was a ten and the face a four.

Mary had no idea what it really meant when the boys called her that. She thought it was the CB radio code truckers used, like "10-4 good buddy." When a boy would say, its Mary 10-4, she would reply "Back at you, good buddy," and the boys would all laugh and the girls snickered.

No boy ever stood up for her except for a sophomore named Brady Michaels. In the Human Studies class they shared, Brady made those who called her 10-4, apologize. "Mary, I promise you no one will ever call you that when I'm around," Brady said.

"It's all right," Mary told Brady. "They're just having some fun and I really don't mind. But I do appreciate you sticking up for me," she told him.

The one true adult friend that she had at school was the guidance counselor, Mr. Jennings. She met with him weekly for her regular counseling session. Jennings always greeted her with a big hug in his office after shutting his door. It was the only human physical contact in her life and she yearned for and needed it.

She told him everything during her appointments with him, including, at his urging and repeated probing, her deepest darkest worries and secrets. Mary felt she had to answer his questions about whether she'd had sex, what her sexual dreams were, and how she masturbated. She told him everything in full graphic detail.

She was smart enough to know Mr. Jennings knew her needs and her family situation. It passed through her mind that he could easily exploit her. Still, he was her only friend. The only person in the world who made her feel good about herself.

Two years after she started seeing him on a regular basis, she didn't think twice when he asked her to touch herself in his office, in front of him, while he filmed her. She did it, but she felt it was an odd thing for the counselor to request.

He must have noticed how uncomfortable the filming made her. "If you want our talks to continue," Jennings told Mary, as he put the movie camera away, "you must swear to keep our special relationship a secret."

She nodded, but felt something had changed between them. She wondered if she could talk to Brady about it. But, she knew she couldn't. It would be too embarrassing.

She soon forgot about Mr. Jennings' strange requests.

At the next session Mary told Jennings about the construction boys she met recently at the deli, he encouraged her to go out with them, if they asked her.

"I am so happy you've made friends with some older boys," Jennings said. "It'll be good for you to get out and have some fun.

I have known these boys for years, they came from good families, you can trust them to be gentlemen."

With Jennings' encouragement and blessing, Mary's mind was made up. If asked out, she would say yes.

That Saturday morning, the boys showed up to get their lunches for the day and it finally happened.

Mark, the tall blond, the one she liked best, approached her. "Mary, we were wondering if you would like to go out with us tonight to a bonfire we are having at the farm where we are staying. We can pick you up if you give us your address say around 7:30 or 8:00."

"Yeah, Mary," Mikey said, "it'll be fun. Lots of people you know will be there from school."

"Old Jennings said he may even stop by," Keith added.

"Yes of course," Mary said, remembering what Mr. Jennings had told her. "I would love to go."

Oh my God, she thought, *I have a date, finally.*

* * *

Mikey, Keith and Mark pulled in to Mary's driveway at exactly at 8:00 PM. They all agreed that Mark, the pretty boy, would go up to the door to get her, in case her aunt answered the door.

Mark knocked lightly on the door, it opened in a flash.

"You're here," Mary said. "I was worried you all had forgotten." She felt half embarrassed.

"We would never forget our lovely Mary," Mark said.

Mary smiled. "I brought something for tonight. Hope you don't mind."

"No problem. It's going to be a great night. All of us have been waiting for weeks to go out with you."

Mary felt flushed and knew her face must be a bright red, and she smiled like she'd never smiled before.

She climbed in the van, and showed them the grocery bag filled to the top with graham crackers, marshmallows and Hershey bars. "We can make s'mores. I've got hot dogs and buns, too," Mary said as she flashed a smile at everyone.

"All right Mary, we love s'mores," Mikey said as he smiled at Keith.

"Yeah, Mary, it will make this night even better around the bonfire," Keith said.

As the van pulled away, Mark opened a cooler and handed Mary an opened beer. "Here Mary," he said, "let's get the party started."

"Hell yeah," all the boys said together. They all started to chant her name "Mary, Mary, Mary."

Not wanting to say no, after all it was her first ever date, she drank it down thinking it's going to be the best night of her life.

The three boys cheered Mary on as she guzzled the beer down. The music was blaring in the van as they drove down Dayton-Xenia Road.

After four beers Mary passed out.

* * *

What Mary didn't know was that Mikey had spiked the first beer with drugs to make her pass out. It was going to be a great night for the boys but not so much for Mary.

The van turned onto a dirt road leading to a housing construction site called Seville Estates. The van stopped next to a large backhoe at the center of the two-hundred-acre development.

When the boys got out of the van a fourth person was standing next to the backhoe waiting for them.

"Did she drink all the first beer?" Ray asked.

"Hell yeah," Mikey said, "every bit of it."

"Okay," Ray said, "that'll give you an hour or so to get her prepared for fun time. When she's ready, Keith, you and Mikey take her to the basement. I'll meet you there. Don't fucking drop her like you did the last one." Ray walked toward the basement.

"Are you ever going to shut the hell up about that?" Mikey yelled back. "How was I supposed to know it'd break her goddamn neck, for fuck's sake? It was an accident."

Mary was like a rag doll as they moved her around in the van cutting her clothes off. First the shirt, then the bra.

"Holy shit, just wait until Ray sees these perfect tits," Mark said. "He'll go to town on these nipples."

Then they removed her shoes and socks and cut off her pants. "For fuck's sake," Mikey said, "this bitch got no underwear on and no hair on her pussy. Look at it."

He touched Mary. "And smooth as a baby's ass."

"When he sees her, Ray is going to give her his special treatment," Mark said. "I told you this girl was going to be a good one. You fuckers never believe me. You never picked out a no panty, shaved pussy girl. Maybe now you two assholes will start listening to me." Mark smiled.

Mikey smiled, too, as he winked at Mark and licked his lips.

Mikey threw all ninety-eight pounds of Mary over his shoulder and climbed down the ladder behind Mark. Mikey was excited beyond reasoning for the upcoming events of the evening.

Doing his best circus-ring-master impression Mikey announced, "Everyone please feast your eyes upon a rare breed of Beavercreek beaver, no panties and a shaved pussy. Never have we found such a fine girl in all our travels, come one and come all see the hairless wonder."

Ray watched silently with an odd look on his face as he thought about how he would prepare this gift for the boys. This was Mikey's favorite part, watching Ray decide.

The three boys howled and clapped with laughter.

* * *

The frenzy of excitement in the freshly dug basement was like electricity in the air.

"Boys, you promised Mary a bonfire and I have made you a nice one." Ray said, pointing to the crackling fire.

"Hell yes," Keith said. "Beer, s'mores, hot dogs with a side of shaved pussy. That's what Saturday night is all about." He laughed.

"Let's get this show started," Mikey shouted as he danced around. He was crazy with excitement and buck naked. "Get the show started," he said again. "It's time for the wicked to fly."

With that all three of the boys were dancing naked around the fire, their bodies soaked with sweat.

"I release you boys," Ray said, holding his arms in the air. "Turn lose the darkness."

The boys took turns sexually abusing her in all ways imaginable. As each performed his own specialty on Mary the others would shout out encouragement. When not performing, the boys ate the hot dogs Mary had brought, and made s'mores over the fire.

Except for Ray. He never joined in with the boys when they partied. He observed the activities while periodically checking his watch.

"Time's up boys," Ray said after about an hour.

They all cheered wildly.

"Now it's my turn," Ray said. "For my Father's Father, I will do what we have always done. I will bring out the darkness, for all to see and witness its glory."

Ray walked over to Mary and knelt next to her. With his left hand, he caressed her breasts. "Boys I got to tell you, you have really pleased me with this one."

"Thank you," Mikey said as he stood, taking a bow for the cheers of the other two.

Ray pulled out two long thin blades from the scabbards on his belt and placed them into the hot coals of the fire. Once the first blade was red hot he knelt next to Mary.

He lifted the first breast and with the skill of a surgeon he sliced off the areola and nipple. The heat of the knife singed the flesh and sent up a small wisp of smoke with the sound of searing flesh. The boys went nuts jumping up and dancing around the fire.

He repeated this with the second blade on the other breast. It was something his father had taught him when he was young. The heat of the blade kept the girls from bleeding out too soon. It cauterized the wound and stopped the bleeding.

The boys howled, clapped and laughed in the light of the bonfire.

"Who wants to roast a nipple on the fire?" Ray asked.

They all did and claimed it was their turn, as each claimed that the other got one the last time. Ray threw a nipple to both Keith and Mikey.

"Hell yeah," Keith said as he skewed it on to the roasting sticks the boys had made.

"Hey Mark," Mikey said. "You can have half of mine."

Mark gave him the thumbs up and smiled. "That's what I'm talking about, cousin."

Ray then turned Mary on to her side. Again, he heated the knives red hot in the fire. A puff of smoke rose as the knife cut into her lower abdomen.

The boys cheered.

"He's doing it again," Keith shouted. "I told you, Mikey. I told you he would do it with this one."

Ray walked away from Mary trailing fishing line he'd tied to a rod in the ground. Mikey and Keith were dancing around the fire half insane hollering as the music blared.

"Now we wait for no-hair Mary to wake up," Ray said. "Mark, get me a beer and a dog, will you?"

* * *

As Mary started to wake up, all four men stood naked around her saying nothing. "What's happening?" She tried to stand.

Mikey poured a cold beer over Mary's head and it snapped her back somewhat to reality. Now Mary realized that she was naked and in pain. She could hardly stand as she swayed, she felt like she was going to pass out.

Mary screamed and the boys laughed and howled.

"Where are my clothes, you assholes? What have you fucking done to me?" Mary screamed. "What the fuck is going on?" She was sobbing. "Why are you all naked?"

Mary ran her hand over her hurting and throbbing breasts. She screamed in pain disbelieving what her fingers didn't feel. Her brain wouldn't let her believe what her fingers knew.

Mary screamed! "What have you done to me?" She vomited.

Mikey walked over to her and poured two cold beers over her head. "Poor Mary, we only did what you wanted and deserved." He laughed.

Ray walked over to her slowly. "My dear Mary, I am going to give you one chance to escape or we'll kill you where you stand."

Mary screamed again. "What are you fucking talking about? Let me go, you freaks. Let me go. Help, help!" she screamed.

"Of course, Mary," Ray said calmly. "I'll help you.

"The boys will give you a ten-minute head start, run to that ladder." He pointed out in the far corner of the basement. "Climb out and run. I promise the boys will wait ten minutes before they come after you.

"Go on now." Ray said smiling. "Get going, RUN!"

Mary was now fully aware that these boys were going to kill her. She looked at the ladder and back at the four boys. Without hesitation, she took off running.

She didn't get to the ladder in the far corner of the basement before a snap was heard, which pulled her backwards. The shock rendered her unable to move. As she laid on the dirt floor of the freshly dug basement moaning, she could see her intestines had been pulled out through a cut they'd made on her side. The steaming grayish white mass was stretched out across the dirt floor.

* * *

Ray had tied fishing line to her intestines through the cut he'd made. He'd pulled them out and then pushed them back in with the line attached. From years of watching his father doing it, he'd learned well. Ray knew she would never reach the ladder.

The boys were cheering "Mary, Mary, Mary," as Ray walked over to her. Bending down he grabbed Mary by the hair and pulled her head up and slit her throat. The blood spilled out of the open wound onto the dirt. The boys cheered.

Mary died that Saturday night never experiencing the date she dreamed of having.

They buried Mary 10-4 in that basement with the backhoe. All traces of what had happened were gone forever.

It was two full weeks before Aunt Clare noticed Mary was missing.

Chapter Two

FATHER BOB

In 1981, Father Bob, the local Catholic priest, looked back at the time when evil was beaten in his town, for a while at least. It happened in 1976, a time when news traveled slowly. There was no internet and no twenty-four-hour news cycle. There were no cell phones. There was one morning paper, the *Dayton Journal* and one evening newspaper, the *Dayton Daily News*. There were only three TV channels and they shut off at one a.m., with a flag waving while the national anthem played.

That was it.

The small township of Beavercreek, Ohio, was its own ecosystem. Not much outside of the township affected the life within it. Children went home during the summer when the street lights came on. They could ride their bikes anywhere in town. When they got thirsty, they found a water hose in someone's yard and drank from it.

Parents didn't worry about where their children were playing or biking around town. It wasn't that they didn't care about their children, it was just a different time. There was no fear of evil in the world. The feeling was that bad things happened somewhere else, not in Beavercreek. The problems of the big cities and the world were not a concern for parents in the smaller townships.

If a teenager went missing, there were no posters, yellow ribbons or milk carton pictures. They were simply deemed runaways. Off to Woodstock, the neighbors would whisper. In most cases, only the immediate family looked for them. Most teenagers disappeared like smoke in the wind. It was understood that they probably went to California, and would show up eventually. Some did, but most didn't. It was a time when moving twenty-five miles away meant you'd left all your troubles behind you.

Beavercreek was a small township in southern Ohio whose only claim to fame was that it was near Wright-Patterson Air Force Base. All the growth over the years had to do with the military moving there along with all the civilians and base contractors who worked at the base.

Father Bob heard the stories about how there were once beavers in every creek in the township, hence the name Beavercreek. But the beavers had long since been killed off. Only the name remained. The only beaver now was the high school mascot, and it wasn't real. It was a caricature of what was part of the township's history that came out only at sporting events and parades.

There was one high school, two junior highs and six elementary schools in Beavercreek. St Luke's was the only Catholic church. A boring but safe place to grow up in, most would say. There was no better place to raise kids. Like most small-town schools across Ohio, September was all about football and girls. However, in 1976, forty-three years ago, everything changed on a cool Friday night, the night of the first home game.

A door would be opened. A light would be shown in the darkness. The events would forever change the way some looked at life.

Chapter Three

THE VISIT

The loud knock on the door startled Father Bob. It was almost seven-thirty on a Friday night, and he wasn't expecting any visitors. He'd just sat down to enjoy a glass of fine wine, a birthday gift from a parishioner the week prior.

He was a bit annoyed at the interruption of his personal time as he walked to the door. "Who's knocking like the parish is on fire?" He mumbled it to himself as he made his way to the door, wishing he could yell out how he felt. The louder they knocked the slower he walked.

A tall priest with a weathered face smiled through the small window in the door. Father Bob was glad he'd mumbled, and probably hadn't been heard.

He stared at the man a little longer before opening the door. The deep lines in the tall priest's face showed he'd seen all that life had to offer. Still, his eyes were a clear deep blue with profound wrinkles at the edges.

Father Bob opened the door with a jerk, wishing he hadn't let the caller anger him. A tattered black leather traveling bag with a large brass locking clasp sat at the man's feet.

All he could get out was, "May I help . . . " before the stranger grabbed the bag and walked in, right past Father Bob, pausing long enough to place his travel bag in the hallway and take off his hat.

He reached out his hand to shake the priest's hand. "Father Bob, My name is Father Anthony. I am from the Vatican."

Father Bob took the older priest's hand, wondering why someone from the Vatican would come to Beavercreek. Could it be because of the letters Father Bob had sent to the Vatican for the last four years? He hadn't received a single reply. Not a call or letter. Nothing.

He'd tried every address he could find at the Vatican. He always addressed it the same. "To the Pope," was the header on every letter. Now, without notice or warning, someone from Rome was here in the rectory.

"I have traveled a long way to see you. I hope you do not mind me showing up unannounced. It is rude, I know, but I hope you can forgive me. When I was made aware of your letters, I got on a plane and came with only the clothes on my back and what I could place in my travel bag. This is how important I found your letters."

Father Bob was speechless for the first time in years. He couldn't utter a word. He was amazed, excited and confused by this unannounced stranger. He stood there and looked the priest up and down from his balding head to his leather shoes.

Father Anthony patted him on the shoulder with an understanding smile. "Could an old priest sit down and have something cold to drink or maybe something a little stronger if you have it. Just no communion wine." He laughed.

"I have been saving a bottle of 1975 Trotanoy Bourdeaux for a special occasion," Father Bob said with eyebrows arched.

"From the Pomerol region, I believe," Father Anthony said with a beaming smile. "I think that will work just fine.

"I would very much like to hear this story of yours in your own voice. Please do not leave out any detail, even if you think it is not important. I want to hear everything, and, by the way, I do not mind telling you I am a very good listener."

This set Father Bob at ease, for his story was a long and detailed one with many parts needing to be told. Parts that might be connected in some way, but he wasn't sure.

"Yes, of course, please come and let's sit down," Father Bob said, his hands shaking from nervousness as he opened the bottle of Bordeaux. "Let me pour you a glass. You must excuse my manners as I'm just amazed someone from the Vatican has come to hear my story."

He found a second wine glass and filled it. "We've got a spare room in the rectory. I'll put your travel bag there."

"Wonderful." Father Anthony sipped his wine.

Father Anthony pulled two cigars from his breast pocket. "You don't happen to a be a cigar smoker, are you?"

Father Bob could feel his eyebrows rising. He was torn between wanting to make his guest feel comfortable and abiding by his no smoking rules.

Father Bob stared at the cigar in utter disbelief thinking no one had ever smoked in the rectory before. With only the shortest delay, he smiled and took the cigar from Father Anthony. "Not usually. But, when Romans are in the house, do as the Romans do."

They both laughed.

Besides, Father Bob thought, nothing was normal about tonight and it was sure to get even further beyond normal before the night ended. "I've heard it's bad manners to let someone smoke a fine cigar alone."

Father Anthony used his silver cigar cutter to clip the end of both cigars, and passed one to Father Bob.

Father Bob rolled the cigar around between his thumb and index finger. "You may have to help me light this thing."

"Here you go." He lit Father Bob's cigar and then his own.

"Thank you." Father Bob took a long draw on his cigar and started coughing. "Oh my, that's strong."

Father Anthony smiled. "Try again. You will like it."

Father Bob took another draw on his cigar, managing to do so without coughing this time.

Over the next three hours Father Bob told the visitor from the Vatican everything that had happened and what he had witnessed in the past five years. Every detail and event spilled out. It was as if he couldn't stop talking.

It was a spectacular tale and Father Anthony didn't speak until Father Bob was finished. And then the only thing the visitor asked was, "Will the boy show up this Saturday?"

"Yes, of course. He's here every Saturday night between eleven and midnight. Has been for almost four years, now. He visits the grotto next to the church, and prays at the statue of the Blessed Virgin in the grotto."

"Where is this grotto?" Father Anthony asked.

"The grotto is a walkout area from the lower church's basement that had been dug out so that the class rooms could have windows. The members of the Parish had placed a large bronze statue of the Virgin Mary there as a place to pray when the church was closed. It's quiet with a small bench to sit on. Quite a lovely place to pray."

"Will he be there Saturday?" Father Anthony asked again.

"Yes, he'll be there. The boy comes like clockwork, without fail. Rain or snow, it makes no difference. We can watch from the window in the church that overlooks the grotto. That's where I observe him and he cannot see us."

"Can it be? We will see the light?"

"It is why I wrote," Father Bob answered solemnly.

Chapter Four

THE BOY

As he turned onto Keller Avenue on his orange ten-speed Schwinn, the last of ten laps this morning, Brady was soaked in sweat. The friction generator light guided his way in the dusk of morning. He rode the three-mile loop through the neighborhoods twice a week, Monday and Friday.

He ran two laps along the loop on Tuesdays and lifted weights on Wednesdays, doing both upper and lower body. Thursdays were reserved for the speed bag, or what his three brothers called the Bruce Lee workout. They would sit and watch him making kung-fu noises while they laughed out loud.

On Saturday mornings, he swam laps at the Kettering Recreation Center from five-thirty until seven-thirty. He'd arranged with the manager to use the pool when no one else was around. He would remind his brothers, who sometimes tagged along, about the advantages of having a neighbor who was the manager. For this access, all it cost in return was for him to take care of his neighbor's cat when he went out of town. His brothers Zane, Caleb and Liam called it pool for pussy, and laughed every time they said it.

Every morning each week, the routine was the same. Up at five to work out and then make breakfast for himself and his brothers. The brothers called it pigs, chickens and toast time.

After Brady had filled his brothers' cups with steaming, black coffee they stood and saluted. "Sir, we thank you for another fine breakfast." They all laughed at the running gag.

"Thank you." Brady would say as he saluted back, laughing.

For all their differences, the four brothers were inseparable and best friends.

But Brady had a secret he couldn't share with his brothers. It was something they wouldn't understand if told and a secret he didn't understand completely himself. It was this secret that made him different from the brothers he loved and kept him from being the brother he wanted to be. He couldn't share a part of his life that he thought they should know.

After eating, he showered, dressed and it was off to school, hauling his pack of goof ball brothers with him. He claimed it was like herding cats.

Only Sunday was their day of rest. The brothers had long ago quit going to mass on Sundays, much to their mother's disappointment.

"If I need to talk with God, I can do it from here," Liam would say and on that cue, the boys would all start to sing Ave Maria in fake opera voices, their saintly routine made their mother smile as she pretended to be angry with them.

Brady played no school sports but was always training. All the coaches were less than pleased at his turning down their repeated invites to join the school sports teams. Brady's response was always the same. "Coach, I thank you for the offer, but sports are just not what interests me."

Because of all the training the boy was doing, even the neighbors thought it odd that he didn't participate in school sports. Rain, snow, heat or cold he was always out there. Some thought he was planning on joining the military and others said he was going to try out for the Olympics.

Whenever the Battling Beavers football coach saw Brady, he would shake his head and wonder: Why isn't he my starting linebacker?

The brothers thought their older brother had a big secret or something. Their theory of what it was changed weekly. Each would come up with some far-out idea, and the rest would shoot it down while laughing with insults. For a while they believed he'd joined the Green Berets and didn't tell their parents. Being the loving brothers that they were, they promptly told their mom and dad of their theory. It was the brotherly thing to do.

His parents dragged Brady down to the Army recruiting office in Xenia and talked with the sergeant there. Brady's parents finally believed him when he said he hadn't signed up. His brothers laughed all day about it, claiming it was the funniest thing they'd done yet.

"Payback is a bitch," was all Brady said, smiling at them and laughing.

This Friday morning was different. The brothers were taking the bus with Big John the bus driver. Big John was the nickname the students had given the quiet driver. None of the brothers were happy about having to take the bus. Not that they disliked the bus driver, far from that, they loved him for how he cared about the students.

It was just that, it wasn't like riding in the Buick blasting their music and talking crap to each other. They would miss their morning routine.

Before Brady started driving, Big John had picked up the boys in front of their house every school day since Brady was in the seventh grade in junior high school.

Brady was oldest at eighteen with brown hair and very athletic. Two dimples burst out when he smiled. The twins Liam and Caleb were sixteen and Zane was the youngest at fifteen.

The twins didn't look or act anything like each other. Liam had red hair, was stocky and had a wickedly fast temper. He was also prone to fisticuffs at the slightest provocation.

Caleb had brown hair and was easy going but loud in voice. He was as strong as an ox for his size. A lady's man his brothers would say. He had this wink he would do that melted all the girl's hearts.

Zane, being the youngest, was what the boys liked to call the crazy one. No bet or dare was too much for him to accept. The boys learned early on not to dare him after he jumped from the roof of the house into a kiddie pool at the age of five. It was the best belly flop they'd ever seen, they told their parents.

The brothers were thick as thieves, their mother would say when they got in trouble. One would never go anywhere without the others, except for Brady. He was the loner, always going off by himself. He needed his quiet time, Zane would tease. That dog and him, who knew where they went for hours on end, his mother would say to their father.

The bus driver smiled as he saw the boys waiting outside for him as he pulled the bus up to the curb. Big John was a quiet man who wore a big smile on his face, a John Deere hat on his head and a silver cross on a leather string around his neck. He told everyone on the bus that it was his mission now in life to drive a school bus and be the best bus driver there ever was. That's why he did it he would say when asked.

The best part of the job, he would say, was that he got to hang out with all the cool kids. That made everyone laugh. When he wasn't driving the bus, he ran a little carryout store he opened when he retired from the air force. It was in the middle of nowhere on Factory Road.

"I was born and raised here and I'll die here," he told the students. "No better place to live. I've traveled the world and let me tell you, if there is a heaven, it's right here in Beavercreek." And then he'd show off that big smile of his.

After the boys climbed aboard the bus, Big John looked surprised. "Holy cow, boys, I haven't seen you guys in a long while. Kinda missed your ugly faces."

The brothers all smiled.

When Brady turned sixteen, he drove the boys to school in Mom's old Buick Gran Sport. It was a cool old fast car. White with knock-off spoke wheels and a 445-wildcat engine, it was a load of fun.

Big John saw Brady's dog Hank sitting by the mailbox. "Is he coming?"

"Not today," Brady said. "And he's not happy about it."

Big John's lips turned down, clearly disappointed.

Normally Hank rode in Brady's car to school and stayed in or around the car until school was out. Brady would feed and walk him during his lunch hour. The two couldn't be separated. Much to the displeasure of his parents, Brady's grandfather had given Hank to Brady on his fifth birthday.

Brady would never forget that birthday. His grandfather told him he'd trained the dog himself, and that he'd always obey Brady. What he failed to explain was that the dog would only obey Brady.

Big John always kept a bag of biscuits on the bus just in case he saw the boys and Hank. He reached over and pulled out a large dog biscuit and threw it to Hank. "There you go, big boy."

The big black and brown dog hopped like a rabbit in glee at having the biscuit.

"That should keep him from being so mad about not coming today," Big John laughed. "Is the car broken down?" he asked as he pulled away shutting the door.

"No, Dad's getting some new tires on it," Brady said.

"Too many burn outs, huh?" Big John laughed.

Caleb jumped in with his loud voice, "Oh hell, yeah."

Everyone on the bus laughed.

"Well, it's true," he said to back up his claim as he flashed his smile around.

"Here's a new tape I got this weekend. Hope you all like it!" Big John cranked up the eight-track tape player as the latest Led Zeppelin tape started playing.

"Hey, it's got your class song on it for all you seniors." Big John bellowed over the music.

How cool was it, listening to "Stairway to Heaven" on the way to school Brady thought? As they drove, Brady's mind was wondering what this day would bring.

Big John dropped Brady and the others off at the high school with his usual, have a good day and be safe. Big John yelled, see you all at the game tonight as he closed the door and pulled away.

* * *

Caleb, Liam and Zane took off to meet up with their girlfriends. Brady called the girls the masters of the uncontrollable. It made him laugh every time he saw his brothers being on their best behavior and manners when they were around the girls. No farting, belching, or cussing. It was almost like they were well mannered. If only the girls knew, he would laugh and shake his head. It made him happy that they were happy.

Brady walked in to the building past the stoners hanging by the back-door smoking weed and watching for teachers who were always trying to catch them. He nodded hello as he passed.

Hey Brady, how's it going they'd asked.

Another day in paradise he'd reply.

It wasn't in his nature, to pass judgment on them for their habits. Brady's only concern was whether they were good or bad. He often told his brothers, that was what was important.

A girl with shoulder length brown hair was leaning against the wall waiting for him. She smiled at seeing him. "Bet the boys loved riding that bus."

Brady smiled. "Yeah, it was at the top of their things to do this morning. But knowing the boys, Michelle, the day will get more interesting if they have anything to say about it."

"Give me a second," Brady said as he headed to the men's restroom. "Too much coffee."

"I'll wait here." Michelle leaned up next to the opposite wall against the lockers.

Calling these restrooms was a joke. A few of the male teachers, who were trying to catch students smoking, thought it would be a great idea to remove the stall doors and in some of the restrooms, the stalls completely. If you ever needed to take the dreaded dump at school, it was to be in front of all who entered. Embarrassing and humiliating doesn't adequately describe the feeling for someone who had to do the deed.

This morning, as Brady walked in, three seniors were throwing wet paper towels non-stop at a poor sophomore who they had caught with his pants around his ankles taking a dump.

The sophomore was covered from head to toe with the white sticky mess. He was dripping wet. It was Matt Beck, a sophomore Brady had seen around the school who was trying to find a way to fit into the social structure of high school. Brady noticed these things about people.

Brady looked at the three seniors and said, "Real tough guys."

The three looked around and were scared shitless seeing the look of displeasure on Brady's face. His brother Caleb called it Brady's *ugly* face. Caleb would say you had better run if you saw that look on his brother's face.

Poor Matt looked like a snowman, they had hit him with so many wet paper towels. What hadn't hit him was stuck on the wall behind him. It was almost like a modernist work of art. From the amount of wet paper towel shots, this attack had to have been going on for at least fifteen minutes.

"Come on, Brady," said Steve, one of the seniors. "He's a sophomore. It's tradition handed down from every senior class."

"Yeah, it's like a rule we must follow," the fat senior named Bob claimed.

"Bullshit, you guys are assholes." Brady said glaring at them.

He had no patience for anyone picking on someone, and they knew it.

The three moved quickly toward the door.

The senior named Chris pleaded with his eyes, while backing up toward the door. "Don't be pissed off at us, Brady. Okay? It's just a joke."

Before Brady could respond, all three seniors left without looking back at their handiwork.

Brady said to Matt, "I'll stay outside at the door so no one can come in while you get cleaned up, take your time."

"Thanks," was all Brady heard.

The poor sophomore didn't look up, but Brady knew Matt was aware of who rescued him and that was enough for Brady.

"What was that all about in there?" Michelle asked.

"Not a great way to start the day." Brady said. "Is it asshole Friday?" he asked Michelle.

He explained in detail what had happened. "I told the kid I'd keep everyone out until he was decent."

Michelle moved up next to Brady and together they blocked the door.

It was common knowledge amongst the seniors not to pick on anyone in Brady's presence. Everyone had heard of the rumors about things that had happened in the past. Stories about a Junior High Principal who had crossed the line. Stories about stories. No one knew what was true or not. The one thing everyone agreed on was to not mess with Brady. Even the teachers kept their distance.

It didn't matter to Brady. It made him friends with those who had no friends. He could come and go, not worrying about the rules of the social cliques in high school. He was welcomed by all and he welcomed all.

It was his nature that attracted those in need to him. He was the sheep dog and the lost sheep flocked to him. And, in the end, these would be the people who would be there when no one else could or would.

Chapter Five

HIGH SCHOOL

Father Bob researched Beavercreek when he first learned he'd be assigned there. He learned the high school was built in 1954 and sat at the east end of the township next to twenty-five acres of woods donated as a land lab. It was a two-story brick building considered quite modern in its day. In 1976, twenty-two years later, the luster had long since faded. It was a cold, drafty building in the winter and an oven in the summer.

Its claim to fame was that on January 3, 1964, a 10-ton Wright-Patterson Air Force Base RB-57 jet flying at fifty thousand feet had its wings ripped off as the plane broke apart in mid-air. The wreckage was spread over a fifteen-mile radius. The fuselage and tail landed in the parking lot behind the school, mere feet from classrooms filled with students.

"Anyone who doesn't believe in God after that day is out of their minds," said Coach Stall.

"It was a miracle no one was hurt. There was only one shattered window," Principal Hess was quoted to have said to the *Dayton Daily News* reporter.

That was the most exciting event in memory and made the national evening news.

In 1976 there were 2,600 students attending the high school and the senior class had a record of 647 students in it. The class colors were blue and silver, the class song was "Stairway to Heaven" and the class flower was the white rose. It was also the 200th anniversary of America.

The teachers were a mixture of people who loved to teach, but there was a large group of male teachers who were the product of the Vietnam War. Some became teachers to avoid the draft, and they hated teaching and disliked the students. Some were using twenty-year-old lesson plans they had purchased from the teachers they had replaced. Many of these student haters were busy trying to become something other than teachers. Some were taking insurance courses or doing construction on the side.

But there was a small group who were there for their own twisted intentions. They would have worked for free, if the truth be told, just to be near the students.

Beavercreek was just like any high school, then or now. The students were self-divided into social groups that hung out at different sections of the building that they claimed as their own turf. Who or what you identified with defined where you gathered in the school building.

The stoners hung out near the back door at the far northeast corner of the building smoking pot. The jocks met in the cafeteria at Weasels' Corner in the center of the building on the north side. The lovers or couples were upstairs near the history classes on the west end of the second floor. Band members met in the hallway near the music room in the northwest of the first floor.

Everyone else wandered the halls like nomads, looking for somewhere to go, trying to fit in or not be noticed until the start of classes.

* * *

Brady didn't belong to any of the groups, but each treated him as if he was one of their own. He could move in and out of the groups without any issues.

He did have a group of friends who found it interesting that he wasn't in a group. Randy had been friends with Brady since the seventh grade. Then there were Greg and Larry. They had meet Brady over the summer between junior and senior year through Randy.

All were Air Force brats, and only hung out with the jocks and honor society crowd. It limited their access to the girls outside of their group. The interesting girls were beyond their reach Greg would say. Being friends with Brady allowed them to talk with girls they would have never had a chance with otherwise. Brady was the ultimate hall pass between the different groups.

He'd signed up for student council to avoid a boring study hall. It was fun, he had to admit. Just goofing off and planning for the weekends.

One of the students in the group was Greg. He was a senior, tall, thin with black hair and had a smile that got him out of trouble every time. If you looked up brownnoser in the dictionary you'd see his picture.

In Greg's mind, it's always about him. The world revolved around what he needed and wanted. It was just his nature. Both

Brady and Randy knew this flaw about him but it didn't bother them as they viewed it as an asset to be used.

The teachers all loved Greg because he was such an insufferable suck-up. Greg was useful for getting hall passes and getting assigned to student council projects. He was the ultimate bullshitter.

Larry, on the other hand, was all business. He played football and was way too serious about everything. He was always afraid of getting into trouble and how it would affect his college chances.

Every girl Larry dated was *the one.* That became a running joke, especially since he changed girlfriends every two-to-three weeks. The good thing about Larry was that if he said he would be there, you wouldn't have to worry about him not showing up.

Randy was tall and he also played football. His mother would say he was as quiet as a church mouse. He considered Brady his best friend. His mom and dad were always happy when Brady visited and never complained about where Randy was going if Brady was with him. Randy liked it when Brady came over with his pack of brothers. Randy didn't have brothers and he enjoyed being considered one of the boys.

Every morning Brady met up with Michelle, Randy, Greg and Larry at Weasels' Corner in the cafeteria. This small student-run store was an unofficial seniors-only hangout.

Coffee, pop, candy and chips were sold along with the latest news and gossip of the day. People went there to see and be seen. The newest couples always made their relationship official with an appearance.

This Friday morning Greg was all excited about the grand plan he'd come up with to paint the bridge. Being the first to paint the bridge senior year was going to be his badge of honor. He had the whole student council crowd excited about his plan.

"Everyone, it's time to paint the bridge," he said.

Brady stood in the back of the excited crowd and listened to this grand plan of Greg's. He knew that when Greg said he had a plan, what that really meant was, others would be doing the hard work and he would be taking credit for it.

On and on Greg talked until he hit a fever pitch that only a born-again preacher reaches. His bullshit was reaching an epic level, even for him.

"We will all be famous. Everyone will talk about us for years," he promised the spellbound crowd as they all cheered him on.

Greg was the center of attention and in his element. The bullshit meter was off the charts but the strange part was they all seemed to believe him. Brady looked at Randy and Randy looked at Larry and all just smiled at this performance. Before the bell rang for the start of first period, Greg had his group of enthusiastic volunteers. They would all meet again during third period student council meeting and smooth out the actual details.

Brady, on the other hand, didn't like being in the spotlight. This worked out best most of the time as Brady's ego had no need for attention.

On the way to class Larry warned Brady and Randy. "You know this is going to go bad. How, I have no idea, but it will all turn to shit. Just you wait and see."

"Yeah," Randy said. "Everything he touches goes to shit."

They all laughed.

Chapter Six

TRADITION

Painting the bridge was a tradition at Beavercreek High School since the day it was built. It happened so often the Beavercreek police turned a blind eye on the bridge every Friday and Saturday night.

The bridge was a train overpass on Dayton-Xenia Road, suspended about thirty feet above the road. The trains that used the tracks sped through the township at scary speeds with usually two engines pulling forty to sixty boxcars. The bridge was built back in the early 1920s and the boxcars swayed back and forth like they could come off the tracks at any moment.

The possibility of danger from the tracks and the trains was well ingrained into the residents' minds. In 1959 a freight train plowed into a car carrying eight girl scouts and two parents, killing all. The car was dragged fifty feet along the tracks. One body was found seventy-five feet beyond the car, the bodies burned and mangled beyond recognition, demonstrating the speed and force of the crash.

The bridge had a lip on the top of the panels about twenty-four inches wide. The space between the boxcars and the lip was about two feet on each side. The panels were eight feet tall but only four feet up from the tracks. The bridge was approximately seventy-five feet long, comprised of ten steel panels about eight feet tall. Just enough panels for painting Beavers '76, Sr Spirit '76 or B Creek '76. It was also perfect for the cross-town rival Catholic high school to paint Carroll '76 or Patriots '76.

It was an every-other-week battle between the rival schools. Beavers '76 could be painted on Friday and changed to Carroll '76 on Saturday. The painting season started the first week of school. There was an unspoken truce that during the summer no one painted the bridge.

The mistakes of youth. "Watch over them, Lord."

* * *

At seventeen or eighteen, not a lot of thought goes into the *what if* part of a plan, especially if Greg had any part in it. Experts claim that the teenage mind is not fully developed, which is the cause of so many bad youthful decisions. In Greg's case, development had nothing to do with it, he was just a dumbass.

By the end of the day there were seven people taking part in the bridge-painting project: Greg, Brady, Linda, Michelle, Dean, Bobby and Sue.

Larry and Randy couldn't participate since they were on the football team. Even though Randy had an injury and couldn't play, he had to be with the team during the game.

"It's crap that you two aren't coming," Brady told them.

"You be careful, Brady. I won't be there to watch your back," Randy warned.

"Hell, I may not even go," Brady replied.

This would be the first time anyone in the group had ever painted the bridge. There was no hand-me-down to-do list from the seniors before them. All they knew was that it had to be done at night and during the first football game.

Greg's plan was for one person, designated the painter, to have a rope tied around his waist and be lowered over the ledge to paint each letter. The painter would have to hold the rope with one hand and paint with the other. A second person would lower a bucket of paint over the ledge for the painter to use. A third person would be tied to the painter and serve as the anchor.

The anchor's job was to keep the painter from falling to the street and being killed by being run over by a car. If a train came, the anchor was to pull the painter up with the rope and both run to safety.

"Don't worry," Greg said. "I know for a fact the trains don't run on Friday nights. The tracks are closed."

Brady knew Greg had no idea what he was talking about. Greg's gift was his ability to lie without getting caught. Brady also knew that if a train came while they were on the bridge, the only exit would be to run if they wanted to live. No ifs, ands, or buts. It was a long bridge, and there was no option of jumping to the ground below if a train came.

Brady didn't like Greg's plan and, as he got up to go to his first class, thought it best to find a reason not to participate.

During third period student council Greg sorted out the details regarding the bridge painting and decided who was to do what. Somehow, he managed to get out of doing anything himself that involved actual work toward the goals he'd set.

He put Linda and Sue in charge of getting the white paint, orange paint, brushes and rollers. Linda worked at the local hardware store and could get a discount on everything. What they couldn't buy they would get out of their parents' garages.

Bobby would get the ropes needed from the farm where he lived.

Greg got Linda to talk Dean into having the honor of being the painter who was to be hung over the edge like a puppet.

At 120 pounds dripping wet, he was the lightest of the guys and the best choice. He had a medium build with a big blonde afro hair do. He'd been infatuated with Linda since the seventh grade and would do anything she asked. He was like her personal boy servant. This crush of his was misplaced as it wasn't a mutual thing between them.

Greg used Dean's love for Linda to further his grand plans. If he'd asked Dean himself, it would have been a big hell no! Hanging from the train bridge suspended by a rope? It was plain crazy and Greg knew it. Proof that love makes people nuts.

The big question was, who was going to be the anchor? Everyone just assumed it was going to be Greg. Randy, Brady or Larry would be best, but Larry and Randy wouldn't be there. Both knew that if it turned to shit, Brady and the others would be on their own. Brady would be the only one who would stay if things took a turn in a bad direction.

Greg would bolt at the first sign of trouble. They knew Greg all too well. It would not be the first time he bailed when trouble started. There was no way Greg would ever put himself at risk. Not until that evening at the bridge would anyone know the rest of Greg's plan. He kept it secret for a reason.

It was decided that everyone would meet up at the football game forty-five minutes early and leave from there. Michelle would be driving since she had the Tuna Boat, an old white Buick station wagon with fake wood panels, large enough to easily hold ten people.

It was just a five-minute ride from the high school to the bridge so there would be plenty of time to paint it and get back to the game before it ended.

At least that was the plan.

There was no rehearsal, no checking on when the trains might run and no escape plan in case the police came. All that was talked about was Greg telling them how they were going to be legends come Monday morning.

"Just wait until everyone finds out who painted the bridge," Greg boasted.

The only one who had grave thoughts over this half-baked plan was Brady. Somehow, it just didn't feel right.

Chapter Seven

GAME NIGHT

It was game night in Beavercreek. The air was crisp and cool with the aroma of smoldering leaves hanging in the air.

Brady shook his head as Caleb, Liam and Zane piled in the car. "I can tell each of you have gotten into my Brut Cologne. Some way more than others. There is a fine line between smelling good and being able to be smelled a mile off." Brady laughed.

"What? You sure as heck can't be talking about me," Liam said.

"Well, he's not talking about Hank," Zane replied as he laughed out loud.

"Should I go back in and wash it off?" Liam asked.

"Naw, too late. And besides, the girls are used to you this way." Caleb smiled.

Brady and his three brothers arrived at the game forty-five minutes early so that all who were going to paint the bridge could get ready. "You guys have rides home tonight?" Brady asked. He knew they did. He was making a point.

"Yes, Brady," said Caleb, "we're riding home with our girlfriends via their parents."

"We told you that ten times already," Liam added.

"Yeah," said Zane, "maybe we should tell Mom your hearing is going so she hauls you off to the doctors to get tested," he laughed out loud.

"You guys stay out of trouble, you hear me?" Brady said as they got out of the car.

"What trouble can we get into kissing girls?" Zane said shoving Liam to get moving.

"Zane, Liam and Caleb, I damn well mean it. Stay out of trouble." Brady shook a fist at them which only made them laugh louder.

"We promise," they replied in unison as they turned to walk away.

Zane pointed toward the ticket booth where their girlfriends waited for them. "Those are *girls* in case you've forgotten, and we have got to go."

"Are you happy now, can we go?" Liam asked over his shoulder.

Now that the boys were gone, Brady turned his attention to Hank.

He put all the windows down. "Buddy, you stay here. I'll be back soon," he told Hank. "Stay in the car, I'll call you if I need you." He patted the big dog on the head, turned and left.

Senior year and having his own car was great, Brady thought as he walked past the ticket booth, handing his ticket to one of the parent volunteers working that night.

He could hear the cheerleaders doing the stupidest cheer he'd ever heard, "I'm a Beaver, you're a Beaver, we are Beavers all, and when we get together we do the Beaver call." Cheerleaders doing the Beaver call, he was sure he wasn't the only one who thought that was more than amusing.

He saw the bridge group gathered next to the concession stand as agreed. The excitement was written all over their faces.

The rule was that once you left the field you weren't allowed back in but as usual Greg had charmed his way through with a lie. He'd spoken to the ladies taking tickets and explained that we were student council members and were going into the school to do a project and would be returning in about an hour.

Michelle parked her station wagon on the other side of the parking lot so no one could see them leave. The girls had packed everything needed in the back of the wagon. Sue had even gotten a cooler of Little Kings beer for the after-painting party celebration Greg had promised them.

"Hey Brady," Michelle called out, "sit up front next to me." She winked at him and patted the seat.

"Sure," was all Brady could say as he got in. Greg jumped in the front seat with them before Brady could close the door, and squished him up against Michelle.

Michelle just smiled, as Brady looked at her and said, "Sorry."

She put the car in gear and pulled out of the parking lot. She turned on radio station WTUE. It was playing Areosmith.

"How appropriate," she laughed out loud and everyone sang along.

Well, on a train, I met a train,
She rather handsome, we kind looked the same
She was pretty, from New York City
I'm walkin' down that old fair lane,
I'm in heat, I'm in love,
But I just couldn't tell her so
I said, train kept a-rollin' all night long

Train kept a-rollin' all night long
Train kept a-rollin' all night long
Train kept a-rollin' all night long
With a "heave!", and a "ho!"
I just couldn't tell her so, no, no, no

The song blared out of the open windows as they headed down Dayton-Xenia Road.

Greg could hardly contain himself talking about the bridge and about how easy it was going to be. It's going to be a piece of cake Greg told the group. Brady just sat quietly next to Michelle, knowing that it was going to be anything but easy.

She squeezed his knee, causing Brady to wonder if she sensed his unease.

He should've stayed at the game. Michelle was the only reason he'd come. He was sweet on her, but in a secret kind of way as was Michelle toward him.

She parked the station wagon on a quiet side street near the bridge, under a large oak tree whose branches hung over the street. The group clambered out and hauled paint rollers, buckets and rope up the steep hill to the field next to the tracks. Once everything had been carried up the steep bank, everyone set about their assigned tasks.

While the paint buckets were being filled, Linda tied the rope around Dean's waist. She talked softly to him. There was no mistaking that look on his face. He was scared shitless.

"Dean, I'm so amazed and proud that you're brave enough to do this," she said.

"Oh, it's nothing," Dean told her as his lip quivered.

Linda gave him a big hug and a peck on the cheek.

In Dean's mind, that alone was worth risking his life.

Brady watched Linda's antics with Dean and shook his head. She's playing him. Everyone knows there is a secret thing going on between Greg and Linda.

"Hey Boss," Bobby called out to Greg, "these rollers don't fit in the buckets. They're way too big."

Laughter was in the air and spilled paint was everywhere.

It was a small detail, but Brady knew it was one that would increase the time they needed to be on the bridge.

"We're really doing this," Greg shouted out in encouragement, pumping his fist into the air.

While all this merriment was going on, Brady went to look at the bridge. As he slowly walked the span, he zoned out the voices of the others.

He could see Mount Zion Church and its cemetery on the east end of the bridge. He turned his head to the west, and saw the open field where everyone was gathered. It was dark now and the bridge looked way different up close. It was ugly and cold looking.

Nothing was like he'd imagined. The bridge was longer and the side panels taller, the spacing between the wood trusses wider. There was a two-foot gap between the walls and the tracks. "This is a mistake," he said softly.

Brady wondered how in the hell could anyone run on the tracks in the dark and not fall. He looked over the edge of the bridge. There was no doubt a jump from the bridge would kill you. If not from the fall itself, getting hit by a car would finish the job.

"Hey, Greg, when was the last train through here?" Brady asked.

Greg replied, "They don't run on Friday nights. Don't worry about it, I've checked it all out."

Brady made his way back to the rest of the group. Dean looked like a puppet on a string waiting for the show to start. He was just standing there trying not to appear scared as he turned toward Brady and smiled.

"What?" was all Brady said to him.

Brady realized at that very moment, he was the anchor.

He looked at Greg. "You've got to be shitting me."

Greg shrugged. "How did you not know. Come on buddy, you know you're the only one strong enough for the job."

"That's total bullshit, Greg." Brady hated it when Greg called him buddy.

"Aw, come on. Don't be sore. It's not that big a deal."

"Don't try your shit with me. You should've asked me."

Brady was now pissed and Greg knew it. When Greg took a step back, Brady knew he must be showing his *ugly* face, or so the brothers had labeled it. But Brady didn't care. He was pissed.

"Greg, you're the biggest pussy ever," Brady said. "You'd never do this yourself. You're always getting someone else to do the hard stuff and then you take all the credit." Brady said it loud enough for all to hear.

He could've punched Greg. He could've walked home. Only one thing kept Brady from walking out. He was the only one who could pull Dean up or hold him in place.

If anyone else tried to be anchor in this group, Dean could get killed. This band of student council misfits were doing this with or without his help.

Brady had to stay.

Michelle placed her hand on Brady's shoulder. "I'm here and I'll have your back," she said as she winked at him.

It made him wonder if she was getting lessons from Caleb.

Brady looked into Dean's eyes. "You don't have to do this."

"Come on Brady," Dean said, "it'll be a hoot, you and me. We will be legends of the class of 1976."

Brady half smiled. "Okay, but it's only because I don't want to hear about you getting killed. You don't want someone else being the anchor and leaving you dangling mid-air or dropping you in the middle of oncoming traffic." Brady looked directly at Greg as he said this.

Dean gave him the thumbs up. "Fucking right, let's do this already."

Brady then took off his Beavercreek jacket and shirt and handed them to Michelle. When he returned her wink, she blushed and turned bright red. She placed his jacket and shirt near the tracks.

With his shirt off it was plain for all to see why Greg had chosen Brady for the anchor. This wasn't the normal body of an eighteen-year-old boy. His lean and heavily muscled upper body was clearly visible as he had on a white wife beater T-shirt. To say his muscles were bulging would not be an understatement.

Bobby picked up Brady's jacket and shirt. "Why is this jacket so heavy?" Bobby asked.

"What are you doing?" Michelle asked.

"I was just moving these things away from the paint."

"Just put 'em down near the bushes." Michelle flashed an angry look at him.

"Okay, okay, just trying to keep from getting paint on them," Bobby said.

While this flurry of activity was going on, Brady became Dean's anchor.

Linda tied the rope around Brady's waist tightly, using a series of knots she learned from her Dad on the family's sailboat. Linda's fingers lingered too close to Brady's muscles as she tied the rope.

Michelle noticed. "I'll finish that, if you don't mind."

"Sure, no problem." Linda said. "He's all yours."

"You got that right." Michelle brushed Linda aside and took hold of the rope.

When she finished checking the knots, she leaned in and whispered in Brady's ear, half hugging him, "I'll be right here waiting for you. If anything happens, I will never leave you, never!"

"I know," Brady said as he looked into her eyes.

The anchor and the painter were now connected by fifteen feet of rope.

As Brady and Dean walked to the center of the bridge the group cheered loudly. "For the glory of the class, we will be remembered!" Greg shouted.

Dean looked at Brady and shook his head. "He really is an asshole, isn't he?"

"Yep," Brady replied.

Brady's mind was on one thing. Could Greg be lying about the train schedule?

Chapter Eight

ON THE BRIDGE

When they got to the center of the bridge, Brady looked at Dean. "Go easy and take your time. I won't let you fall."

Dean looked over the side of the bridge. "This is far scarier than I ever imagined."

"Don't be afraid, Dean. Look at me." Brady pointed at his eyes. "You can trust me."

Dean nodded, but he was trembling.

"Focus only on my face," Brady continued. "I won't let anything happen to you. Nothing. Look at me and tell me that you believe me."

Dean made eye contact with Brady and held it briefly. "I believe you. I have no fucking idea why, but I believe you!"

Dean seemed calmer until he climbed onto the lip of the panel and looked over. "Oh shit, this is way higher than I expected." He turned to Brady. "I can't do this."

"Yes, you can," Brady assured him. "Have faith in yourself and in me. I know you can do this."

"Well, you're the only one up here that fucking thinks that." Dean shouted back from the edge of the top lip. Fear was all over his face and his body shook.

"If you drop me, I'll be pissed." Dean was hyperventilating.

"No, you'll be dead."

"Nice." The start of a smile washed over Dean's face.

Linda yelled to Dean. "You're the man."

Brady shook his head. "She's as big an asshole as Greg. You know that, right?"

"Yeah, I know."

Brady looked back at the group cheering them on from the safety of the field. Everyone, that is, except Michelle. She was standing at the edge of the tracks with a worried look on her face.

Dean looked at Brady. "If this rope wasn't tied to you, I'd never be doing this."

Brady smiled. "You're the only reason I agreed to do this."

Michelle walked up carrying a five-gallon bucket of white paint with a rope tied to the bucket's handle.

"What are you doing here?" Brady asked.

"I took this job over from Bobby." She looked Brady straight in the eyes. "You didn't think I was going to let you have all the fun, did you?"

He knew exactly what she was up to and there was no amount of arguing with her that would change her mind. It was too late.

Bobby's job, now Michelle's, was to lower the paint bucket to Dean once he was over the edge and in position to paint.

Dean turned toward Michelle. "Don't hit me in the head with that bucket, okay?"

She smiled. "Don't worry about that. All you need to be concerned about is how fast Brady can pull you up when the cops come."

Brady and Dean looked at each other, no one had talked about the cops coming.

Dean started over the side, but paused and looked at Brady directly in the eyes. "Don't fucking drop me." And over the lip he went.

The rope tensed in Brady's hands. Dean wasn't as heavy as Brady had feared. Still, he wondered if he could pull Dean up fast enough if there was a need to.

Michelle lowered the bucket of paint over the lip and it bounced, hitting the panel hard enough to spill paint on Dean. This caused a rant of cussing to erupt from Dean. Paint covered his afro hairdo and plastered his face.

"Sorry, couldn't be helped." Michelle yelled down to Dean just barely able to suppress a giggling fit that was about to erupt out of her. Her control didn't last long. She burst out laughing uncontrollably upon seeing Dean's face.

Every time she looked down and Dean looked up, she howled with laughter. This caused everyone on the west side of the bridge to come see what was going on. The whole group had made their way onto the tracks and were now spread out along the bridge.

All were laughing and trying to direct Dean where to put the paint. That just pissed him off further. It was a full five minutes before he could wipe off the paint from his face enough to see the roller that was tied to his waist and start to paint.

This was taking way longer than Brady was comfortable with. He started to express doubts about the plan and that he wanted to pull Dean up.

It was then he heard what Linda asked Greg, "Does a train have one or two headlights?"

"That's not funny," Greg said.

"No, really. Look." She pointed to the west.

At that, all turned to look toward the west.

Bobby screamed, “TRAIN!”

“Train, train, fucking train!” Someone said.

It was a damn choir of people screaming, “TRAIN, TRAIN, TRAIN.”

Everyone on the bridge broke out into a run trying to get off the tracks.

“Let go of the bucket.” Brady yelled at Michelle. “Drop the paint and run . . . Michelle RUN.”

She hesitated looking back at Brady.

“DO IT NOW, RUN,” He yelled.

“What about you?” she yelled back.

“GO,” was all he said.

Michelle let go of the bucket’s rope and ran, hitting Dean in the head and spilling more paint on him, this time from head to toe.

Dean was cussing like a drill sergeant, he was now talking fluent ‘sailor’.

Brady could hear nothing but the sound of the train’s engines and wheels on the steel tracks and the repeated blast of its horn.

Dean wiggled like a fish on a hook. This jerking on the rope made it next to impossible for Brady to pull him up. The lip on the panel and the angle of the rope caused him to have to use all his strength to pull Dean up.

The train was near the bridge; its lights flooded the area. The horns were one long loud screaming of sound. The bridge trembled from the rippling vibrations from the oncoming mass of energy hurling toward the bridge at a high speed.

Everyone screamed for Brady and Dean to run, but he tuned out the sound.

The muscles in his arms were burning as he pulled with everything he had, causing the ropes to bite into his hands.

He'd made a promise and he was going to keep his word.

How could they run?

They couldn't.

He wouldn't leave Dean. Besides, he knew that these were not the type of knots that could be quickly undone. In a split second, Brady decided his plan.

When he'd pulled Dean up to the top lip of the bridge railing, Brady reached over and grabbed him. Brady half pulled and half threw Dean onto the twenty-four-inch lip of the top panel.

It was too late to run. The train was on the bridge, its horns continued to blare. The bridge trembled fiercely as the train placed its weight on it.

"The train is here." Brady yelled in Dean's ear. "Hold on tight and don't let go."

He jumped up onto the lip and laid down. He grabbed one of Dean's legs with one hand and the outer lip of the panel with his other. He barely made the transition from the track to the lip. Brady's mind told him the train was there with only a twenty-four-inch island of safety. Screaming voices, blaring horns, the terrifying sound of steel wheels on steel rails, amplified by the tall steel panels of the bridge all blended into one terror-filled roar of deafening noise.

With the train just inches away, sticking out a finger just an inch might cause it to be lopped off. The steel of the lip was freezing cold with the rushing of the air from the speeding train. The forward motion of the train created a vortex with the steel panels, that sucked them away from the ledge and toward the side of the train.

Dean wouldn't be able to hold on. Brady grabbed Dean's foot firmly and made the bond, then called for the light.

It happened in an instant. The light hovered over them as they lay on the edge. There was no sound, no sense of hot or cold and no sense of the train. Only a feeling of peace and safety. There was no fear. Time stood still as it always did when he called the light.

After almost ten minutes, the train passed. The light was gone; time and sound returned. The screaming of voices returned.

Chapter Nine

THE AFTERMATH

Michelle stood in the field with Greg, Linda, Bobby, and Sue in disbelief. She feared they would find the dead bodies of their classmates littered across the tracks after the train passed. Michelle was bawling, but at the same time angry and pissed off.

"It was Greg's fault," multiple voices said at once.

Linda gave Greg an ear full. "You fucking caused this. I told you Dean couldn't do it. You're a coward," she screamed. "You lied about there being no trains on Friday nights."

Michelle was now in Greg's face, pointing a finger at him. "You got your best friend killed, you asshole." Her other hand was buried in her purse. "You should have been the one up there."

Greg just stood with his head bent down staring at his feet as if he knew it was true. For once he had nothing to say.

Michelle saw over Greg's shoulder what appeared to be two figures coming toward them. Out of the darkness, walking slowly and still tied together, were the two people everyone thought had been killed.

Is this a dream? Michelle thought.

She was frozen where she stood.

Michelle could only yell out, "BRADY!"

Everyone turned to look. Michelle couldn't believe what she was seeing. What they were seeing wasn't possible. A look of astonishment and utter disbelief showed on her friend's faces.

Dean and Brady were alive and walking toward them. The group ran to the pair yelling and swearing. How the train had not killed them, Michelle didn't know.

Once they reached the pair, there was hugging and patting of backs. The relief she felt seeing the two alive was an adrenaline rush for Michelle and she was sure it was the same for all.

Dean let out a soft whimpering cry. He was having none of this celebration. "Get this fucking rope off me," he said staring at Linda.

Greg came over to him and started to speak but Dean cut him off. "You son-of-a-bitch, fuck you, this is all your fault. No trains, you said. FUCK YOU, you prick."

Dean started sobbing uncontrollably. Linda touched his face softly with her hand like a mother would to calm a frightened child. She put her arms around him unconcerned about the paint. "It's okay, I'm here, Dean. You're okay now."

Linda was taking the blame because everyone knew Dean had agreed to be the painter because of her. Michelle suspected Linda was ashamed for using his feeling for her to take advantage of him. Linda continued to talk softly to Dean as she untied the knots.

Once freed from the ropes, he fell to his knees, still sobbing, with his arms wrapped around his chest.

* * *

Brady had just gotten out of his ropes with Michelle's help, when he first heard the police siren. It snapped him back to what was happening. He looked at Michelle, Greg looked at Linda, Linda looked at poor Dean and Sue looked at Bobby.

"Oh, Lordy Jesus. Could this night get any worse?" Bobby said.

Brady knew what was *really* wrong with Dean. He knew what had terrified Dean. It was the bond he'd made by touching him when he called the light. Dean was traumatized, almost in a state of shock. He wouldn't understand what had happened, and was probably afraid of Brady being near him, probably fearing he would touch him again. Dean had not only seen the light, he'd felt the terrifying pull of the darkness.

The sound of the police car approaching snapped everyone out of the *you lived* moment. Greg yelled, "It's time to get out of here. Leave everything and run to the car. I'm not going to jail tonight."

Bobby turned to leave, but stopped. "Brady, is that your dog there?" He pointed at the dog standing at the base of the hill.

"Thanks, Bobby." Brady motioned for Hank to come to his side. No one asked how the dog got there or why it was there.

Brady could see the police car's flashing lights and knew running to the car would be a waste of time; he could see the police car was parked next to the Tuna Boat.

* * *

The police waited at Michelle's car. Officer Hickey stood, leaned up against the front of his patrol car. He was one of the two officers on duty that night. It was a small police department filled with rookies just starting their police careers.

The look on his face wasn't the usual smile he had when he worked the football games. He meant business. Normally, all the students knew him as a nice guy and easy to talk with. But tonight, he was pissed off.

When the students walked up to him, he addressed them. "We just had a radio call from a train conductor who passed over the bridge saying he thought a couple of kids had been hit and killed there. The poor man is in a fucking panic about it."

Hickey shined his flashlight up and down each person. He knew they had been painting the bridge since most of them had paint on them.

Then his light shown on the dog. "Whoa," he said as he jumped back two steps.

Hickey had seen Hank before but was scared shitless of the dog. Why, he had no idea. "Kid, keep a hold of your dog," Hickey said.

"Don't worry, he's a big teddy bear," Brady said.

Hickey just shook his head and said, "I'm sure he is. Just keep him away from me."

Hickey looked up at the bridge and asked, "Are there dead bodies spread from here to Xenia up there?"

Silence.

"Tell me the fucking truth." He used his drill sergeant's voice, causing everyone to move back a step.

"No, no, no. We're all okay," everyone said at once.

Again, he asked and again the answer was the same.

He then shined the light on Greg who was carrying the cooler with the beer in it.

"So much for leaving everything," Michelle said loud enough for Officer Hickey to hear. "You're such a dumbass, Greg."

Officer Hickey walked over to Greg and opened the cooler. "Been drinking, dumbass?" he asked.

"Why no," Greg said. "But we were going to celebrate painting the bridge afterwards. I won't lie. But the train came and changed our plans."

Officer Hickey just stared at him, debating on whether to lock that dumbass kid up. But then he remembered how Greg had caught him butt naked in the cruiser with Greg's neighbor. Guess this was Greg's *get out of jail free card* night.

"Most people paint the bridge, not each other," Hickey said, half smiling. "You sure no one's been drinking?"

Sue spoke up, "I can assure you, Officer Hickey, no beer has been opened or consumed." She flashed him her best student council president's smile.

Hickey looked at her. "You're as big an asshole as Greg, aren't you?" That wiped the smile right off her face.

Hickey shook his head and turned back to Greg. "That cooler is police property now. Put it in the backseat of the cruiser."

Hickey looked around at the students and no one objected. It was a fair price to pay for being underage and getting caught with beer.

Hickey had the girls talk with him without the boys to get the real story about what had happened. They assured him that no one had been killed, contrary to the reports from the train.

"Stop the bullshit," Hickey said. "No one could lay on the ledge of the bridge and live. The men on the train were one-hundred percent sure they had killed two people who were on the bridge as the train passed through."

He took the girls back up to the bridge to look around. Afterwards, Hickey tried to get the boys to go, but Dean was in no condition to do anything.

"There's no fucking way I'm ever going back up there," Dean yelled. "You can arrest me before I go back to that evil place. Fuck all of you." Dean sobbed.

Maybe it was the paint that Dean had from head to toe that caused Hickey to pity the kid. He almost burst out laughing just looking at Dean. The kid did have the balls to say "fuck you" to a cop. No matter the real reason, he allowed all the boys to stay at the car with Dean.

Once satisfied there were no bodies plastered all over the bridge or on the road below he said the girls could go. That was, after they all promised to clean up the mess and take it with them.

Once the girls finished gathering up the buckets, brushes and rope, they hurried down to get in the station wagon. All the boys were still standing outside of it waiting for them.

* * *

"Brady, you and Hank can get in front with me," Michelle said. "Let's get out of here."

"Yeah," Linda added, "let's get the hell out of here."

"Yeah," Greg said, "before Hickey changes his mind and takes all of us to jail."

"Come on." Everyone except Dean chimed in.

Dean was sitting in the back seat next to Linda staring blankly up at the bridge. He looked frightened.

Brady walked over to Michelle's window. "I have a few things to do here. I'll meet you at the game."

Michelle gave Brady a worried look.

"It's fine. Don't worry. Hank's here. Go on now or you'll miss the game. You must leave now."

Brady watched as the tail lights of the station wagon flashed, turning onto the Dayton-Xenia Road heading back to the game.

"Come on Hank," he said as he headed back up to the bridge.

CHAPTER TEN

THE RULES

Brady learned to call the light at the age of five when he first heard the voice of the Lady. A soft, sweet voice had called him into the field next to his house on that warm summer morning. From that moment on, he could summon the light at will. Brady would call out to it daily and spend hours in the field with his new-found teachers.

When he turned thirteen, everything changed. That was when his grandfather began to pass on all that he knew of the light. From that day forward there were rules to follow when the light was called. The prayer of vengeance had to be said at the very spot the light was called. It was the first of seven rules. Calling the light went from being a secret child's game to something much more. After the change, there was a price to be paid each time the light was called.

Brady walked out to the middle of the bridge, knelt, held his arms out with his palms up. Hank stood guard as Brady floated into the air looking toward the church to the east and the field to the west. Neither man nor Beast would be able to get near his charge as Brady recited the prayer aloud with a familiar cadence.

"Oh, Queen of the blessed Rosary, I beseech thee to grant me the vengeance for which I seek, to send the evil before me back into the darkness, from which it has come. For I am the sword and the shield, with my voice, I speak the authority that which you have bestowed upon me. For the serpent fears you above all others. Generation to generation we have served you, honoring a promise made on the hill at Calvary. I honor my forefathers' pledge to seek out the darkness. Make my hands fast and accurate. When I call out to you, I beg of you to heal those who have suffered at the hands of this evil. I freely accept the pain and will endure the suffering of the innocent, as my honor to you. Being one of the righteous, I rejoice when vengeance is done, for it is my reward."

When the prayer was said, Brady walked off the bridge thinking about how poor Dean would be changed forever. It wasn't Brady's fault. The light had to be called if Dean was to live. But, in doing so, Dean got a glimpse of, and felt, the darkness that it called. It was the essence of this pure evil that scared Dean to the core of his beliefs and had marked him.

This feeling was one Brady knew all too well.

Rule 2: There was a price for calling the light, he just didn't know when. But it would be coming soon, he felt. It was coming, it had been called.

Once the light was called, the darkness would follow like a moth to a flame. It was the price that had to be paid. Brady could feel the darkness and to what degree it had taken over the soul of a person, animal or object.

It was like trying to touch two magnets of opposite polarity. The resistance or push of the magnets is what Brady felt toward the darkness. He'd been told it was his warning.

There was less push in some situations and more in others. Sometimes it was so strong he could hardly be in the same room with a person who was corrupted by the darkness.

This darkness was what took over a person's soul. It could make a person feel anger and ill-will toward the one who called the light. It was all consuming in its evil. Even though the person affected had never met or crossed paths with the caller of the light. It was instant anger, rage and possession.

Rule 3: The darkness hunted the light. Brady could sense the push of the darkness before it arrived. Sometimes there were days or, at times, mere seconds of warning, but it was always sufficient to mount a defense against whatever the darkness had sent to do its bidding.

Rule 4: A bond must be attempted to heal the broken soul and deliver them from the darkness. The caller's hands must be placed on the forehead and the light called. There is no guarantee that the lost soul can be saved. Some are damaged beyond forgiveness.

Rule 5: If the bond fails and the soul is truly lost, it must be ended and sent back to the darkness from which it came.

Rule 6: Pain and injury inflected by a servant of the Beast upon an innocent victim can be healed by calling out to the light. The pain and suffering will be transferred to the caller of the light and all will be healed.

Rule 7: The darkness cannot enter the holy ground of the church. This was the only place where the light could be called and shielded from the darkness. This was the last and final rule that Brady learned when he turned thirteen. His lessons had ended and the task he was trained for began. Before that the light could be called anywhere without fear of the darkness coming. The protection of the light was all encompassing.

When he turned thirteen, there was no longer protection when he called the light.

The darkness would seek out its caller.

The student became the warrior.

Chapter Eleven

THE FIGHT

Brady and Hank walked down from the bridge, through the weeds, and back on to the road. "It's going to be a long way back to the high school to get the car," he said to Hank.

He thought about hitchhiking, but knew no one was going to pick up someone with white paint all over their clothes and a big black and brown dog that was more than a bit scary.

As they headed east on Dayton-Xenia road, a car slowed, and its lights flashed as it stopped just in front of them. The door opened and a man with a smiling face wearing a John Deere hat leaned out. "You two need a ride?"

It was Big John.

Brady smiled. "You couldn't have had better timing. Yes, thank you. We *do* need a ride. We're going to the high school. My car is there. But, we'd be happy to go as far as you're heading."

Big John looked at Brady and the white paint on his pants. "Let me guess, painting the bridge tonight, are we?"

"Yes, and it was a disaster." Brady decided it was best to leave out the details.

Big John got out and opened the trunk of his car. He took out an old tarp and placed it on the front seat for Brady to sit on.

He also handed Brady some rags to wipe off the excess paint he had all over him. "Here, use this and try to clean up some of the paint. You're a mess." Big John smiled.

Big John looked at Hank. "Damn smart dog. No paint on him!"

Hank walked over and leaned on him as Big John petted him. "Go on, get in." Big John said as he opened the back door and put the window down. Hank jumped in and placed his big ol' head out the window. It was his favorite thing to do during a car ride. It made Big John smile seeing that big head sticking out looking so happy.

Big John looked at Brady. "How are you doing over there?"

"It's about as good as it's going to get," Brady said as he finished cleaning up what he could of the paint, put the rags in a sack in the trunk, and closed the lid.

Brady climbed in the passenger front door, being careful not to get any remaining paint on anything except the tarp Big John had placed on the seat. "I really appreciate you giving us a lift. It's not a long way to walk, but I'm anxious to get back to check on my brothers."

"I understand. Don't worry about it Brady, it's my pleasure. I'm heading to the game myself. Now buckle up so we can get going or we're going to miss the last quarter of the game."

Big John's CB radio was alive with chatter.

Someone named Flatfoot wanted to know if BJ had found what he was looking for. Strike Eagle answered, saying BJ was busy and that he had.

"Sorry about all this noise, it's one of my hobbies."

Brady found all the CB radio code talk hard to follow, let alone understand.

Big John reached down to the controls. "Let me turn this down and I'll find something you'll like better."

He turned the radio to station WTUE and "Stairway to Heaven" was playing. "Hey, your class song's on. I'll turn it up."

The drive to the high school took about ten minutes with traffic. With the music up loud, there wasn't a lot of talking along the way. That was fine with Brady. He had a lot to think about.

When Big John pulled in to the parking lot, he saw Brady's car and drove over to it and stopped.

"Thanks for the ride Big John, you saved Hank and I a long walk back."

"No problem," Big John said. "If you need anything else, I'll be at the game."

Brady waved goodbye as Big John pulled way.

Brady gave Hank some water from the jug he kept in the car. "Stay here, Hank. I'll be back soon."

He patted Hank on the head, turned, and walked toward the front gate.

He never made it in.

There was a large group of people between Brady and the gate.

It hit him like a brick. The darkness was here.

He felt the *push* from multiple directions. It was so strong he knew there was something very wrong happening nearby. He didn't know who or where it was, but it was close and getting closer. He sensed it in the group of people in front of him.

Brady suddenly heard a familiar voice. It was his brother Caleb yelling, "Get the fuck off me."

He heard another brother, Liam, yell, "Oh, hell no you don't."

That's when he saw what was going on. A group of three men had surrounded his youngest brother Caleb. Brothers Zane and

Liam were there too, trying to stop the three men who half dragged and half pulled Caleb through the parking lot. These were grown men and the boys were no match for them.

Brady pushed through the crowd, like a hot knife through butter.

He was now engaged in the fight.

Blocking the blows from the men with his body, he pulled his brother out of harm's way. At that very moment, Hank appeared at his side barking, growling and showing his large white teeth.

The hair on the dog's back was standing up and he was postured to maul the men when released to do so.

"Hank stay, guard the boys," Brady yelled out to his dog.

The darkness was here now in force and ready to do battle.

This was the price to be paid for calling the light to save Dean. One of the rules. There was no turning back. These were not students, but men who reeked of weed and beer. Human bodies filled with the spirit of the Beast, to do the bidding of evil.

There was an anger about these three that was different than what he'd experienced before. This was personal somehow. The rage was directed at him.

Things happened quickly with no words being exchanged.

There was to be no warning of what Brady was about to do.

It must have looked like a blur to those watching in the crowd.

Brady's movements were fluid and lightning quick as he moved from one man to the other. The sound of fists hitting flesh, of bones breaking, it was a sickening sound of damage being done.

There was a raw beauty to this dance of carnage that played out in mere minutes. Bodies fell to the pavement. When Brady finished his dance of destruction, three twisted bodies were on the ground groaning in pain.

A girl in the crowd screamed for someone to get help.

A wooden handled buck hunting knife with blood gleaning on its steel blade was on the ground.

People were yelling and screaming all around the brothers.

This confusion was the cover Brady needed to finish what had to be done. He went from man to man, knelt, and placed his palm on their foreheads.

No one noticed what he was doing except Michelle. He caught her eye and saw that she had her hand buried deep into the cloth purse that hung from her side.

Those nearest to Brady, would be able to feel something strange in the air, and hear the electric static popping sound.

There were rules that had to be followed, but this time he couldn't follow them. These souls couldn't be saved. They were forever lost. He couldn't send these souls back to the darkness in front of all these people. He would find them later and finish what he was bound to do.

* * *

Michelle had felt the energy before and knew Brady was trying to save their souls.

It was at that exact moment she made eye contact with one of the men and recognized him as the driver of the car on the night she'd been taken, years before.

Michelle was filled with hatred. "Kill them," she shouted out to Brady.

* * *

Brady looked her way and shook his head no. He saw she had her hand in her purse and understood what she intended to do.

He knew what these three had done in the past to her.

To show Michelle he understood, he broke the fat man's left leg with a swift heel kick as he moved away from him. The sound was like a bat breaking. People in the crowd moaned at the sickening sound. A sophomore girl who was watching became sick and threw up.

From his mere touch, Brady knew of the darkness that dwelled in their souls. All their darkest secrets were shown to him. The evil they had done over the years, he knew it all.

This was the darkness he'd been told would be coming for him by the light. It was what he'd trained for. It was time. The lessons were over.

Brady never knew what happened to Mary Wright. But in that split second, he saw her ravaged body; he felt the full force of her tortured agony; he knew that she, too, was awaiting vengeance.

He would follow the rules, but at a time of his choosing.

These hunters of the darkness would become the hunted.

He would find them again. "Let's get out of here," Brady barked to his brothers and Michelle. "Now!"

Chapter Twelve

MICHELLE'S STORY

Michelle had just turned twelve and was a tomboy who loved horses. Her love for her horse consumed her free time. Riding him, feeding and washing her horse was what filled her life.

It was just like any other day. She was walking back from the stables where she boarded her beloved horse, Jackson. He was a brown quarter horse about eleven hands high. Michelle had gotten Jackson as a colt and had hand-raised him. Working at her dad's car repair shop all summer, she'd saved every penny to buy Jackson.

It was about a mile walk from her house to the barn. Every morning she would arrive to feed and water her horse. She arranged to catch the bus on school days at the barn. In the evening she would ride, brush Jackson and clean out his stall.

Seven days a week this had been her routine every year since she'd gotten her best friend.

On her way home, on a Tuesday night, a van stopped next to her.

The driver, who had a beard, asked her if she needed a ride.

"No thanks." She knew better than to get in a stranger's car. Too late, she learned he wasn't alone. While the driver had distracted her, a man came around the back of the van behind her. He hit her in the face with such force he knocked her to the ground. She was dazed and disoriented from the blow. She felt her limp body being pulled into the van. She heard the door slam and the motion of the van moving. Soon, her hearing faded and she blacked out.

* * *

Brady got a call from Michelle's frantic father. The Wolfe family lived about a block from where Brady and his family lived. Some nights Michelle would have some excuse to stop and talk with him. Still, she would always call her dad and tell him that she was at Brady's.

"Brady, this is Michelle's dad."

Brady could tell by the man's voice something was wrong. "Yes?" He waited.

"I guess she's not there, is she?" Hope mixed with fear.

"She was at the barn, but she should've been home by now. I went to the barn, but they said she'd already left. I searched everywhere between the barn and home. I know she always calls if she stops at your place, but I . . . I just had to check."

"I'm sorry, sir. The last time I saw her was when she got off the bus after school. I'll go look. I'll call as soon as I know something."

Brady wasted no time in leaving the house to help look for his friend. He called out for Hank and they walked to the barn.

Brady wondered if Michelle had taken the short cut to get there faster. It cut through a two-hundred-acre corn field that ran next to the road to the barn. When they were halfway there, Hank took off in a full-out run. “Hank stop,” Brady yelled, but the dog didn’t even turn his head. He was running toward an old abandoned farmhouse instead of the barn.

Brady yelled again for Hank to stop, but the dog refused, continuing to run at full speed, barking all the way. By the time Brady got to the farmhouse, Hank was nowhere to be seen. Brady saw a broken window on the first floor and assumed Hank had entered there.

Brady listened. Hank voiced a dangerous growling type of barking. Brady knew why when he sensed the lingering effects of the darkness. It had been there.

From the sound of the barking he could tell that Hank was on the second floor. Brady shoved and kicked the front door open and called for Hank.

“Come now, Hank,” he ordered.

For the first time ever, Hank didn’t obey his command.

The dog barked with such force it hurt Brady’s ears and shook the loose and broken panes of glass in the windows.

Brady made his way to the second floor and found Hank standing guard over a half-naked body crumpled on the floor. There was blood everywhere. There had been evil here this night that he didn’t want to think about.

Revenge was all that filled his mind, but he had to focus on his friend who was on the floor before him. He knelt and softly touched the blood-streaked cheek of his friend. She slowly opened her eyes and spoke.

“Brady, is that you?” Michelle whispered as a bloody foam came from her mouth and oozed down her chin.

Brady’s heart fell into his stomach. “Yes, yes, it’s me Michelle.” Tears fell from his eyes as he looked at his friend.

A rush of anger filled him.

He brushed the blood-matted hair out of her face and mouth. "Where are you hurt?"

"It all hurts, Brady. I can't breathe." She gasped for air. "They stabbed me. Help me Brady, I'm dying." Her voice was only a whisper. Her eyes showed hopelessness.

She wept.

Brady picked her up off the ground and pulled her in to his lap. He looked directly in her eyes as he held her. "It's going to be all right. I am here to help you. Do you believe me?

Michelle could only mouth an unsaid yes.

Sitting on the floor, he held her in his arms, bent his head to the ceiling and called out.

* * *

What Michelle heard next would stay with her forever.

Brady's voice was strong and clear, booming in the still of the room:

To me, to me. Bring it to me.
Bring me the pain and I will suffer it.
For I am the sword and the shield.
I beseech thee, oh Blessed Mother,
Queen of the Holy Light
Grant this request for which I pray.

He'd called the light.

The upper room filled with a blinding white light.

At that very moment, Michelle felt a sense of calmness. She felt no pain, there was no sound. It was as if time had stopped and she was not of this world.

There were people around her she thought, not real people but shapes of people. All talking but she couldn't understand what they were saying. They were laying their hands on her. They were talking with Brady and he was talking to them.

As her wounds healed, they reappeared in the same spots on Brady's body.

In an instant, everything changed back.

Michelle sat up.

She looked over her body and saw that all the wounds had healed.

She could breathe without effort.

She wanted to ask her friend how this could be.

The sight before her caused her to find her voice and scream out loud. Laying behind her was Brady, in a pool of his own blood, with her wounds, dying.

She turned around and dropped to her knees screaming, "What is happening?"

Brady said in a whisper, "It will be okay. I have taken the pain and wounds that you couldn't bear."

"What are you talking about?" she pleaded. "What is happening?" she cried.

"Just stay here with me for a while, Michelle," he asked.

Bloody foam coming from his lips.

"What if the men come back? Oh, Brady, what can I do to help you?" she begged.

"Don't worry, Hank won't let anyone hurt you again."

"Hank will protect us," he said. This prompted the dog to growl an ugly sound that she'd never heard before.

"Michelle, please look at me."

He made sure she looked before he continued. "Don't be afraid at what is about to happen."

"What do you mean? What's going to happen?" She looked around the room.

"Promise me, Michelle. It will all be fine. You must trust me. You trust me don't you?"

Michelle was shocked and confused by everything. "Yes," she whispered. "Yes, yes, I trust you, you know I trust you."

Brady struggled to stretch his arms out, with his palms up.

At that moment, he called the light a second time.

The energy was so strong around him that she was forced to move back.

Instantly, he rose in the air.

Michelle couldn't believe what her eyes were seeing.

Her friend who was bleeding and dying, had risen in the air.

As she watched spellbound at this amazing and beautiful sight, she saw the wounds on his body gradually heal. There was a sound like electric static popping in the air engulfing Brady's body. Approximately twenty minutes after it started, it was over. Brady was on the floor, not moving.

Hank walked over to Brady and started licking his face, nudging him to get up. Hank barked a soft bark for his master to get up. Brady slowly sat up.

"Good dog," he said as he patted Hank on the head.

Michelle walked to him and dropped to her knees, sobbing.

Brady took off his shirt for her to wear.

She slipped it on and hugged Brady.

During the walk home, Brady tried to explain what she'd seen and how it was possible. "Don't worry, Michelle, I will tell your mom and dad everything."

Michelle walked into the house through the front door and saw her mom.

She'd been sitting on a chair in the front room. At the sight of her daughter, she cried out her name and collapsed to the floor.

Michelle had forgotten about how she looked. Her blood-stained, ripped clothes and her blood-matted hair must have horrified her mom. She was wearing Brady's bloody shirt. Her father rushed into the room at hearing the scream, and pulled his daughter into a giant bear hug.

By the end of the evening Brady had explained everything to Michelle and her parents. Hands were held, and it was agreed no one could know the truth about what had happened that night except for Father Bob, the parish priest. The story they decided on to tell others was that some men had grabbed Michelle as she walked home from the barn and then let her go. The one detail the parents couldn't tell anyone, including the priest, was Brady's name.

As to the truth of what really happened, Michelle and her parents would become Brady's secret keepers.

On Brady's birthday that year, they gave him a special Beavercreek school jacket. Michelle left it on his door step wrapped in a box with no note early one morning before he'd come out for his run. Michelle knew that he'd always wanted one but didn't have the money to purchase it. She knew he would try to refuse it so this was the only way to make him keep it.

This was no ordinary school jacket. Michelle's dad had made some modifications to it with the help of her mother. He'd made formed fiberglass panels to be put in the forearms of the sleeves at his auto shop. He also put the panels into the chest of the jacket with a metal plate over the heart area. Michelle's mother then expertly sewed them into the inside of the jacket. It was their way of thanking him and helping to keep him safe.

They would be forever in debt to this hero boy who had saved their daughter. He'd touched their daughter with the hands of the angels.

Michelle and her parents had been allowed to see the light that night and with that had also felt the darkness lurking in the background.

It was this, that kept Michelle's parents up at night, ever fearful for their daughter's safety.

Michelle's father gave her a snub nose 38 detective special which she hid in a special pocket her mother had sewn into her cloth purse. She never left home without it.

Never again, would she be unable to protect herself.

Chapter Thirteen

HOKEY POKEY

By the time Beavercreek's finest had arrived on the scene in the parking lot at the football stadium, Brady and his brothers were gone. Only the three injured men and the onlookers remained.

After making sure the wounded were cared for, Officer Hickey and Officer Brown asked for witnesses to come forward. They were looking for anyone who saw everything from the start to the end of the fight. They wanted to know the names of everyone who were involved.

"Please come talk with us. Any information would be most helpful," Officer Hickey shouted out to the crowd.

A skinny kid stepped forward. "I saw it all, it was amazing."

The student gave the officers a detailed statement about how the three wounded men had started a fight with three students.

The witness pointed to one of the men lying on the ground. "The fat one with the beard over there pulled a knife on the student who came to help the other three students."

The fat man on the ground sat up. "I didn't have no knife. That fucking kid broke my leg. If I'd had a knife he wouldn't have gotten away."

Officer Hickey made a note of what was said and turned to the man on the ground. "I'll deal with you later."

The police officer went back to talking to the student. "So, there were *four* students?"

"Yes, the fight was between those three there . . ." He pointed at the three men on the ground. ". . . and four students."

He went on in great and glorious detail about how the fourth student did a "fucking blender" on them. "You should've seen it. It was like a fucking Bruce Lee movie except real. It was unbelievable the way one student beat the snot out of all three of those older guys at once."

A crowd of students gathered to hear the story. This animated tale of the ass-whipping of the year went on for almost ten minutes, with full sound effects and body motions. By now all three of the men who'd allegedly been knocked unconscious by the lone student were awake and asking for medical attention.

When Officer Hickey asked the names of the students involved, the witness stuttered to a stop. "I have no idea. Looked like some seniors, maybe. Never seen them before."

The student pointed at Hickey's feet. "Hey, you know you got white paint all over your boots?"

"Shit," Hickey said under his breath, as he looked down at the mess.

"Son, what's your name and don't give me some fake bullshit name either."

"Matt, Matt Beck," the witness said.

"You remember every detail of the fight, but you don't recognize the students involved?"

"Yes, sir." Matt's eyes were wide open as he moved away from Hickey.

Hickey took him roughly by his collar and placed him in the back seat of the patrol car. "Maybe you can remember the names of the students involved after sitting in here for a while." Officer Hickey slammed the door shut.

* * *

Matt knew what he had to do. He remembered how his new friend Brady had helped him when he'd been pelted by wet toilet paper in the boy's restroom. Now, Brady needed more time to get out of there and Matt was determined to give it to him. He jumped up to the front seat, glad there wasn't a cage between the front and back seats, and locked all the doors.

Seeing the keys in the ignition, he said, "Nice." Matt started the car and pressed on the gas pedal revving the big block V8 engine. To put the cherry on the sundae, he turned on the lights and siren.

"Oh, hell, yeah. Now we got a party," he yelled out.

Hickey came running back and was pounding on the windows. "You dumbass, you had better open this damn door now, you hear me? *Now*, I said."

Matt just smiled and mouthed at him, "I don't think so."

Matt's next trick was to turn off the siren and turn on the public-address system. "It's now time for an adult swim. All those under the age of eighteen must leave the water."

The students in the crowd roared in laughter. They went wild cheering him on. It was all the encouragement Matt needed.

He then started calling out the "Hokey Pokey", at which the students followed his instructions.

Hickey was pissed, but at this point, he almost broke into a smile.

After about five minutes Matt opened the door to the cheering crowd.

Hickey dragged him out of the cruiser by the collar of his jacket. "That was the funniest thing I've ever seen, kid," he whispered to Matt. "You're still getting arrested, but that was laugh-your-ass-off funny."

Matt took a bow and waved at his adoring fellow students.

As Hickey placed the handcuffs on him, all Matt could think of was Brady, and how they were now even.

The crowd had started chanting, "Matt, Matt, Matt." He bobbed his head to the beat of the chant.

* * *

With Matt securely in the back of the patrol car, Officers Hickey and Brown asked for more witnesses to make a statement. That turned out to be a waste of time. None of the students wanted to follow the Hokey Pokey routine.

Officer Hickey had about given up on finding another witness when a big man wearing a John Deere hat quietly approached him. He said he'd seen it all. His statement was just like Matt's down to the detail of not knowing who the students were, but since he was a bus driver, the officers believed him while they'd doubted the clown handcuffed in the back of the cruiser.

Big John added an additional detail. "There was a fourth man who tried to enter the fight with the students. I put the guy in a head lock and held on to him until it was over. When I let him go, he took off into the crowd. I wish now I'd held onto him until you got here. There was something wrong about that guy."

Big John nodded at Hickey. "The one thing I can tell you, those four are not from around here. Not with those thick West Virginia accents."

Hickey nodded back.

After Big John departed, Officer Hickey opened the trunk and took out a rag and wiped the paint off his shoes. "You ready Mr. 'Hokey Pokey'," he asked as he climbed into the car. "Time to go to the Pokey, Pokey and call your mom." Hickey laughed finally.

It had been one hell of a night.

CHAPTER FOURTEEN

RAY JOHNSON

Watching from his white Ford van in the parking lot, the anger Ray Johnson felt was uncontrollable. It was sheer rage. "What the fuck just happened?" he yelled out as he pounded the steering wheel. "Who the fuck was that kid who destroyed my crew tonight? How was it possible? There were three of them up against one high school kid."

He shook his head and kept talking aloud. "My guys will be in the hospital tonight, probably go to jail. Tonight, of all nights.

"Fuck me." He screamed.

They had made plans for tonight's party weeks ago. They had all followed the plan up to this point. So why did these assholes have to get into a fight?

He was pissed. This wasn't the first time his crew hadn't listened or followed his instructions. They'd once gone out hunting on their own while he was back in West Virginia, tending to the family farm. It was a disaster. They'd killed a girl and had almost been caught.

"It was like herding rabid dogs going after a bitch in heat," he muttered out loud.

His father never would have approved of these dumbasses. A drunk and two druggies, what could he expect?

Ray was a basement digging subcontractor by trade. He and his three-man crew would dig the basements at new construction sites all over Ohio, Kentucky, West Virginia and Tennessee.

Ray had started working with his father, Earl, at an early age. Ray's earliest memories were being at the job-site digging with his dad. His father homeschooled him as they traveled from state-to-state. Ray had never been to a real school. They don't teach you in school what you really need to learn, his dad would say to his son.

It was much easier to keep secrets, too, if you didn't go to a real school.

He was always with his father on a job site. He had no mother that he remembered or knew of. His father was mother, teacher and best friend.

Builders called on them frequently because they were considered the best basement digging teams in the four-state area. This gave them their choice of all the prime job sites.

The father and son were not only a money-making business team, they were also a hunting team.

The father taught his son everything he knew. He'd always told Ray, if anything ever happened to him, Ray must take care of the crew, all three of them the same day. His crew wouldn't be loyal to Ray and could no longer be trusted if anything happened to his dad. Don't hesitate, his dad had said. Just do it. Then get your own crew.

His dad called it cleaning up loose ends. "Son, you never leave loose ends." He'd said that on several occasions.

"You have a greater purpose. This is just the beginning of what you are meant to accomplish."

When the time came, Ray knew exactly what to do. The crew all lived in trailers spread out across the farm. They had been with his dad for as long as Ray could remember. The three-man crew hadn't only been part of the construction business, but were also his dad's hunting buddies.

This was the one secret that bound the crew together. Their financial and sexual needs were met through the relationship with his father.

Ray was twenty-one years old when his dad was killed in a head-on drunk-driving accident. He took care of the crew and dumped their bodies in the spot his dad had shown him. He called it "the door to what lies below". With that one act, all his dad's secrets went with them.

Now, as he sat in his van in the high school parking lot, his thoughts returned to the boy who'd beat up his crew. He watched as the boy walked toward the stadium. He looked wounded. Good. But, something was wrong. Strange things and ugly feelings overwhelmed him. The voice in his head talked to him.

"You need to hunt this one," the voice told him.

An odd excitement filled Ray's body.

"We've been looking for this one," the voice in his head said. It was the legacy from his father. He would now take over the role his father had.

It was the darkness that talked to him.

He would stalk this one. He would find out everything about him. He would need a plan.

He remembered his father's old friend at the high school. The school counselor would know who that kid was.

The counselor was the one who told them about the troubled girls and their secrets. The girls would confide in him during his counseling sessions and he would then share the information with his dad, then with Ray after his father died.

It made Ray smile to think about how the students were duped by the school counselor. The very person they trusted with their deepest darkest secrets was the one who would betray them.

His father had met Jennings in a bar called the Road Runner Lounge on Dayton-Xenia Road one Saturday night. Earl had plied him with whiskey and drugs to learn his deepest darkest secrets.

Jennings invited Earl to a party he was having the next Saturday night where there would be several of the girls he'd befriended for a private party. Once there, drugs and alcohol would be provided. The girls had no idea it was a trap.

Once drugged they were stripped naked, abused sexually and photographed. The Polaroid pictures and 8mm films would be used to blackmail them from ever talking. Jennings had done this for almost twenty years.

Earl had told his son, everyone had their price and the counselor and his friend's price was our ability to make a girl disappear if she couldn't be controlled.

Jennings helped the coverup by claiming that the missing girl talked about running away to California or Florida in their sessions together. Jennings never asked questions about what happened to the girls. He simply didn't care.

This was how Jennings and his teacher friend, Brooks, made extra pocket money, as they called it. They sold the pictures through coded ads placed in European newspapers using a P.O. Box address. That was how he made five times his teaching salary on the side and lived way beyond his means.

The hardcore pictures were a big seller to collectors in Europe. Their best customer was Wolfgang Gerhard, who lived in Austria. He paid in cash bundles sent through the mail.

The voice in Ray's head told him, "It would be the best hunt yet. Dad will be so proud. Finally, someone worthy of our talents."

He started the van. He needed his release soon. It would be a good night to dig.

He turned on the eight-track tape player, "There's a sign on the wall but she wants to be sure cause you know sometimes words have two meanings" was blaring through the speakers.

The music muffled the sound of the girl tied up in the special box in the back of the van. She'd been drugged earlier that day with horse tranquilizer and was now coming out of it. It was to be a dream of terror and the thought of it excited him even more.

Ray had learned to hunt and stalk from his father in the back woods of West Virginia. "Patterns of behavior" was what his dad said was most important. To find your game, you had to know where they would be when. You had to have a plan. Always follow the plan he would lecture his son.

While they did hunt deer, their preferred prey was teenage girls. Not in the woods but at the local high schools, teenage hangout and parties. From father to son this dark and twisted enjoyment was passed down.

These were the type of girls some might call party girls or stoners, the ones who were always in some sort of trouble at home or at school. Running with the wrong crowd is what would be said about them.

They would just turn up missing, and, often, no one cared.

Most were deemed runaways due to drugs or family problems. They were never heard from again. No one ever looked for them. No posters, yellow ribbons or pictures on milk cartons.

The hunt was far more important than the actual killing. How you get rid of the body was the key to not getting caught, Earl had taught his son.

Conversion vans were all the rage and this helped with the key part of their plan. Earl had designed a special "holding compartment" inside their van that they used at the work site. Covered in carpet it was made to look like a bench seat. It was there that the girls were placed. Once drugged, they could be kept unconscious for hours and no one would know.

The bodies were always buried in the basements of the houses on the construction sites. His father taught him to put them in the sweet spot, where the stairs landing came up from the basement to the first floor. It was dug five feet deeper than the rest of the basement and the body would be placed there, covered with lye and leveled with the rest of the basement. When the pea gravel and cement was poured it would always be protected by the stairs landing. It was the one spot where no one would think to look.

Earl was quite proud of his hiding place.

In almost thirty-eight years he'd never been found out. More than four-hundred girls were buried in the basements of homes spread out over four states. Never more than one girl taken per small town, per season. But there could be multiple girls buried in the same construction site.

That was the most important of the rules, his father had taught him. This night would be no different. He would place the girl in the sweet spot.

The party was about to begin and Ray was beyond excited.

Chapter Fifteen

AFTER THE FIGHT

Brady's three brothers tried to hold still as their girlfriends tended to them with ice and napkins they had gotten from the concession stand. The girls were still trembling and scared about what had happened. Unlike the brothers, the girls didn't see any humor in it. As the brothers joked about their latest adventure, they couldn't help but notice that their older brother was nowhere to be seen. They said nothing about his absence to the girls.

"How's the eye, Liam?" Caleb asked.

Liam had taken a fist to the right eye during the fight with the three older guys in the football parking lot. It was swollen and red, but the brothers knew from experience the bruise would turn blue then purple in a day or so. It'd be a lovely purple-green color by day six.

"It's okay." Liam winced. "How about you, are you hurt?"

"Naw, just a bloody lip," replied Caleb as he spat blood on the pavement. "Those guys were a bunch of fucking pussies. They hit like girls." He grinned.

The joking and tough talk was all show for the girls.

The old fuckers *did* hit like grown men and had hurt the brothers. Not that they would ever admit it to the girls. It was a matter of pride. If it wasn't for their oldest brother showing up, who knows what would have happened.

"Yeah, real fucktards," Zane chimed in. "Good thing Brady showed up. I would have destroyed the asshole with the beard who was holding you."

"Did you see what Brady did to that idiot who pulled out the knife?" Liam asked. "One second, the knife was in his hand and the next Brady was breaking the arm that held it."

"What happened to the knife?" Caleb wanted to know.

"No clue," Zane said. "It all happened so fast."

"I saw Officer Hickey pick it up," Liam said. "It had blood on it."

The brothers looked at each other with a look of worry but said nothing more. They knew someone had been stabbed, but the question was who.

Liam rubbed his swollen eye. "Do you think anyone will tell the cops it was us fighting with those guys?"

"Naw, once that kid got in the cop's car and started raising hell, that's all anyone will be talking about," Zane assured them. "No one is even thinking about us. I'll have to find out who that guy was so I can thank him properly for the distraction."

Caleb's girlfriend, Marybeth Kline, had gotten her dad out of the bleachers when the trouble started. He'd been sitting at the far end of the stands near the top, making it hard for her to find him. By the time they got back to the parking lot, the fight was over.

* * *

At six-feet-four-inches, Mr. Kline was a bad attitude, take-no-shit, muscled bricklayer. When he saw his daughter crying and screaming for his help, he came running, no questions asked. The crowd in the stands parted like wheat in a tornado. Someone was going to get 310 pounds of whoop-ass opened on them.

All his daughter had to do was point out the unlucky sons-a-bitches. Kline was coming and he was bringing the attitude of a pissed-off father with him. There was going to be hell to pay.

"You boys all right?" he asked, out of breath from the run to the parking lot. His face was bright red and angry. "What the hell happened?" he demanded, looking at the brothers leaning on the old Buick.

He turned to the girls. "Give me the truth. No bullshit. I'm going to rip off someone's head and shit down their necks."

He looked around. "Where are those men who were beating up you boys?" His face was red. "Men beating up boys, I'll show them, let them try that shit with a grown man."

"Point out those fuckers now, Marybeth," he demanded.

"Dad listen," she pleaded, "please listen to me just for one minute, please. You must calm down. Brady took care of them. Look over there," she pointed. "The police have them now. It's those men groaning on the pavement."

Marybeth, Julie and Angie then explained how they were all waiting near the ticket booth just outside of the gate as agreed for the ride home. All three couples were going to Marybeth's house where they were going to have a bonfire and hang out together.

"Dad, we were just talking and these three guys came up to Julie. Then that creepy guy over there..." Marybeth pointed to the one with the beard. "...put his arms around Julie and grabbed her boobs."

"Are you fucking kidding me?" Kline asked.

"The other two men started laughing when he did that," Marybeth said.

"That's when Liam clocked the asshole in the side of his face." She let loose of all the emotion that had built up inside her. Crying, she said, "The boys were just protecting us Dad, honest."

Kline looked over at the brothers and nodded his approval and added two thumbs up.

Marybeth continued. "It all exploded as the other two grabbed Caleb and started dragging him into the parking lot punching and kicking him." Marybeth had tears streaming down her face.

Angie was crying, too. "Mr. Kline, we don't even know these people. They aren't students, we've never seen them. Everyone was fighting and the boys were losing..." Her voice choked. "...until, until Brady and Hank showed up."

Julie told in graphic detail how Brady had "fucked these guys up" not realizing what she had said until it was already out of her mouth.

"Sorry for the language," she said, "but that's what he did. I was cheering him on, we all were. It was terrifying and beautiful at the same time."

Kline just shook his head at the look of satisfaction and anger on her face.

"Did that dog bite anyone? Mr. Kline asked.

Marybeth shook her head. "No, Brady had him guard all of us. Hank wouldn't let anyone in the crowd come close to us. He didn't even let the cops get near us to ask questions."

"So, where is Brady now?" Mr. Kline asked.

"We don't know Dad, I think he may be waiting for the cops to go."

"Was Brady hurt in the fight?" Kline asked.

"I asked him and he said he was fine," Liam said. "But he'd say that even if he wasn't fine. That's just his nature."

"Yeah," Zane said. "He must be okay. If Hank is here...," Zane pointed to the front seat where Hank had his big head sticking out the window, "...Brady can't be far away. Hank is his shadow, hell they even sleep together."

Caleb patted the big dogs head. "Good boy."

Mr. Kline looked at each of the six kids. "Marybeth, here are the keys. I'll meet you girls at the car. Boys, do you want me to take you home or are you still coming over to eat all the food the girls prepared for tonight?"

The brothers looked at each other and nodded in agreement. "If it's all right with you, we still want to come over," Caleb said.

"Okay, fine." Kline was glad.

After the boys and girls headed for the car, Mr. Kline went over to where the police and ambulance crew were tending to the three men.

When he got closer he could see that the men were not going to be causing any more trouble tonight. He listened to one of the medics as she called in the injuries to the hospital over the radio.

The one with long blond hair had a broken nose and one broken arm in a splint. The fat one with dark hair and a beard, had a broken right arm, broken ribs and a possible broken lower leg bone. The third man, the one with the flat top haircut, had four broken fingers on his right hand and a broken wrist on his left arm.

"Are you sure?" was the reply from the radio operator at the hospital.

"Yes, positive," the medic said.

Mr. Kline smiled for the first time since his daughter had called for help. Julie was right, that boy did fuck up those guys. In a way, it made him proud that those boys had come to the defense of the girls against such odds.

As he walked past the police car he nodded to Hickey, who tipped his hat back. Kline saw someone in the back of the squad car in hand cuffs. It wasn't Brady. Kline made a mental note to ask who Hickey had arrested and why. But, now it was time to get these boys out of here before anything else happened.

Kline's CB radio crackled to life as soon as he started the car.

Someone named BJ was saying the Brick has the puppies, followed by Strike Eagle asking if the Judge had seen the boy. Mr. Kline reached over and turned the CB radio off.

"How about I turn on the radio instead of listening to all that noise on my CB?"

"Good," Marybeth said.

As he drove home he knew the others would find what they were looking for. He'd have to wait until later to get the full story.

Chapter Sixteen

COLONEL HALL

Father Bob gestured toward the round table in the kitchen of the rectory and Father Anthony took a seat.

Father Bob placed two shot glasses and an unopened bottle of Laphroaig single malt whiskey on the table.

"Is it possible to interest you in shot of scotch whiskey?" he asked. "Or is that frowned on at the Vatican?"

"We do like our whiskey, but you'll never see me turn down a taste of liquid gold," Father Anthony answered with a smile. "And I can assure I am not alone in the sentiment."

"Then let me pour us as a glass before we tell the rest of our stories. I have the feeling this is going to be a long night." He poured two healthy measures of the whiskey and raised his glass in a silent toast.

"That is an excellent idea." Father Anthony moved his whiskey glass in closer to where he sat. "Nothing better than a fine whiskey and a good cigar to go along with an amazing story."

With that the older priest pulled out two Cuban cigars, cut the tips off with his silver cigar cutter, and passed one to Father Bob. He lit his, drew in a long puff and exhaled a stream of sweet-smelling blue-tinted smoke into the kitchen. Father Bob did as well, without coughing this time.

"Now, before I begin, I want to hear the parts of your story you said were not in your letters to the Vatican," Father Anthony said. "Please do not leave anything out for fear of me thinking ill of you. I need to see the complete picture because, somehow, I believe your story and mine are intertwined."

Father Bob cleared his throat and stared at the ashes glowing on his cigar. "It all started four-and-a-half years ago on a Saturday when I was hearing a confession. It was the last person of the day, after hearing confessions all afternoon. The parishioner asked if he could talk to me privately and I, of course, said okay.

"He and his wife had just lost a daughter. I had said the mass for them. It was quite sad and just about her whole high school class attended. She died much too young; it broke my heart seeing her at the viewing.

"His name was Colonel Hall, and he was an Air Force doctor at the base nearby. He seemed to be a quiet man. I didn't know him well. I would see him when he came to the church for mass on Sundays and on Thursday nights. We have a small group that prays the Rosary every week and he would join in.

"He said he had a story to tell me that I'd find hard to believe. I answered by telling him I was in the GOD business, so believing in the unbelievable was what I did. I also told him that whatever he told me would stay between the two of us.

"When his daughter, Cindy, was sick, in what turned out to be the last week of her life, his twelve-year-old son Randy had a friend over for the night. Randy had talked his friend into helping him dig a drainage line from the house's downspouts to the street. It was busy work the colonel had given Randy to keep his mind off his sister's illness. That evening, after the boys finished their task, Mrs. Hall cooked dinner and they invited Randy's friend to eat with them. He was a polite boy and well mannered.

"Randy had told his friend about Cindy and the boy had asked if he could talk to her. Colonel Hall had mixed feelings about it, but said yes, anyway. The boys were up there about twenty minutes and then came down. The colonel didn't think anything of it at the time. The boy and Randy came into the kitchen to see if they could get a pop. Randy's parents said yes and they sat at the table.

"Randy's friend warned Randy and his parents it might seem odd, but he wanted to know if they would join him in talking with Cindy.

"Colonel Hall said that caught them by surprise, and they didn't know what to say. The boy smiled assuredly and asked them to trust him.

"Something caused the colonel and his wife to stand. There was a feeling that made them feel the need to do what the boy asked. The three of them followed him to Cindy's room. When they opened the door, Cindy was sitting up in bed resting on pillows that had been placed behind her, smiling. She'd not sat up in weeks. Mrs. Hall started crying.

"The boy walked over to her bed and sat on the edge of it and took her hand. He asked Randy and his parents to sit on the bed, too.

"Colonel Hall said they did, still not knowing why they did as the boy instructed. The boy took the colonel's hand and he asked that they form a circle holding hands with Cindy. When the circle was made the boy called out something and everything changed. What Colonel Hall didn't realize at the time was that the boy had called the angels.

"The bond made between the five of them holding hands allowed the light to show what was and what will be, and it showed that what was to come need not be feared. It was beautiful and the angels said they would all be together again. They said Cindy was going to be just fine. But her time here was ending soon. The boy allowed them to say our goodbyes as a family.

"The colonel said he had no idea what the boy did, but they were not in this world. It was a world of light and angels. Not like the angels in pictures or the movies, but forms of beings that were pure energy. He said it was beautiful.

"Colonel Hall described it as being like time stood still. The angels spoke with them and they spoke with the angels. They told him Cindy would be without pain and not to worry because they would be with her. The colonel was told his parents, who had passed, were there, too.

"Colonel Hall broke down and softly cried after telling me this part of the story," said Father Bob. "After a while, he was able to continue the story.

"He said it seemed like days that they were there, but according to his watch, it couldn't have been more than fifteen minutes.

"The colonel said that as the boy left the room, he said that this was his gift to the Halls. When Colonel Hall asked what he meant by gift, the boy said Randy had described all that their family had been going through, and the boy knew he could ease the sadness for them.

"The boy went on to tell them they needed to know that there was still good in the world and that there were reasons to believe. He told them their faith wasn't misplaced and that She'd heard their prayers."

Father Anthony held up a hand. "He said *She*?"

"Yes. I asked about that. He was very clear about it." Father Bob said.

Father Bob continued telling what Colonel Hall told him.

"All the boy asked in return for this precious gift he'd given them was a promise that they would never tell his name to anyone. It was to be their secret and he had them make a holy vow.

"The colonel told me he'd seen men die on the battlefield, men he couldn't save, men suffering pain no person should ever suffer. He always wanted to believe that this would not be the end for his poor airmen, but he was never sure. Not until the experience with Randy's friend.

"The colonel told me to go to the grotto next Saturday night and wait. The boy will be there. When I asked how he knew that, he said the boy had told him that's where he would be if he ever needed him again.

"I asked Colonel Hall what I would see Saturday night. He said he'd see me Saturday night and I could tell him what I witnessed. After that, he said he'd tell me the rest of the story.

"As a priest, I had no idea what to do or say," Father Bob said. "This was more than a story. It would be a miracle on a scale equaling anything I have ever read. A boy, in my parish could call the angels, now that was something no priest is prepared for.

"And yet there was still more to the story to come," Father Bob told the older priest. "I had no choice but to go about my duties in the church that week and wait for the day to arrive.

"What I saw that evening, will be what you will see when the boy comes." Father Bob said.

"I prayed for guidance for twenty-four hours straight. I lit every candle in the church. I needed answers but none came."

"And what about the rest of this tale?" Father Anthony asked.

Father Bob poured himself another glass of whiskey and took a long puff on his cigar and let out a trail of blueish smoke. The kitchen was filled with a haze from the smoke of the cigars.

"It's your turn for an amazing story," Father Bob said, as he looked over his whiskey glass, "then I'll finish mine."

* * *

"Okay, that is fair," Father Anthony replied. "My story began sixty-two years ago in a small village in Italy. It was 1914, I was twenty-two and assigned my first parish in a small town in Sicily. I was to be taking over for a priest who was retiring. I was less than thrilled about being assigned to this small village church that was clearly quite poor. I had hoped to be assigned to the Vatican, to help set church policy and maybe be an adviser to the Pope. Lofty goals, I must admit, but it was my failings of youth. I had come from a well-to-do family and my mother had groomed me to be a priest from the time I could talk.

"But I was also raised to not question God or those who were his servants. I was determined to make the best of my assignment.

"The first order of business was to go out and meet the families who attended the church. The old priest, who had been there for the last thirty years, would be taking me around the village to meet everyone. I dreaded the task of meeting the parish members.

"The priest I was replacing was Father Vincenzo. He was retiring and looked forward to having a young priest with the energy he lacked to take over the church he loved and looked over. He knew I was not pleased to be there but he was sure I would change. In fact, he knew I would, he told me much later.

"We walked the winding dirt roads, passed fields of wheat, olive groves and fig trees. He stopped suddenly and looked me in the face as if he had made up his mind he could talk to me.

"He told me right there that the parish had a secret, one that no one outside of the parish knew of.

"I looked at him and asked what he was talking about. His response was that the secret was guarded and treated as one would a golden treasure.

"He had decided early on that he would never betray this secret to any of his superiors in Rome. His lips were sealed with a promise he had made to the Blessed Mother, the boy's parents and to his parish. He explained that he feared the Vatican would want to claim this as its own. This was what the church had a history of doing and he would have no part of it.

"I was truly puzzled by his story. The day was long and hot as we continued to walk. He said nothing more about the parish secret.

"Up and down the hilly terrain to each farm house we walked and talked. Most of the poor farmers grew olives, figs or vegetables. Many raised goats, pigs, sheep and a few had cattle. The largest farms were the ones with cows. What they had in common was that they were all poor and barely making ends meet. Even so, Father Vincenzo told me, these farmers shared amongst the parish so that no one went without.

"Everywhere we traveled, the priest was greeted as an old friend. Everyone loved him. Each family invited us in for food and wine. There were bowls of olives, fresh bread, fruit, dried meats and vegetable dishes.

"It was no wonder that Father Vincenzo was a bit on the rotund side. By mid-day I could eat and drink no more. As the miles wore on, my opinion about this place changed. These people were poor beyond belief, but they had the kind of faith and hope I had never seen.

"While we rested in an olive grove on the way back to the rectory, Father Vincenzo talked about another family he wanted me to meet. He explained that the family had a son, a very special boy. He told me not be surprised if they refused to meet me or let me into their home. He said if that happens, I should just listen and smile. He went on to say he would explain everything on our walk home.

"When we reached the last farm, the priest stopped and said, this is where the Ventura family lives. Then he looked me in the eye and said I should remember what he had told me about the boy.

"Father Vincenzo walked up the dirt path to the front of the small stone house and knocked on the wooden door. As with every house that day he was greeted warmly and asked inside.

"However, when they saw me standing behind him, everything changed.

"A look of worry appeared on the parents' faces, voices grew angry and hushed between Father Vincenzo and the parents.

"Father Vincenzo then turned to me and said he was going inside to sort things out with the parents. He pointed toward the road and told me to go stand out next to the road and wait for him.

"I sat on the field stone wall that surrounded the small house for about thirty-five minutes when I noticed a boy about seventeen years old with a large black and brown dog walking straight toward me. The boy stopped directly in front of me. He tipped his hat and said I must be the new priest. He went on to say he had heard about me all over the village, and that everyone liked me.

"He spoke softly as he introduced himself as Giovanni Ventura. He reached out his hand and shook mine slowly, holding it longer than was commonly done. As he did so, he looked directly at me, I felt a strange sense of calm and peacefulness come over me. My hand was hot when he finally let go.

"I had no idea what he had done and why it would affect me so greatly in the coming weeks. At the very moment he let go of my hand, the door to the house opened and Father Vincenzo appeared, shutting the door behind him. He looked over and saw the two of us and smiled.

"Father Vincenzo greeted Giovanni and said something about his meeting me, his replacement.

"Giovanni said he had met me, then said my feet looked too small to fill Father Vincenzo's shoes.

"Father Vincenzo laughed replying, his feet will grow larger with your help.

"I said nothing as it took me a minute to realize what had just been said and what was happening and by then the boy had left.

"As we walked back I asked Father Vincenzo if he knew the boy would not be at the house. He nodded as he said there was no other way for you to meet the boy. The parents would never have allowed it.

"Forgetting my manners, I asked him how he knew all this, especially what time the boy would come home. His reply was that he knew his parish and that a good priest knows his flock.

"But he did not leave it at that. He explained by telling me Giovanni trained every Saturday by running for miles through the country side. His routine was such that anyone in the village could tell you where the boy was at any time of the day. All

Father Vincenzo had to do was make sure we were there around 3:00 PM.

"He added that he also had to distract the parents. He knew that once they saw me that would be easy, hence the argument that he had to have, with no intention of winning.

"He told me he knew the boy would walk up to the house at some point while I was at the road. What he did not know was if the boy would talk with me. That would be entirely up to me. Father Vincenzo said the whole point of today's journey was to get everyone to tell Giovanni about the new priest who was replacing him and how nice I am.

"I had to agree the old priest's plan worked quite well.

"He smiled as he turned to finish our walk back to the church. As I walked with him, I sensed that the old priest was deciding if I could be trusted with what he was about to tell me. It was going to be a long quiet walk.

"When we finally reached the church, we went inside and he motioned me to sit down. He then asked what I felt when Giovanni shook my hand. The feelings I felt spilled out of my mouth before I realized I was talking. I told him calmness, happiness and joy. I had this need to express what had happened to someone but I did not realize it until I entered the church.

"I felt the Holy Spirit, I think, I said to the retiring priest.

"Father Vincenzo smiled and I knew he had made his decision. He announced that he wanted me to come to the chapel that night with him around eleven to see with my own eyes what secret treasure the parish guarded. He ended our conversation by saying he needed to rest and asked me to wake him at ten-thirty."

Father Anthony took a deep breath, remembering that day so long ago. He looked at Father Bob and saw by the expression on his face, he could hardly wait to hear more.

Father Anthony continued. "The clock could not move fast enough for me. I woke Father Vincenzo at the exact time instructed. We then went to the chapel. Once inside he led me behind the altar to a small room in the back. He said we would wait there until it was time. When I asked time for what, all he said was wait and see.

"At about eleven the front door of the church opened and I could see a boy with a dog walking to the far corner of the chapel. They walked over to a statue of the Blessed Virgin ringed with candles. The room glowed in the dark from the candles lit in Her honor. The boy, who I could now see clearly, was Giovanni. He knelt in front of the Blessed Virgin Statue, stretched out his arms, turned his palms up and bowed his head.

"At that very moment, he rose in the air. I gasped and fell to my knees."

"What!" said Father Bob. "You saw what I saw here? And, so long ago. How could that be? It's not possible."

"That is what I thought, when I read your letters. But before I go any farther with my story, Father Bob, it is your turn to finish telling me yours."

Chapter Seventeen

THE TRAINER

Randy was getting medical tape and other supplies in the trainer's room to take back to the stadium in case he needed to wrap a sprained ankle of one of the players. The room was small and smelled of old socks and damp towels.

He should've been playing, but had hurt his knee in a preseason game. Until it's healed, the coach said he was the team's medical trainer.

It sounded important, but it was a glorified title for a guy who taped up hurt players. Randy figured it was better than just sitting on the bench the whole game. As he was gathering supplies he wondered how it was going painting the bridge. Since he couldn't play in the game, he would've rather have been at the bridge with his friends than being a glorified water boy for the team.

Randy's dad had been a field doctor in the war and had encouraged Randy to take a class on what to do in medical emergencies. He'd said it would be good training for Randy and would look good on his high school transcripts since he planned to pursue a medical degree. Like his father he wanted a career in the Air Force.

Out of the corner of his eye he saw someone walk in. It was Brady.

"Hey Randy," Brady said with a slight grunt. "I've got a slight problem and I could use your help." Brady opened his jacket and showed Randy the red stain that was all over the front of his shirt. There was blood leaking down his arm and dripping from his hand to the floor.

"Holy shit. What happened?" Randy demanded.

Brady took off his shirt. "Got into a fight in the parking lot."

"Fuck me," Randy said. There was a deep puncture wound in Brady's upper shoulder that was oozing blood. With every breath Brady took, blood streamed from the wound.

Randy grabbed a chair. "Sit here and don't move," he instructed Brady. He grabbed a towel and pressed it on to the wound. "Hold this here and put pressure on it while I go get help."

"No." Brady said quietly. "Calm down, Randy. Everything is going to be okay. All I need for you to do is watch the door and make sure no one comes in."

Randy was far from calm. "Are you out of your mind? You're going to bleed out in a few minutes." Randy was in full panic mode now. He knew what was happening from his medical training and from talking with his dad. This was a kill wound; an artery had been nicked or severed.

Before Randy could say anything else, Brady slid out of the chair dropped to his knees. He held out his arms with his palms raised and called out to the light.

The room exploded in white light, the air was hopping with static popping and electricity.

Brady rose in the air.

At this sight Randy gasped and made the sign of the cross. He didn't understand what was happening but now understood why Brady had asked him to make sure no one came in.

He raced across the room and locked the door to the trainer's room. He watched in utter amazement. The wound on Brady's shoulder was healing right before his eyes. He tried to move closer, to touch him, but could not. It was as if an electrical field blocked him from getting closer.

He always knew Brady was different after the night with his sister, but he had no idea he was this kind of special. This must be why his dad and the men at the church were keeping such close ties on Brady.

This was a secret his dad had been made to swear never to tell his son, now he knew.

In less than five minutes it was over.

Randy could only stare at his friend kneeling there.

Brady looked up. "Can you get me a clean shirt and some sweat pants?"

Randy was way ahead of him and had put clothes in a pile on the chair. As Brady held up the shirt he read out loud, "Home of the Battling Beavers."

"Nice," he said, "how appropriate."

"Beggars shouldn't complain," Randy fired back, "it's all I could find."

Brady just smiled and put on the clean clothes. "It's fine. Thank you."

"How about we go back go back to my house," Randy suggested. "I'll get my mom to clean up the paint and blood on your clothes. Plus, she's made food expecting me to bring people, meaning you and Hank, home after the game. You know how she is."

* * *

Brady knew Randy's parents wouldn't ask any questions. It was part of their unspoken understanding that was the bond between all of them.

It was an old Air Force policy, everything was on a need-to-know basis, Colonel Hall would tell them. If Brady shared what was going on, that was great. If he didn't, that was okay also.

"Can you also fill me in on all the shit that happened this evening?" Randy asked. "Did you guys paint the bridge? Why do you have paint on you? Who in the hell did you get into a fight with and how did you get stabbed? The one night I leave you by yourself and things go to hell in a handbasket."

"I promise to tell you everything. I'll also try to explain what you just saw. Just give me some time. Before the night is done, all your questions will be answered."

"Okay," Randy said, "that's more than fair."

With Hank in the back seat of the Buick, his head hanging out the window, the boys pulled out of the parking lot. The Beavers had lost the game and the crowd of people leaving the game were backed up in the parking lot waiting their turn to leave.

As the car turned on to Dayton-Xenia Road, Randy picked out an eight-track tape and put it into the player. Grand Funk Railroads song "Train Kept A-Rollin" blared out of the car speakers as they headed to Randy's house.

Brady shook his head. "Really, of all the tapes in that glove box and you put this one on. By the end of the night it would be all too clear to Randy the irony of his song selection.

Chapter Eighteen

RAY WITHOUT HIS CREW

Ray pulled into the empty construction site and parked next to the basement they'd dug that morning. Everything had been prepared for tonight's special guest.

It was something he'd done dozens of times the past year. Always the same, he followed the rules set down by his father.

He opened the van's side door and turned up the eight-track tape player. Led Zeppelin filled the air. Ray had no worries about the noise, they were on a two-hundred-acre construction site and there was no one around to hear anything. He stripped off his clothes and folded them neatly, placing them on the van's carpeted floor.

He walked over to the box and unlocked it. Blinking up at him, trying to focus her eyes was Sally Jane, the girl that they had met at a party the week before. She was like all the others. Her mistake was sharing her secrets with the wrong school counselor.

This was a girl who wouldn't be missed for days or weeks. A stoner and chronic runaway. Ray's crew had talked her into skipping school that Friday morning to go partying with them. They had drugged her with a shot of horse tranquilizer after they'd gotten her drunk and high on weed. She never saw it coming.

For the crew, it was one of their favorite things to do, stripping the girls naked and tying them up to be placed in the box. Ray would not allow any sampling of the goods until it was time for the party. That was one of his father's rules.

Without his crew, things were different. Ray pulled her out of the box. Sally Jane was naked, with her mouth taped, hands and feet bound with wire. She smelled of urine since she'd peed all over herself in fear while in the box for so long. He pulled her out of the van by her arms, and dragged her to the edge of the basement hole. He forced her down on her knees and pushed her over the edge into the basement with a muffled scream.

His release wasn't in the physical act like his halfwit helpers. It was in the pain and suffering he would inflict on the girl. The longer it lasted, the more pleasure he got.

It was all about the screaming and terror each girl expressed. If they begged, it was even better for him. Oh, how he loved it when they begged.

The darkness overwhelmed Ray as he set about his slaughter.

Her screaming only heightened his enjoyment as he pealed the skin off her left breast with his red-hot knife. It sizzled and a puff of smoke rose when it touched her milk-white skin. He held up a small piece of flesh saying, "body of Christ" and laughed out loud as he placed it in his mouth and swallowed.

This wasn't something that would be over quickly. Ray was in no hurry for Sally Jane's life to end this night. It wasn't long before she was begging him to kill her. Poor Sally Jane's little heart could take no more of the punishment that was being brought upon her body and she died before Ray was finished. That pissed him off.

"I'm not finished yet my sweet Sally Jane," he yelled out into the night. In an act of rage, he leaned down and slit her throat from ear to ear, almost severing her head off her neck. He dragged her by her right foot over to the corner of the basement wall where the landing of the stairs would be. He threw her in the hole and climbed up the ladder.

Using the excavator that was at the site, her body was covered in less than fifteen minutes. He scraped the whole floor of the basement leaving no sign of the evil that had taken place there.

The eight-track was playing "Stairway to Heaven" as he finished putting back on his clothes. He started the van and pulled out of the job site, without looking back.

There was one thought on his mind, as he drove back to the trailer, going to the hospital to get his crew.

Chapter Nineteen

SECRETS REVEALED

Brady pulled in the driveway at Randy's house and shut off the engine. He lived in a tri-level house in a new subdivision called Spicer Heights Estates. The house was at the far end of a quiet, tree-lined street. Their neighbors were mostly current or former Air Force and civilian employees of nearby Wright-Patterson Air Force Base.

"I love coming over to your house," Brady said as he got out of the car with Hank. "Coming here at night always makes me smile. Your mom has every light in the house on, plus all the outside lights."

Randy laughed. "Yeah. Dad says you could probably spot the damn house from space."

His laughter subsided. "Since my sister passed, Mom does this every time I'm out. It's her way of showing me the way home in the darkness of night."

Hank jumped out of the back seat and was already barking at the front door announcing their arrival.

"Looks like he's ready for his dinner and treats from Mom," Randy said.

Randy's mother, Becky, loved the big dog. But, it hadn't always been that way. Hank could be very intimidating when you met him for the first time. The first time she met Hank, she was terrified of the black and brown dog. Later, she told Brady she'd never seen such a well-mannered dog, one that would follow any command given to it.

The dog had won her over with his gentle nature. She confessed to Brady how she'd always wanted a dog as a child but, since her father was an Air force general causing them to move frequently, it wasn't possible. It'd been the same since she'd married Randy's father. Every couple of years he'd get a new assignment and they'd move to a new base in a new town.

Hank became the dog she never had.

"Hank," Brady commanded the first time Randy's mother met the dog, "whatever Mrs. Hall asks you to do I want you to do it."

Brady explained that Hank would only listen to his commands unless told otherwise. He would not eat or drink without his command. Mrs. Hall and Colonel Hall found this amazing and a little hard to believe.

"Ask him to do a trick," Brady said to Mrs. Hall.

"Any trick?"

"Yes, any trick."

For the next fifteen minutes, she asked the dog to sit, stay, come, lay down, bark, growl, smile, shake, fetch an item and the dog obeyed.

Mrs. Hall laughed out loud with the delight of a child.

When Colonel Hall asked Hank to sit, shake or come, the Dog did nothing.

Mrs. Hall giggled with joy at this. Colonel Hall was amazed.

From that day on, Mrs. Hall kept a cabinet full of treats for Hank and spoiled him as if he were a favorite child.

Colonel Hall didn't know Hank had been told to follow Mrs. Hall's commands only. It delighted her so that only she could ask the dog something and he would do it. She wanted to keep that special privilege all to herself.

Brady smiled and agreed to their little secret.

As soon as Randy opened the door, Hank rushed past them barking as if looking for Mrs. Hall.

"You know," said Randy, laughing, "Mother likes that damn dog better than she likes me. And, Dad threatened to turn my room into a dog room for Hank when I go off to college."

"Boys, I didn't expect you back so soon after the game," Randy's mother said.

She nodded at the bundle of clothes. "Does that need washed?"

Randy looked at Brady.

"Come on, hand them over," she said. Instinctively she reached out taking them from Brady.

"By the way, you're never going to get a girlfriend dressing like that." She winked at Brady about his mismatched outfit.

"You two go sit in the kitchen. I'll wash and dry these in no time. I've got snacks and cold pop in the fridge. Go eat and I'll be back shortly."

That was one of the truly great things about Mrs. Hall, there was always something special for the boys to eat and lots of it.

"For a boy to grow into a man," she often said, "he needs to eat like one."

* * *

In the laundry room, Becky undid the bundle of clothes and gasped. Her knees weakened. She leaned on the washing machine for support. She was taken aback by what she saw. It wasn't the paint but the wet blood soaked on the T-shirt and pants that took her breath away.

On the T-shirt, there was a jagged rip in the shoulder she knew instantly was from some sort of stab wound. She put the pants, socks, and shirt into the washer. The jacket, she set about cleaning with a brush and a rag to get off the paint.

Why there was white paint on his Beavercreek black and orange jacket, was beyond her wildest imagination. As she cleaned the jacked she noticed something that she'd never noticed before when Brady wore it. There were what appeared to be some sort of metal or plastic panels that had been sewed in the arms and chest of the jacket.

She found a hole in his jacket just above the right chest panel. She took the T-shirt out of the washer and laid it on the jacket and the holes matched up. There was blood on the black fabric she'd not noticed until then.

She decided she needed to get a hold of her husband right away. She opened the door from the laundry room that led into the garage. She opened the garage door and started her car and turned on the CB radio.

"Strike Eagle, this is Mother Hen, you must come back to base. Strike Eagle we have an issue, come back at me. The boy is here and there's a story that needs told. Strike Eagle, do you copy?"

"Mother Hen, Strike Eagle here, already on it. Will be home shortly. I'll fill you in then. Strike Eagle out."

After she headed back into the house she heard a girl crying and sounding agitated. She walked toward the sound and found the familiar face of Michelle Wolfe in the kitchen. She'd been to the house many times with the boys and Mrs. Hall liked her.

Michelle was in a heated conversation with Brady, but she quieted down when she saw Mrs. Hall. "Oh, hello, Mrs. Hall," Michelle said, unable to hide her angst.

"Is everything all right, Michelle?" Mrs. Hall asked.

"Everything's fine." Brady answered for Michelle. "We just had a small problem at the game tonight."

"From the looks of your clothes, I would say *small* is putting it lightly," Mrs. Hall said. "Colonel Hall would say it's a damn understatement of events." She tried to lighten the mood and failed miserably.

"Everyone, I've made all of Randy and Brady's favorite snacks and there are cold drinks in the fridge. Get some food in you and you'll feel better. I'm sure Colonel Hall will be home shortly and I'm certain he can help sort out whatever is going on."

The three young people looked at each other as if they knew the conversation was over until Randy's dad got there.

Michelle shook her head at Brady, doing all she could to control her emotions and sat on a bar stool at the kitchen counter.

The boys followed her lead.

Mrs. Hall placed food and drink in front of them and in her best military mom voice, she said, "Chow is served. EAT, and that's an order."

She put the plates down in front of them knowing it was going to be a long night. She walked out of the room and called the Wolfe's house to let them know that Michelle was there with the boys so that they would not go into a panic if she was supposed to be home.

Colonel Hall walked in the front door just as Mrs. Hall completed the call to the Wolfe's. "Where are the boys?"

"They're in the kitchen. Michelle Wolfe is here, too."

He looked at her, confused.

"I know," she said. "I called her parents. Now tell me what happened tonight." She spoke softly, but forcefully.

"Come into the kitchen with me. I'll tell you what I know. I think I'm going to need you there," Colonel Hall said.

They walked in together. He hugged Randy and then greeted Brady and Michelle.

He got a plate of food and took a seat. He ate everything on his plate and only made small talk with Randy and his friends.

Mrs. Hall had seen this slow dance dozens of times over the years. It was her husband's way of comforting airmen who had been in a bad situation. Only when he was finished eating would the real discussion start.

He got up from the counter and placed his dish in the sink. He then walked over to the fridge and got out a six pack of beer.

He opened five of them and handed them out.

"I think we're going to need these to tell the story of what happened tonight. I want to know everything, and don't leave out a word. The truth is what I need to hear.

With that he turned to Michelle and said, to her relief, "I need to hear your story first."

With that Michelle started sobbing and everything from painting the bridge, the train, to the fight tumbled out of her in rapid detail. She even shared her secret.

Her rage at seeing the men who had raped, stabbed and left her for dead was uncontrollable. Her hands moved over her body pointing out where there were once wounds.

Her hands shook.

She told how she screamed for Brady to kill them at the fight. She wanted justice to be done there, at that moment, for all to see. She said she always carried a gun and had almost killed them all herself, right there in the parking lot. She touched her purse as she talked about her gun. Her boney knuckled fists were clenched bare white, in front of her. She was shaking with rage.

When Michelle finished, Mrs. Hall had her arms around her, crying with her as she stroked her hair. Colonel Hall had a single tear that streaked his cheek, he was angered beyond anything that Mrs. Hall had ever seen.

"I had no idea," was all Colonel Hall managed to say.

Michelle was whimpering and seemed spent of emotion.

Colonel Hall looked at his son and said, "Now, your story."

Randy told him everything that had happened from the moment when Brady came to him in the locker room. He didn't leave out a word.

Mrs. Hall almost fell to her knees when Randy told of Brady calling the light and healing himself.

Michelle looked at Brady sobbing, "I didn't know you'd been hurt. You were bleeding," she sobbed again. "I would've helped you. Why . . . why didn't you tell me. I would have helped you," she pleaded. "I would have helped you," she sobbed. "I should have killed them, I would have if I'd known." Her lips quivered.

At that moment, Mrs. Hall knew, Michelle was in love with her hero.

"Why is this happening again?" Michelle said repeatedly.

* * *

"Michelle, I'm fine, please stop crying. I'm okay. You're going to make me cry, too, if you don't stop. That's why I didn't tell you. Don't you understand?"

Michelle just looked at him and nodded her head.

Brady looked at Colonel Hall. "It's all true what they've said. But there's far more going on and I'm not quite sure how it's all tied together yet."

"Tied together? What are you talking about?" Colonel Hall asked.

"This is all part of something very dark and ugly. The darkness was at the game tonight." Brady paused. "Please don't ask me for details since I'm just not sure. When I have it figured out, I promise I'll explain it all to you."

Colonel Hall walked over to Brady and placed his hand in Brady's. "Please." His intentions were clear, he wanted to see it all.

Brady called the light at that very moment. It lasted for just a few minutes and then it was over. Still, the darkness would know. Brady wasn't concerned. Not now. Now, he was the hunter and not the hunted. The colonel needed to see the truth of what they were facing.

Brady could see Colonel Hall was flushed and sickened by what he'd been shown. Brady kept an eye on him as he walked over to the sink and threw up the plate of food he'd just eaten.

Colonel Hall rinsed the sick out of the sink before he turned to look at Brady. "I've been through wars and I've never experienced anything so evil. Find these bastards. Find them and we will kill them all."

There was a shocked look on Mrs. Hall's and Randy's faces. It was if they were afraid of the rage in Colonel Hall's voice, and

Brady concluded Randy and his mother had never seen that side of Colonel Hall, a side of him only his men had seen in war.

Michelle was no longer crying. She had a look of rage and revenge on her face that no one saw but Brady.

"I must go," Brady said. "I still have things to do tonight."

They all understood and didn't protest.

"Randy and I will see that Michelle gets home safely," Colonel Hall said.

"Thanks," Brady said. "That's one less thing to worry about."

When Brady got to the front door to leave, Mrs. Hall handed him his Beavercreek High School jacket. "I'll have the rest of the clothes ready tomorrow."

Brady put on the jacket. "Thank you, ma'am."

"You be careful," she said, hugging him longer than normal. "Promise you'll call us if you need anything."

Brady nodded.

She looked at Hank. "You bite anyone who tries to hurt Brady."

Hank barked as if to say okay. It made her halfway smile.

Michelle threw her arms around Brady and hugged him. "I'll always have your back." She kissed him on his cheek.

"I know, Michelle. The same for me."

Mrs. Hall turned and walked away. Brady noticed she had started to cry.

Brady was heading to church. He needed answers to what had happened tonight. Things had changed. Never had the push been so strong and with so many lost souls of the darkness.

Had the rules changed?

What was this *evil* that had found him?

Chapter Twenty

FATHER BOB CONTINUES

"Something happened to a young girl a few years back," Father Bob said. "She'd been abducted by a group of men and later found in a farm house reportedly roughed up but basically unharmed.

"Her parents, Charlie and Ann Wolfe, were members of the parish along with their only child Michelle. Upon hearing the terrible news on TV, I went to visit the family.

"When I talked with them, the girl seemed to be fine by all appearances. But there was something strange and out of the ordinary about her. After a short time talking, the girl went upstairs to rest and I continued talking with her parents.

"We went into the kitchen for coffee and for what I assumed was conversation that they didn't want their daughter to hear. Something was odd but I couldn't understand what it was at that point. Clearly, the parents weren't telling me everything. I could tell they wanted to, but just couldn't seem to talk about what was bothering them.

"I asked them if we could pray together, hoping that might help. It did. Before I could start praying, Charlie confessed that they hadn't been completely honest with me. When I asked what he meant, he said they'd been bound to keep a secret.

"Charlie looked at his wife and they nodded in silent agreement. He said they would tell me what they could without violating their vow of secrecy.

"He began by saying they had seen and experienced a miracle last night.

"I was startled, and wasn't sure I'd heard him correctly. I asked if he'd said *miracle*, and he said yes.

"Ann got up and left the room without saying a word causing me to wonder why. She returned in a matter of seconds carrying a box. She handed it to me, saying I should look inside.

"There was an odor of earthy dampness and the sickening smell of dried blood coming out of the box. It overwhelmed my senses. I almost gagged, I felt bile rise in my throat.

"When I asked what was in the box, she said the box contained the clothes Michelle had on when she got home last night.

"Naturally, I was confused since Michelle hadn't appeared to be harmed when I talked with her and the bloody clothes didn't match what had been reported on the news.

"I asked them how that could be since she didn't appear to be hurt when I talked to her.

"Ann said what I saw wasn't how Michelle was found by the boy in the farm house. Michelle said she'd been stabbed repeatedly and was dying when she was found. Ann's voice trembled.

"Charlie wrapped an arm around his wife and added, Michelle's clothes tell the truth of what happened at the farm house. Look with your own eyes, he told me. Touch them with your own hands.

"I hesitated, but realized it was important to these parents who'd experienced such tragedy. I did what was asked. I pulled out a ripped shirt, jeans with holes in them, torn underpants and socks. All were blood soaked. I was sure I was going to be sick, but I managed to continue to examine the contents of the box until I had seen each item."

Father Bob paused and took a deep breath. "Pardon me. The memory is painful."

"I understand," Father Anthony said. "Take your time."

"I was confused when I found a second pair of bigger jeans and a shirt, both covered with blood. Two people? How could this be, I asked them. I had just talked with Michelle and she was fine. All this blood . . .

"Ann interrupted me, and said her daughter was fine . . . *now*.

"Charlie took the box and said they were going to tell me the truth about what happened, but they were going to leave out one detail, one they can never tell me. If I agreed, he said I would hear something that only a priest could believe or would believe.

"Of course, I agreed to their terms. I was mystified and intrigued with the story I heard, to say nothing of the soiled clothes before me.

"Charlie said a boy, one of Michelle's friends, had found their daughter that night. She'd been raped, stabbed and left for dead, dying alone in that abandoned farm house. The boy had knelt, cradling our daughter in his arms and called upon the angels to heal her. I sat there listening in shock.

"They then said that their daughter had told them in doing so the boy took on her pain and suffering. He took her actual wounds. The boy was covered in blood and had stab wounds. The wounds that were once on her body were on his. He became the one dying.

"Once she was healed, she sat up and heard the boy call out again. When he did, the room filled with light and he rose into the air, floating. As she watched, his wounds healed before her.

"Michelle had told them the boy *called the light*.

"How could this be, I asked them, not believing a word of what I had just heard. What do you mean, he *called the light*, I asked? I had heard some crazy things in confession but this was off the charts of my experiences.

"Angels, he called the angels, was their answer to me.

"They went on to describe how this boy who found her had walked her home. Charlie then described what happened next. The boy walked in behind Michelle, he told me. He didn't see the boy at first. Charlie went on to say, Ann was waking, half sitting, half laying on the floor. Michelle was covered in blood, Charlie said, as was the boy, who he'd yet to recognize as Michelle's friend.

"Charlie continued, Michelle was crying and trying to assure me that she was fine, but his mind couldn't focus on anything but the bloody clothes she had on. Only when he saw this big dog standing next to the boy did his head start to clear. Something about that dog was reassuring, Charlie said.

"The boy told Ann and Charlie that everything was all right. Before Charlie could say anything, the boy reached out and took his hand, and then reached out and took his wife's hand. Michelle then finished the circle by holding her father's and her mother's hands.

"Charlie said it was as if the world had quit turning. He wasn't in his house, but he didn't know where he was. That was when the boy talked about the angels. Ann and Charlie were shown everything that had happened that night, but it didn't anger them. But, it let them understand what the darkness had done to their daughter. He saw what he thought were angels. The angels talked to them. The angels were so unlike the ones you see in the pictures. The angels comforted them. It was as if time had stopped. They felt calm, safe and didn't want to leave that place where they had been taken.

"Charlie said that when the boy released his hand, Charlie's sense of the world all around him returned. His hands were hot to the touch. He said again that everything would be all right.

"Charlie told me he believed without question. He felt a deep faith like he'd never felt in all his life. The only thing the boy asked in return for saving our daughter was that we keep his identity secret."

Father Anthony smiled and nodded.

"I didn't know what to believe," Father Bob said. "It was the most amazing and scary story I had ever listened to.

"The blood on the clothes didn't lie. I felt like St. Anthony who had to touch our Lord to believe. Was this a true miracle? Was my faith being tested? If it was a test I surely passed.

"Not until my talk with Colonel Hall did I make the connection and truly believe both the stories.

"I had a boy in the church who could heal the dying and call the angels. My prayers were nonstop for help and guidance. It was then that it came over me to do what most would think crazy. I began writing the letters to the Vatican addressed to *he who believes in miracles.*"

"Letters that were delivered to me," Father Anthony said.

Father Bob nodded. "It was also the time when I put together a group of the faithful to keep an eye on our gift from the angels."

Chapter Twenty-One

FATHER ANTHONY CONTINUES

Father Anthony offered the younger priest another cigar. "One more of these and my story should be done."

I do need another glass of that wonderful Scotch. Maybe a wee bit less this time. Will you join me?"

Father Anthony pushed his empty glass toward Father Bob. "Certainly." He clipped off the tip of his cigar and lit it with a wooden match. He took a long draw and let out a cloud of blue smoke. He looked at the foot of the cigar to see if it was burning evenly and blew on it a couple of times.

Father Bob filled his guest's glass and then his own. "Now, let's see, you were telling me you saw the same boy and dog many years ago. What happened next?"

"Ah, yes. Well, it was not the *same* boy, but they did look a lot alike. Right? The dogs, too."

Father Bob nodded and took a sip of whiskey.

Father Anthony checked his ash once more. "Now, let me tell you the rest of this amazing story.

"Father Vincenzo said nothing to me the whole time we watched the boy. His silence was what told the story. What I saw challenged everything I believed and had been taught. It made me questioned everything I had experienced up to that point in my life.

"Time seemed to stand still, but according to my watch, it was all over in about twenty minutes.

"The boy and the dog got up and left as quietly as they had entered. As the door to the church clanged shut Father Vincenzo motioned for me to sit next to him on the pew.

"He told me I must never tell anyone outside of the village what I had seen. He asked me to swear to keep the secret. I agreed and swore to the Lord, our Father himself, that I would keep the secret. I made the sign of the cross to seal my pledge.

"The boy's parents had told Father Vincenzo what I saw had been going on since the boy was five years old. It was a secret only his parents knew. The parents were afraid that, if the church officials heard of it, their son would be taken away and they would never see him again. They were also afraid of what others would say about the boy or might do to him."

Father Anthony paused and looked at Father Bob. "Vincenzo said everything changed on a Sunday in the month of June, about seven years before."

"What happened?" Father Bob asked.

"As everyone was leaving church there was a scream in the crowd on the stone steps outside the church. Vincenzo heard the commotion and ran to where the people were standing and shouting.

"Joseph Franchina was bleeding on the steps. He was twenty-two years old and lived on a farm on the outskirts of the village. He was a handsome boy who had fallen in love with the wrong girl. This girl was above his lower-class farmer status.

"Father Vincenzo said the girl was from a family who had big plans for her, plans that did not include a peasant farm boy. Her family was one that ruled with a Black Hand. They were forbidden from seeing each other by her parents, but as love would have it, they continued to get together secretly.

"This was the kind of disrespect that could get you killed in Sicily. The family of the girl soon found out the boy had not heeded the warning and decided to send a message to the whole village with a public death for all to see.

"Vincenzo explained the assassins were from a family who, for two generations, were contract men, who worked for Black Hand families across the country. They had been instructed by the girl's father to make his death painful and drawn out. For this reason, he was shot in the stomach three times with a small caliber pistol. Joseph was then dumped on the church steps on a Sunday morning before Mass was to let out.

"It was a warning and a punishment. It would be a slow and painful death for all to see what happens when you cross the Black Hand."

Father Bob shook his head slowly.

Father Anthony continued. "Joseph's mother Elena, father Francesco, two brothers and three sisters were all crying out for someone to save him. His mother screamed out for help as his father held his son's head in his lap. The dying boy tried to speak to him. Blood came out of the corner of mouth and ran down his neck. His shirt had been torn off and the red wounds were visible to all.

"The cries of the family echoed in the plaza off the cobblestone streets and stone buildings.

"Giovanni walked up to Joseph and looked at him in the eyes, then asked his own father to take Joseph into the church. His father desperately shook his head saying no, apparently knowing what would happen if he did. But, Giovanni pleaded with him, and told him it was time for all to see.

"The crowd watched as Giovanni's father took Joseph out of his father's arms and carried the dying boy into the church. Father Vincenzo said he tried to help, but Giovanni's father would have none of it. He carried the boy over to where Giovanni was standing in front of the Blessed Virgin's statue.

"The whole parish followed them back inside along the trail of dripping blood, mortified at what was happening. Giovanni knelt and motioned for his father to place the boy in his arms.

"This part, Vincenzo told me verbatim. He said he'd never forget the words. Giovanni called out in a loud voice, *to me, to me,* his voice was strong and clear.

"His voice boomed and echoed in the still of the church as he said:

Bring it to me, bring me the pain and I will suffer it.
For I am the sword and the shield.
I beseech thee oh Blessed Mother,
Queen of the Light
Grant this request for which I pray.

"He had called the light and the church instantly filled with white light. There was a popping static sound and a feeling of energy in the air. Some onlookers screamed in terror.

"The body of the boy started to heal, his wounds disappeared. He had been healed for all to see.

"Instantly the wounds started to appear on Giovanni. He was now bleeding and dying. His father knelt next to his bloodied son and helped Joseph stand.

"Giovanni asked his father to help him to his knees. Then Giovanni struggled to stretch his arms out, with his palms upward. That's when he called the light again.

"Father Vincenzo said the energy was so strong around them that Giovanni's father was pushed back. Giovanni rose in the air off the floor of the church. The amazing and beautiful sight of the wounds on his body being healed caused those watching to drop to their knees and make the sign of the cross.

"A boy who was shot and dying was healed by a mere child who took on the suffering of the boy and then healed himself. Giovani had called the angels that day and it was witnessed by all. From the back of the church a prayer was being said over and over.

"Hail Mary, full of grace, the Lord is with thee;
blessed art thou amongst women,
and blessed is the fruit of thy womb, Jesus.
"Holy Mary, Mother of God,
pray for us sinners now
and at the hour of our death.

"It became a chorus that went on for almost an hour.

"Everyone stayed in the church all day until nightfall. The women went home and brought back fruit, meat, cheese, olive oil and bread to share. Homemade wine was also shared by all.

"It was a spontaneous celebration, for this small village of poor farmers had witnessed a miracle by the Blessed Mother. She had chosen their church above all others.

"In a time of poverty and hardship this proved that their faith and prayers had been answered. It meant they were not alone.

"Father Vincenzo decided that no one should know of the events that happened that day. Giovanni's parents, who had protected the secret all these years agreed and were pleased by the decision. Father Vincenzo made every adult and child to place their hand on the *Holy Bible* and swear a holy oath to be a keeper of the secret."

Father Anthony paused, looked again at Father Bob. "As Father Vincenzo told me about everyone who had been there that day taking the oath of silence, I realized the flaw in the plan. I knew that children had also witnessed the miracle and expecting them to keep it a secret was unrealistic.

"It was something that children had to share. It would be a matter of time before the story of a boy who could heal the dying and could call the angels would be told.

"Perhaps that was why the church elders agreed to send Joseph to America to live with relatives so no one would know he was still alive. They had a funeral later in the week and a burial. To further hide the truth of what had occurred, they also agreed the girl he loved, Maria Longo, would go with him.

"They would make it look like she threw herself into the sea in grief over the death of the boy she loved. It was a plan that would work until the story got out. Then all hell would break out.

"As I sat in the wooden pew, I was stunned at what Father Vincenzo had told me. Since what I witnessed was true, this story I had been told had to be true also.

"Less than a month after I arrived and heard the story, Giovanni came to the church on a Saturday morning to see me. He said he was leaving in the morning and he had things to tell me and discuss with me.

"As he spoke, my world changed forever." Father Anthony took a sip of whiskey and paused.

"He told me things I needed to hear and put into motion events that were yet to happen. My whole life's journey was laid out before me. I can remember what he said as if it were yesterday.

"Father, it was not your fault that you could not save your friends at the lake. You tried and that was all you could do. You have carried this burden for far too long. They are with the light and are the guardians who watch over you. You were spared because you have many things yet to do before your last days."

Father Anthony locked onto Father Bob's eyes and paused. "My knees became weak and I had to sit down in a pew. I was overwhelmed. How could he have known about my friends who had drowned that warm summer day when I was seven? It was the saddest moment of my life, watching my friends go under as we tried to swim across the lake to the swim platform. It was farther than we had guessed and the water far too cold. Each had begged for me to help them but I could not. I could barely save myself. When I finally made it to the platform, sitting there, my friends were nowhere to be seen. To this day I can hear them pleading and crying out my name to save them.

"After all those years, I had not found the forgiveness in myself or through the church that could lift this burden.

"Giovanni reached out and touched my forehead with his palm. He had called the light. It was beautiful. He allowed me to be with my friends one final time. I talked with them for what seemed like hours. I found the peace and forgiveness that day that I had prayed for all my life, it was his gift to me.

"He then spoke to me. He said to take a letter to the Pope and tell him all that has happened here. The look on my face betrayed what I was thinking. As he handed me the letter he said, *do not doubt what I am telling you. It is from Her lips to your ears.*

"When they call you to Rome, tell them everything you witnessed here. Leave out only my name. It is time for those who preach the word

of God to believe again. It is at Her request that you do this for there is a battle coming for our very church and its teachings.

"Father Vincenzo will attest to all that you claim happened here. From these letters, they will know that this is the word of the Blessed Mother. He then handed me a stack of envelopes.

"The Pope must follow what has been asked and foretold.

"You will fill those shoes of yours before this has ended. We will meet again but not until many miles have been traveled and we are but old men.

"It is then that we will finish the journey that started in this small church.

"When they demand to know who I am, and they will, tell them that I am the sword and the shield of the light. That, from my lips, speaks the word of our Blessed Mother.

"Later, much later, I learned that before Giovanni left the country, he brought an end to the reign of the family of the Black Hand murderers who had tried to kill Joseph.

"It was done in such a way that no revenge could be taken. Those who saw the carnage he left behind were shaken to their core. He put the fear of God into those whose very business was crime and murder. He left an image of the light burned into the wall of the house for all to see.

"It was his last gift to the village that had protected him."

Father Bob shook his head in disbelief. "Amazing."

Chapter Twenty-Two

CHURCH WITH GRANDPA

A white car pulled up next to the stairs that led down into the grotto. Its lights flashed into the rectory kitchen window where Father Anthony and Father Bob watched. After a few minutes, the car door opened. A boy and a dog exited and walked down the stairs.

Father Bob looked faint. "Hurry," Father Bob exclaimed. "We must get inside the church if you are to see what is about to happen. "He's a day early."

The boy wore a Beavercreek High School jacket. He had the face of seventeen-year-old teen, but his broad shoulders and large arms made him look older. Father Anthony strained to get a look at the boy's face. As he approached the statue, the boy turned in a way that allowed the old priest to see his face clearly.

In a loud disbelieving voice, he exclaimed "Giovanni! How can it be?"

"Quiet," Father Bob said, looking with astonishment at Father Anthony. "Have you lost your mind? The boy will hear you and you'll miss what you have traveled so far to see."

At that moment, the big black and brown dog got to its feet and slowly turned their way looking up.

The dog knew, Father Anthony thought to himself.

"That boy's name is not Giovanni," whispered Father Bob. "His name is Brady and the boy's family are members of the parish."

Father Anthony stared at the younger priest. "Go on."

"I started looking for the boy in the grotto about four years ago," Father Bob explained in a hushed voice, "after hearing the confession of another member of the parish, an Air Force colonel. It was such an amazing and unbelievable tale, I had to find out if it was true."

He paused.

"With my own eyes. You understand, don't you?" Father Bob half pleaded for approval.

"I waited until the next Saturday night and the boy described showed up as Colonel Hall said he would. This part of the story was true, but I didn't know whether the rest of what Colonel Hall had told me was true or not. So, I started keeping a log of what I witnessed."

Father Anthony whispered, "And, what did you learn?"

"Every Saturday night the boy would show up and go to in the grotto and pray. It was always between eleven and midnight. When I first started watching him, he appeared to have walked here. In the last year and a half, he has driven here. And now he's here a day early. There must be something wrong."

Father Bob continued, still speaking softly. "He always has that big black and brown dog with him. It's a breed I've never seen before. Not the kind of dog you want to pet, if you know what I mean. It's a scary looking dog, but it never barks or makes a noise. It's as if that dog is standing guard over the boy."

Father Anthony turned his head and looked at the priest. "Where I am from, we call them butcher's dogs. All the farms that raise cattle kept them to protect the herd and keep robbers away. It's an ancient breed the Romans used."

"Interesting," said Father Bob in a whisper as he looked back at the boy and the dog.

"Please, Father, finish your story," said Father Anthony.

"As I was saying, they go down to the statue of the Blessed Virgin and the boy kneels with his arms out stretched and his palms up. There, he's doing it now. Watch for yourself and you'll see what I have seen!

"It's happening!"

The light rain had turned into a slow hard rain.

The boy knelt, bowed his head and stretched out his arms with his palms up. As he did so he was lifted off the ground, a foot into the air. There was an electrical popping, or buzzing sound coming from the grotto. The hard rain that fell did not fall on the boy.

The two priests blessed themselves and kissed the crosses that hung from their necks as they witnessed this event. The priests looked at each other, one frightened and the other amazed.

The priests were spellbound as they stood there gazing on its wonder and beauty. This glorious event lasted over an hour.

Then it was over.

The boy got up and turned, leaving with the dog. But as he did, the boy looked up at the window where the priests were standing.

They knew that he now knew.

"Come," Father Anthony said, "let's go back to that good bottle of whiskey you were going to enjoy before I interrupted you. I will tell you my story and why I have come so far."

Father Bob didn't move. "I must confess I haven't told you all the story. I feared that whoever read my letters would think *the cheese had slid off my cracker*, if you know what I mean." He looked at Father Anthony with a half-smile.

"Well, that would be something I also feared with my own story," Father Anthony assured him. "I will not judge you if you do not judge me."

* * *

Brady stood in the grotto, trying to sense any change that might be there. As he looked around, all seemed as it had always been. This was a protected holy ground so, according to rule seven, the light could be called and shielded from the darkness. There would be no push within it. The guardians would never allow it.

Still, he felt something was different. He didn't know what, but he needed to find out. He would call the light for the answers he needed. The events of this evening were beyond anything he'd ever dealt with. He needed guidance and answers. The pure evil he'd encountered was like nothing he'd ever felt before. It was as if they knew of him and had been looking for him.

While Brady looked at the statue of the Holy Mother, Hank started barking at the stairs. Brady turned his head slowly in the direction of where Hank was barking, not sure what he was going to see. Had they followed him here? He felt no push, but was ready just the same.

His heart raced slightly, there was someone there. As the person slowly came into view Brady could only smile. Hank stopped barking and wagged his stump of a tail excitedly.

Brady had experienced the miraculous many times, but he was still awe-struck at the unfolding vision. Out of a swirling mist a shape appeared and took form. It was Grandpa Ventura.

"Grandpa, you came," Brady said.

"Of course, I came, I felt your guardian call out to me. Are you okay, I understand you and the boys had a bit of a problem tonight."

"We're all okay, Grandpa, but something has changed and I need guidance."

"Show me."

The two knelt, clasped hands and Brady called the light.

It was over as soon as it had started. Grandpa gently let go of Brady's hands and looked into his grandson's eyes.

"That is the Beast I have told you about. You are right, everything has now changed. Do you understand me?"

"Yes," said Brady. "It has found us."

Brady looked up at the window. "That priest you told me about is here. He's watching us from the church with Father Bob."

"I know," his Grandpa answered. "I can sense him. Call the light and find your answers here in the grotto while I go talk with the priests." Grandpa Ventura turned to leave, but stopped to pat Hank on his head as he spoke to him in Italian. The dog responded with a low bark.

* * *

It was then that Grandpa Ventura's dog became visible to the two priests looking from the window.

"He's coming up here," Father Bob said in a near panic.

As the man and the dog climbed the stairs heading to the church's front doors, a plan laid out decades before started to unfold.

CHAPTER TWENTY-THREE

THE REUNION

Giovanni reached the front door of the church and pulled open the door. The priest from his small village so many years ago stood facing him.

"Father Anthony," said Giovanni as he reached out and shook Father Anthony's hand. "It has been a long journey and many years for you to arrive at this church. It is as I promised you. I hope you are ready for what is about to transpire."

"Yes," Father Anthony said. "Have you met Father Bob?"

"No. But I know of him." Giovanni shook hands with Father Bob.

"Nice to meet you." Father Bob shook the man's hand and then turned to leave. "I'll leave you two alone to talk."

"No. You need to hear what we have to say." Giovanni's words were more of an order than a suggestion.

Father Anthony put an arm on Father Bob's shoulder. "Yes. Stay."

The three sat.

Father Anthony turned to Giovanni. "What is happening here? I have followed the path you set for me more than sixty years ago and it has not been easy. I have given each of the seven letters to the Cardinals that you addressed, on the dates you had written on each letter. To this day, I do not know what was inside the letters. I have never questioned anything. What I do know is that each person who received a letter became Pope, as you foretold. I have done everything that you instructed, I have seen things that have changed how I view the church and my faith. I have traveled the world searching out visions, separating the true from fraud."

"Yes, yes you have," Giovanni said, "and for that you have been blessed."

"Keeping your identity a secret has been a bigger burden then I could have imagined," Father Anthony explained. "If not for the Pope's favor, I would have been banned from the Vatican and placed in some small parish in the middle of nowhere.

"My enemies within the church are many. You warned me that would be the case, but I had no idea of the battles that would be going on inside the Vatican for control and direction of the faithful. The very survival of the church hangs in the balance for this is the battle that has been spoken of by all who have heard Her voice. She has warned of this moment in time within the church.

"My office is in the deepest bowels of the Vatican. For all this time, I have been alone in this task you have laid out for me," Father Anthony sighed.

Giovanni placed a hand on the old priest's shoulder. "You have never been alone. She has always been by your side."

Father Anthony continued. "With each new Pope, the mystery surrounding what I was doing drew unwanted attention from those who were worried that it was their power or authority that I was after. They could not have been more wrong.

"I was there at Fátima and witnessed how the children were treated by the church skeptics. The secrets they were told frightened the church to its very core. I went to Lourdes and found what you had described. Everything that you foretold has come true. With each task you had set, my faith grew stronger.

"You told me, only those who are chosen would be able to receive the messages She had for the world. This I have proven.

"That is what frightened the powers in the church most. That the least of those amongst us would be chosen, mere uneducated peasants who attended their churches. That She would show herself to them.

"To see the light, you do not need the church or a priest, this fact is what has divided the powers in the church.

"Neither prayer nor self-sacrifice would get you the vision the faithful pray for. Some in the church grew bitter by this fact. They had dedicated their lives to the church yet did not have visions or hear the voices of the angels.

"I kept the secret of the boy who could call the Blessed Mother and the Angels. The one who could heal the dying with just a touch. Not even the Popes asked your name as I am sure that was part of your instructions in the letters," Father Anthony said as he looked at Giovanni.

Giovanni only smiled.

"Giovanni, I am afraid there is a group within the church that would do you great harm if they ever found out your identity."

Giovanni shook his head slowly. "She has made me aware of this. This evil in the church will be purged. Those who wear the cloth of religion are not always as they appear."

Giovanni continued. "There is the evil of darkness within the church as I told you. I fully understand and realized at the time it would not be easy for you. You were chosen just like I was chosen. The same with my grandson. You have made them believe. The good in the church, you have strengthened and the evil you have frightened to its very core. You can feel it, it is a part of me I gave to you. You can feel the push when in the presence of evil.

"While you have been chasing down visions of the light, I have been tracking down the truly evil in the world. You have not been the only one on a mission."

With that Giovanni handed him a letter with the name of a priest in Poland. "This is the first of the last three letters that you will deliver and they are the most important ones I will give you.

"The two others are addressed to a former governor in California and a stateswoman in England. These three leaders will come together and change the world as we know it. From the ashes of the church in the east will rise an ally who will join with the west to fight the false prophet and religion of the darkness.

"This is the same battle that has been fought over the centuries. The events that we are setting into motion will lead to the final battle between good and evil."

The look on Father Anthony's face was of resignation to a task that he could not say no to. There were no questions.

Father Bob looked at Giovanni. "How about we take this reunion into the rectory where I have the feeling a long conversation is overdue. Wine is on me and cigars are on Father Anthony."

"Not yet," Giovanni said, "I must show Father Anthony what has happened tonight and what happened long ago. He must see the evil that is upon us now."

With that he walked over to the statue of the Blessed Virgin in the alcove in the church and knelt. Without being asked Father Anthony and Father Bob did likewise.

Giovanni reached out his hand to Father Anthony who clasped it without hesitation. He then did the same to Father Bob.

Giovanni called the light.

Chapter Twenty-Four

FATHER BOB'S TRAINING

"Father Anthony and Giovanni, please follow me," Father Bob said as they entered the rectory. "Let's sit in the kitchen. I'll get the wine out. I need something to calm my nerves." He was unsteadied and weak-kneed from what had just taken place in the church.

"Please explain again what just happened," Father Bob pleaded. "That calling of the light."

"Exactly as I have already explained to you," Giovanni said. "The answer is not going to change."

When they got to the kitchen, Father Anthony excused himself. "You two go ahead, I have to go to get something from my room," Father Anthony said.

"Do you like cigars Giovanni?" Father Bob asked.

"Well, yes, yes I do. It is a pleasure I have enjoyed over the years," Giovanni smiled.

"Well then, you're going to like the Cuban cigars he's bringing down, they made me lightheaded." Father Bob laughed. "Felt like I'd had a tad too much wine. It's not like that ever happens," he grinned.

Father Bob had poured wine into the three glasses when Father Anthony returned with three cigars along with an object wrapped in a red velvet cloth under his arm. He placed the object on the table, still wrapped, and made the sign of the cross.

They enjoyed the wine and the fine Cuban cigars silently for a time before Giovanni nodded toward the object wrapped in red velvet. "Is that what I think it is? What I requested so long ago?"

Father Anthony let out a long blue stream of smoke. "Yes, it is. It is truly magnificent and my honor to deliver it to you. The Pope had the finest craftsman at the Vatican do all the work as per your instructions."

Father Bob looked at Father Anthony and then at Giovanni. "The Pope? This is from the Pope?" Father Bob had no idea what was about to happen. He was both excited and afraid by what was in the package. He could tell by how it was packaged and reverently handled that it was of great importance.

Father Anthony placed his cigar in the ash tray and stood. He picked up the package and lightly kissed it in reverence, and made the sign of the cross again before he handed it to Giovanni.

Feeling the gravity of what was happening here in this small rectory kitchen, Father Bob took a deep breath to prepare himself. He tended to hyperventilate, but had learned to control it.

Giovanni kissed the cloth and made the sign of the cross as he started to unwrap the red velvet wrapping.

In the light of the kitchen a weapon appeared.

The handle was of the finest hard wood and leather. The blade was of iron and appeared to be as sharp as the day it was forged.

Giovanni looked at Father Bob and explained. "Some call this the Holy Lance, the Spear of Destiny or Spear of Christ. This is the

Roman lance that pierced the side of Jesus while he was on the cross."

Father Bob fell back into his chair in shock and disbelief as he clasped his hands to his mouth. "The spear that pierced the side of Jesus? It can't be." He reached out to touch, but quickly withdrew his hand.

"Yes, Father, it is the lance of legend," Father Anthony said. "The Vatican has always had it. It is one of many secrets hidden there. All other lances that have appeared over the ages were merely fakes. The Pope himself had the handle made for the lance as per the instructions given to me years ago by Giovanni. The handle is needed so Brady can use the lance as a weapon.

"The lance is one of only a few Holy relics that can send the demons back into the darkness never to return. Giovanni's grandson must use the Holy Lance when he faces the Beast if he is to succeed.

"It is the same demon Giovanni faced the night at the farm house before he left Sicily years ago. He killed the father and his sons but he could not send the demons back to the darkness that controlled them.

"He surprised them that moonless night. That will not happen this time. They have been looking for his light and the guardians ever since."

"What fight? What guardians?" Father Bob felt ill as he looked to Father Anthony then to Giovanni. Father Bob drank down the wine remaining in his glass in one gulp, refilled his glass and did it again.

"Is that what has been going on for so long?" Father Bob asked. "It's all tied together! They have been trying to find him all these years."

"Yes," Giovanni said. They have been looking for my light ever since that night sixty years ago. What they do not understand, is that the light they have found is that of my grandson.

"They do not yet know there are two of us. I have not called the light since I left Italy except in a church where the Beast cannot see and is forbidden. This storm has been decades in the making.

"Did you bring the crosses?" Giovanni asked.

"Yes." Father Anthony reached into his travel bag and lifted out another package. He opened it on the table and revealed twelve crosses. "These crosses are simple small wooden ones that have been expertly lacquered and attached to a simple gold bezel with a handmade gold link chain. The wood was taken from the cross where Jesus died, found by St. Helena around the year 324 and secretly stored in Vatican vaults."

Father Bob stared at the crosses.

Father Anthony picked up one and kissed it. "Over the years pieces of the original cross were given to the powerful all over Europe as gifts, and some slivers have been stolen."

Giovanni kissed one also. "They are beautiful." He turned toward Father Bob. "You need to give one of these to each of the seven guardians you have gathered. You need to also get a cross to Michelle Wolfe and Randy Hall."

Father Bob was surprised at first, then it hit him and he understood. By calling the light in the circle, he knew everything.

"I will give one to each of my three other grandsons," Giovanni said.

Father Bob was shaking with so much to comprehend. "Did I hear that right, they're made from Christ's cross?"

Giovanni held up a cross and looked at it with respect. "Yes. Father, you must tell everyone not to take it off, ever. It will keep the darkness from being able to touch them. You may tell them the secret, that it is from the cross of our Lord and will protect them."

"Father Bob, are you are hearing all this?" Father Anthony asked.

"Yes, yes, I'm listening."

"It is important they understand the dangers involved in helping Brady," Giovanni said. "They must know helping Brady will draw attention to them from the darkness. The darkness is hunting Brady now."

"Yes," Father Bob repeated. "I'm listening."

* * *

Father Anthony and Giovanni looked at Father Bob as if wondering what was wrong, why he repeated himself. The priest didn't look well. His face was chalky white, soon his eyes rolled up in his head and he passed out, hitting his head on the table as he fell.

They both stood to help him. Father Anthony said, "This one is going to be zero help, I am afraid."

Giovanni nodded his head in agreement. They laid Father Bob on the couch in the TV room to recover and walked back to the kitchen.

"Polpette, come here," Giovanni said.

Father Anthony stared at the dog. "This cannot be the same dog Polpette you had as a boy? Is it? Please tell me it is not the same dog!"

Giovanni smiled. "The darkness can instill itself in people, animals, houses and objects. As you well know, Father. What the church does not like to talk about is that it can also happen with the light.

"The light does it on a much grander scale. Meatball, as my grandson calls him is my guardian from the light. He has never left my side since I left Sicily.

"Hank is my grandson's guardian."

With that, Father Anthony plopped into the chair and poured himself a glass of wine. "So many surprises in one night. It is almost too much for this old heart of mine."

"If you are going to pass out like our friend in the TV room, could you at least sit on the floor first." Giovanni flashed a wide smile. "I am too old to pick you up by myself."

Father Anthony laughed "In all the years of doing your bidding, I have seen the unbelievable. I have talked to those who were truly touched and could hear the voice of the Holy Mother. I have met with the Sisters from Fátima and learned of the three secrets and their meanings. I traveled to Brazil and met the Padre with the stigmata, witnessed all that he could do. I have visited with dozens who have heard the call of the light around the world.

"I have even talked with a false mystic who made a pact with the devil. I have witnessed demonic possession of children, women and men. I have seen the demons cast out before my eyes.

"Everything you said would happen has happened.

"But this, this one fact, is overwhelming. I thought I had seen and heard it all. That nothing more would surprise me.

"Is the dog what I think he is?"

"Yes," Giovanni said. "There is much more you don't know yet and so much more for you to see. You need to leave soon and get those letters delivered. The future of the world is at stake."

Giovanni continued. "You have been setting events into motion all these years that will save mankind. You have been chosen by God's providence to help consecrate Russia in union with all bishops to the Immaculate Heart of Mary. World peace depends upon this because the conversion of Russia is the victory over Satan.

"The Eagle and the Bear must unite to defeat the false Prophet Mohammad and the religion that the darkness has brought.

"After almost fourteen-hundred years the ending is almost at hand.

"Everything you have been doing is part of a puzzle that fits together leading up to this.

"My small part in this grand plan is to be the sword and the shield of the light, to return the demons that roam the earth to the darkness.

"It will be the same with my grandson. His part in this grand plan has only just begun.

Giovanni placed an arm around Father Anthony's shoulder. "Father, our time here together is almost over but I will tell you that we will meet again."

Father Anthony hugged Giovanni. "Until then."

"Yes." Giovanni smiled. "Until that glorious day, let us smoke these fine Cuban cigars, drink this wine and tell me the stories of your travels over all these years."

Chapter Twenty-Five

AT THE HOSPITAL

Ray was at Miami Valley Hospital early Saturday morning just as the sun was starting to rise. He had to make sure his crew members were all right. More importantly, he wanted to make sure they kept their mouths shut. Had they followed the plan and given the police the fake names they were supposed to if they ever got arrested?

If they hadn't they wouldn't leave the hospital with him.

They would *never* leave the hospital.

It was one of the rules he had set for them to follow. Never have any identification on them when they were out hunting. They were to claim to be from Atlanta, Georgia, living out of a motel, working construction in a nearby city.

The story was always vague enough that it couldn't be easily verified. There was always some truth mixed in with the lie.

Don't trust them, his father had ground it into him. Only trust yourself, Earl would tell his young son. If things go to shit, kill everyone so that there is only one story. He could hear it as if his father was whispering into his ear as he walked into the hospital.

They had a girl in the van, the night of fun and excitement was all planned. Why they decided to screw around at the football game with those kids was beyond his wildest imagination and it pissed him off.

They were only supposed to be scouting girls for future parties. They knew the routine, act like students and don't stick out. The dumbasses were supposed to be hunting, not getting into fights. If his dad was here, he'd bury them at the farm.

It may come to that.

He approached the reception desk to find the hospital volunteer reading, *Interview with the Vampire*. The title made him smile.

"May I help you?" she asked.

"I'm looking for three men who came in last night by the names Gaul, Sharon and Bauer."

She looked at her chart. "They're in Ward B on the third floor."

"Thank you, miss." Ray turned and walked away, looking for the elevator.

He was pleased to hear they weren't in some sort of police custody at the hospital. Why had the police not arrested them? Maybe they were waiting for them to leave the hospital?

Ray got off the elevator on the third floor and looked around. If he saw any sign of police, he'd walk away and never return, except maybe to silence his crew.

The hallway was completely empty except for the one nurse sitting at the station near the elevator. He approached her quietly and noticed she was asleep. As he walked past her, he smiled that smile of what could have been. She was pretty, the type he enjoyed most. *Later*, he whispered to himself.

He'd only walked a short distance from the nurse's station when he found a sign with an arrow pointing to Ward B.

He entered the room, but immediately wondered if he was in the right place. All three of his crew members were on white hospital beds bandaged and wrapped like fucking Christmas packages.

They didn't seem to know he was there. He wondered if they were drugged up or sound asleep. They looked like they'd been in a car accident.

He couldn't believe the damage each had. They wouldn't be able to work for weeks.

"Fuck me," he said out loud. "What the hell am I going to do?"

He walked over to the closest bed and shook Keith.

"Wake up, you asshole," Ray said. "Wake the fuck up."

Within a minute or so Keith was talking and telling him all that had happened from the start of the fight, to when they were put in the ambulances and taken to the hospital.

He described in detail the damage that kid did to them.

He told Ray the cops didn't come to the hospital at all last night and he didn't think they would be coming.

"How's that?" Ray asked.

Keith explained. "I heard one cop talking to another cop as they loaded me into one of the ambulances saying they thought we'd been punished enough by whoever gave us this ass whipping."

Keith looked at his boss. "Ray, I didn't start that fucking fight. I fucking swear."

Ray knew it was a lie since he'd been there watching, but he kept quiet.

"Look what that fucking kid did to us," Keith said as he pointed to the cast on his left arm, his taped-up ribs, and his broken leg. "We need to fucking kill that kid, we need to find that fucker and skin him alive."

"Shut up, asshole," said Ray. "I need to get all of you out of here now before anyone finds out who you really are."

At that point, Keith's cousin Mikey spoke. He must've been listening the whole time to the conversation between Ray and Keith.

"Ray, you need to know, this kid knows everything. He fucking knows everything about us." Mikey was wide-eyed and looked scared shitless. "I don't know who this prick is but he knows our secrets."

"Are you drugged out of your hillbilly mind?" Ray asked.

"No. You gotta believe me. That kid knows."

"Shut the fuck up," Ray said. "SHUT UP!" He pulled out his blade and pointed it at Mikey.

"No, no you have to listen to me," Mikey pleaded. "That kid touched my head and got into it. He read my mind or something. All the girls, everything we have ever done. He fucking knows. It was painful as he sucked and burned it all out of my head. I couldn't stop it."

"I said shut up or I'll shut you up." Ray flashed the blade mere inches from his neck. "I'll cut your tongue out and shove it down your lying throat."

"Ray, how is it possible? I saw a girl there we killed. You know that *girl* from a few years ago we grabbed leaving the horse farm. She was there at the school parking lot screaming for this kid to fuck us up. We killed her, I know we stabbed and gutted her. How is she fucking still alive? I saw her with my own eyes bleeding on the floor in the farm house. What is going on Ray?" Mikey pleaded. "Cut my throat if you want, but it's the truth."

"Shut your mouth." Ray's face was red.

"Ask them, go on ask them," Mikey demanded. "That kid did the same thing to them. Fucking tell him, Keith, before he kills me in this fucking bed. You know exactly what I'm talking about. Tell him the fucking truth."

Ray looked at Keith, but before Keith could say anything, a voice in the far bed next to the window said, "It's all true. That kid knows everything. Mikey ain't fucking crazy."

It was Mark. He must have been listening the whole time.

"He knows everything bad we've ever done. We must get the fuck out of town, now," his voice shaking. "Fucking NOW, all of us before that kid talks to the police."

Ray felt his world was crashing down. The voice in his head was talking and telling him what to do, now. It drowned out the voices of those in the room. Ray just stood there in a daze and said nothing for a full two minutes.

Then Ray spoke.

"Everyone shut the fuck up, stop your crazy ass talking, we are leaving now. Get your asses out of bed and get your clothes on now."

They left the hospital, walking past the sleeping nurse and down the elevator. Once on the main floor, they left through a side exit and hobbled out to the van. As they turned onto US Route 35 heading east, Ray was wondering if it was time to clean up the loose ends.

The voice in his head said, not yet.

If things blowup on you, get rid of the crew first thing, Ray could hear his father talking in his head. The truth dies when the crew dies.

He would make his decision in the five-and-a-half-hour drive back to the farm in West Virginia. There was someone at the farm he needed to talk with first.

Chapter Twenty-Six

THE CREW

During the drive to West Virginia with his injured crew, Ray Johnson remembered how he'd met each one, and why he'd selected them to work with him.

Keith Gaul made it to the ninth grade, which was a family record in Hico, West Virginia. He was product of a dysfunctional, alcoholic family, that lived in a trailer with no running water, on a shutdown farm, in the back holler of a valley along the mountains.

Each member of his family tree was a loser of one type or the other. The marrying of first cousins was the norm for them. The adults abused the kids and in time the kids became mirrors of those who raised them.

The bullied became the bullies.

Drugs, alcohol and sex was on the menu every day.

Keith had long stringy brown hair and a face that was pockmarked from years of drinking RC Cola and eating MoonPies. Since there was no running water, washing up happened sporadically and only if the weather permitted it. The nearby creek was the preferred method. Poor hygiene was all part of growing up in the Gaul household.

In his warped mind, Keith thought of himself as a lady's man. However, most girls were put off by his complexion, poor hygiene, bad odor and rotten teeth. To compensate for his poor complexion, he grew a beard to hide the blotches on his face.

His first cousin, Mikey, was the same age with like education. One day, when Mikey was two years old, his mother dropped him off at Keith's trailer for them to watch him and she never returned. What happened to her? No one ever said nor seemed to care. It's how things happened in the back hollers of West Virginia.

Mikey was short and squat in stature. He wore his hair in a flat top style and looked far better to the girls than his fat cousin. This helped a lot when they went out cruising for chicks.

But the cousins had their ace in the hole, their buddy Mark.

To round out Ray's group of losers was Mark Sharon. Mark lived along the same back dirt road that the Gauls did. He had long blond hair, and was tall and skinny. He was "beautiful" as his uncle used to say. As a small boy, he was passed around among the uncles and family friends to do with as they pleased.

This stopped the day he turned fourteen. He hit his uncle square in the head with a shovel when he was sleeping. It split his face open ear to ear. Killed him dead as a door nail. It was his last day in that trailer of horrors. From then on, he stayed at the Gaul's.

The cousins called him their fishing "spinner bait".

Mark would lure the girls into partying with the three of them with his charming good looks and drugs. All the while the girls had no idea what this trio had plans on doing. They would get the girl drunk and high so she would have no way of stopping them or telling what had happened. They would take their "date" in their car to a quiet area in the back woods and "party" with her until they were finished.

The trio would always dump the girl off near where they had picked her up. Most times they just left her in a field naked with her clothes in a pile and no memory of what had happened.

It was during one of these backwoods parties that Ray came upon them. For over four hours he observed them, deciding that he needed to find out everything he could about them. He knew right then and there that he could refine their methods. He could teach them to be his own crew.

He stepped into the clearing and scared the shit out of the three boys. They stopped their fun and gathered around the stranger naked as jaybirds, that is except for the knives in their hands.

"Calm the fuck down," Ray said. "I've just been admiring your work."

It was then that they saw the Smith & Wesson 9mm pistol in his hand.

"Mind if I join in on the party? I'll show you how it should be done and how to finish it properly."

With that he tossed a quarter-pound bag of weed to the kid with the beard.

"Let's just say that's payment for my share of your party."

That was all that was needed. The party resumed but finished in a way that changed everything.

Within the year Ray had moved them onto the farm near his house on the back forty acres of the three-hundred-acre farm. Each had his own trailer to live in with running water and a flush toilet.

For the first time in their lives they were earning a salary. They were taught the family trade, digging basements and growing pot. Both of which allowed them to make more money than they had ever seen.

They also learned what was allowed and not allowed.

One rule that was strictly enforced was that they weren't allowed to bring anyone they knew to the farm. They paid for everything with cash. They had access to one girl each at the barn to do with as they pleased but only Ray could do the finish.

They were taught the rules of hunting and keeping the barn stocked. It was beyond anything that their sick and twisted minds could have ever hoped for.

They became the crew that Ray needed.

Chapter Twenty-Seven

GREG'S FAILURE

The great celebration Greg had envisioned when he returned to school Monday didn't happen. No pats on the backs from his fellow seniors. He knew why, of course. There was nothing to celebrate. Greg's idea for his team to be the first seniors of the year to paint the bridge failed. No one would heap glory on him today as he had hoped, all due to his lack of any planning.

Most of the bridge painting team avoided him, too. Because of the failure Friday night, his reputation for being a dumbass had hit a new high.

Dean wasn't even at school, and Greg suspected he'd be out all week. Only Linda knew why Dean was out and she refused to talk about it. All she would say was that he was going through some stuff and when he'd sorted it out, he'd be back. Her cryptic language made the rumors about him worse.

There were whispers about what had happened in the parking lot, but no one wanted to talk openly. It seemed no one wanted to risk being the one who spilled the beans of who the students were. Some kept the secret because they wanted to protect the brothers. Others were just simply too scared after what they had seen or what they had been told happened. The Bruce Lee description, in all its glorious details, being told by a sophomore, didn't help. The story got better each time he told it.

The snapping of some guy's leg was too much for most of the students. The part about the girl puking at the sound of the leg breaking was repeated in hushed tones all day in every class.

And then there was the star of the night.

It wasn't a football player.

Everyone talked about Matt Beck and his "Hokey Pokey" arrest. He was an instant celebrity. He'd gone from the snowman crapper to instant legend status in one night.

Greg didn't think it was fair. At least he'd tried to paint the bridge. All this Matt guy did was get arrested for singing.

Everyone who had heard about his arrest agreed Matt was the most talked about sophomore ever to walk the halls at Beavercreek since it was built twenty-two years ago.

Matt's story had now taken on a life of its own. It was blown way out of proportion as these things tend to be. The more it was told, the better the story got. Fact and fiction became one, the way all legends began in high school.

Between class changes Matt's fellow sophomores would sing the "Hokey Pokey" song as he walked the halls and everyone would do the dance. Even some of the teachers joined in singing the song before the end of the day. It was laugh-out-loud funny and amazing to hear.

Truth be told, Greg was more than a little jealous of Matt. He was pissed off.

* * *

No one in Greg's bridge painting group bragged about what they had attempted to do. And, for good reason. Brady felt they must have all gotten together and agreed not to tell anyone about the events of Friday evening.

For some it was shame of failure and for others it was faith-shattering fear. For Michelle and Brady, it was a secret about the light and the darkness. Both knew all too well the danger that was there at the bridge and what followed at the game was all because of it.

Brady could tell it would be a long day for this group of would-be bridge painters. Seeing each other in classes and in the hallway was a constant reminder of what should have never happened. Their experience together on the bridge changed everything for this small group and it would probably take years for some to come to terms with what had happened.

Brady walked over to the table where Matt was sitting at lunch. He was retelling the story of his arrest in graphic detail to an eager group of sophomores. Everyone had stopped laughing before Matt realized in mid-sentence Brady was standing behind him at the table.

"Matt, can I talk to you?" Brady asked.

Matt turned around and stared at Brady. The look on Matt's face showed that he was both surprised and concerned.

"Sure," was all Matt could get out. He stood.

Brady walked up to him and said loud enough for all to hear, "that was the best 'Hokey Pokey' I've ever heard. Thanks for your help."

With that Matt rushed over and high fived Brady. "Anytime. That's what friends are for."

"That's right," Brady said, "we *are* friends and if you ever need me for any reason just call out and I will be there."

Brady put his arm around Matt's shoulder and, in an awkward motion, laid his hand on the side of Matt's head. Softly, so that no one else could hear, Brady said, "just call out my name if you're ever in need and I will find you."

Matt wobbled from the mere touch of Brady's hand, he seemed dazed and confused. Brady kept an eye on him to make sure he didn't pass out in front of all his friends.

Brady helped Matt to his seat. "Matt is now the legend of the sophomore class."

Everyone clapped and cheered, "Matt, Matt, Matt, Matt."

Brady couldn't help but smile. On his way out, he could hear the first few lines of the "Hokey Pokey" starting up again.

* * *

Jennings, the school counselor, had heard from the football coach that bloody towels had been found in the locker room after the game. Jennings told Brooks about it and they both believed the towels had something to do with the student involved in the fight. If so, he must've gotten hurt. And, he must be the one their business partner asked about. They pulled some of the students they knew they could bully out of class and interrogated them about what they knew about the fight.

They weren't doing it for the good of the school and its students. This search was prompted by an emergency call on Sunday from their business partner. He'd said someone had been stabbed Friday night and he wanted the name of the student. He also wanted them to check to see who wasn't at school Monday, to narrow down the list of who might have been stabbed.

By the end of the day they had the name of a student. The problem was, this student was at school and couldn't be the student they were looking for. No one who had been stabbed in the chest, possibly multiple times, with an eight-inch hunting knife could be at school.

They pulled the suspect student's class schedule and made plans to confront him at lunch the next day. Their plan was simple. They'd catch him in a restroom alone, and accuse him of having drugs on him. That would give them an excuse for an un-authorized strip search to see if he had injuries similar to what the student involved in the fight probably had.

Chapter Twenty-Eight

THE BROOKS AND JENNINGS TEAM

Linda Barr volunteered in the high school office rather than take study hall her junior and senior year. It gave her something to do and she got one credit hour toward college for it. In addition to that, she got to eavesdrop on everything said in the office.

That Monday, after the big fight Friday night, she noticed Mr. Jennings, the guidance counselor and Mr. Brooks, a teacher, sneaking around the office acting odd. That is, odder than they usually acted. They seemed to be on some sort of a mission they didn't want Mrs. Neal, the office secretary of twenty years, to know about. Whatever they were up to, they wanted it kept secret.

"Linda, could you be a sweetheart and do me a favor?" Mr. Jennings asked in his nasally tone of voice. "Mrs. Neal is so busy today, I don't want to bother her. You understand, there's no need to add to her work load. You know how they overwork that poor women."

Linda knew right then and there, that was a lie. Jennings could care less about Mrs. Neal. "No problem. What is it you need?"

"Could you pull the class schedule for Brady Michaels and copy it down for me?" Jennings half ordered with that fake smile he flashed at all the students. "Oh, and no need to say anything to Mrs. Neal, I'll tell her later why I needed it."

Yeah right, sure, asshole, I'm not only telling Mrs. Neal as soon as you leave but I'm telling Brady, she thought to herself as she flashed her best fake smile right back at him.

She couldn't quite figure out what he was doing, but she knew something was up.

The pair of them creeped her out.

That night she called Brady.

* * *

"Hello," Brady said as he answered the phone.

"Brady, this is Linda Barr. I just thought you should know Brooks and Jennings had me pull your class schedule today."

"Did they say why they wanted it?"

"No. Said not to tell Mrs. Neal and that they'd tell her why they needed it later. Those two losers give me a bad feeling. They're up to something and it somehow concerns you. Maybe it's about Friday, if you know what I mean."

"Yes, I know exactly what you mean. Thanks for the heads up."

"Sure. You be careful, now."

After Brady hung up the phone his mind continued to go over the conversation. What was going on? He had a hunch, but wasn't sure if this was the connection he was looking for.

On Tuesday, as he pulled in to the parking lot, he told his brothers to stay away from Jennings and Brooks. If they say anything to you at all about Friday night say nothing.

"I want to know at once if they approach you. Come and get me out of class if you have to."

"Sure, no problem," Caleb said. "Everyone hates those two jackasses."

"Make sure you have someone with you anytime you're not in class," Brady added.

"Okay, now you're making me wonder what's up and don't tell me not to worry as usual," Liam said.

"Do you want us to hold hands and skip to class like good little boys?" Caleb asked.

"Yeah, Brady, this is bullshit. Tell us what's going on," piped in Zane.

"It's probably nothing. I'll explain it all on the way home."

"See what I mean, we're never told anything. Bullshit," Zane said.

Brady watched as his brothers all gave him the finger then joined hands and walked toward their classrooms.

"Real funny," he shouted. Even after they were out of sight, he could hear the laughter of his brothers and it made him smile.

Brady made his way to Weasels' Corner where Michelle and Randy were waiting with scowls on their faces.

"Hey guys, why the welcoming committee?" Brady said half laughing.

"You know fucking why," Randy said. "You're not the only one who talked to Linda. We have instructions to not let you go anywhere by yourself today."

Brady noticed the glint of the gold chain with the wooden cross around Randy's neck but said nothing. "That's just great, I have babysitters now." Brady shook his head.

"Yes," Michelle said, smiling, "I wore my best babysitter jeans just for you."

"Okay," Brady said, "let's get some coffee, I'm buying for my sitters."

Randy and Michelle took turns being his escort between classes. As they walked the halls, Brady was waiting for any sense of the push. But he didn't sense anything. The two teachers Linda mentioned were nowhere in the halls so far and now it was time for lunch. As they headed to the lunch room both Randy and Michelle were with him. They ate, talked and played cards, their usual routine.

"Michelle, please pay attention to the game," Randy said. "It's like your head is on a swivel turning in all directions looking for something that's not there. Chill, please."

When their lunch period ended, Brady said, "you two are going to have to excuse me but nature calls."

Michelle and Randy both looked at him and then each other.

Brady said, "Really, it's the restroom I don't need a helper in there."

"Okay," Randy said. "We're going to wait over there for you." He motioned down the hall toward where their next class was."

The push hit him strong as Brady entered the restroom and he instinctively moved to his right before Jennings could grab him. His movement was so fast Jennings was taken by surprise. Brady was now standing parallel to the teachers.

"We have information that you have drugs on you," Brooks barked at him.

"We need to search you," Jennings demanded. "Take your shirt off."

"Let me think about that for a second." Brady surveyed his options in the restroom. "Yeah, I don't think that's going to happen."

"You will do what we fucking tell you to do." Brooks moved toward Brady.

Brady felt the push coming and moved to his left, hitting the teacher with a blow square in the middle of his chest. Brooks was caught off guard. The force of Brady's first strike knocked Brooks off his feet and stole the air from his lungs. He landed on the tile floor with a thud, gasping for air.

When he tried to get up, Brady leaned in and hit him again. This time with a blow across the side of his head, a right cross, that made it lights out Brooks. Jennings glanced down at his partner on the floor a couple of times as if willing him to get up and help.

Jennings must have figured out that wasn't going to happen. He turned and ran toward the door. Brady quickly turned on the spot and moved quickly toward Jennings causing him to howl for help like a stuck pig.

Randy and Michelle ran into Jennings as he was attempting to leave. The impact knocked him to the floor next to his pal Brooks.

Jennings was at a boiling point. His scream was loud enough to be heard down the hall. "Get the fuck out of the restroom. Do as I say. Get out of my way."

Brady couldn't help laughing. The funny thing was, all the time Jennings was ranting, he was still on the floor.

Jennings tried to get up and make his escape about the time Brady's three brothers and Hank entered with the force of a hurricane.

The cavalry had arrived, set for all-out battle.

Zane ordered Hank into position. "Wait outside the door and don't let anyone come in."

Jennings crawled toward the door. The brothers blocked him and pounded the living shit out of him, using hammer fists Brady had taught them.

Only when Michelle told them to stop, in her best mother's voice, did the brothers pause and look up.

"Boys, boys enough, you can stop now," she said, holding a gun in her right hand.

"I have you all covered," Michelle said.

"Now that's what I'm talking about!" Caleb stood and moved next to her.

"It's Annie, Fucking Oakley," Zane proclaimed.

Michelle just smiled at the brothers as she looked over her shoulder to Brady, as he nodded his approval.

Brady looked at his brothers. "How'd you guys get here so fast?"

All three looked a little sheepish. Liam answered. "We've been ditching classes all day to keep an eye on you. We have a detailed plan to follow in case of trouble."

"Yeah," Zane added. "We got Hank out of the car and had him moving around the outside of the building. Right now, he's stationed outside the restroom door."

Brady worried about his brothers at times, but no one could call them stupid.

Caleb chimed in. "When Grandpa gave us the crosses and the instructions, we knew that shit was going to be hitting the fan soon. We didn't want to miss the action."

Zane added. "Besides, we're not going to ever abandon you, Brady, especially after what happened Friday night. We always knew you were special, but it wasn't until then that we knew just *how* special. Grandpa promised a full explanation soon, but that only piqued our interest in what was going on."

Just then, they heard Mr. Bortz, another teacher, saying, "Hank damn it, let me in. Boys, call off this dog."

Brady called Hank and Mr. Bortz came rushing in.

"Oh, Lordy Jesus," Mr. Bortz said. "Is everyone all right? Is Brady okay?"

He looked toward the teachers on the floor. "Shit balls. Are they still alive?" He shook his head. "I don't want to know."

Bortz looked over at Michelle holding the gun. "Please, Michelle, put that away."

"Yes, they're alive," Brady said. "They tried…," was all Brady could get out before being cut off by Bortz.

"No time for the story, no time," Bortz said. "Everyone get out, get out now. I'll take care of this mess." He made a shooing motion with both hands toward the door. "Get out quick, now!"

Jennings moaned before all the kids could leave. He tried to get up off the floor. Mr. Bortz walked over and kicked him straight in his nose, knocking him out cold. He hit face first on the tile floor, making a sound like a wet sponge dropping onto a hard surface.

"Damn, that was great," Zane said.

Mr. Bortz smiled. "Not bad for an old guy."

"Hell yeah, not bad at all," Zane added.

Brady placed his hand on Jennings and Brooks, and got the truth he looked for. He finally had the truth about Mary 10-4 and the evil these two had done over the years. Everyone watched in amazement as he did this, but said nothing.

"Brady hurry, before anyone comes, get out." Bortz ordered, breaking the silence.

"All of you need to get off school grounds. Get to your car and leave. We're all meeting at the church, be there around 4:00. I'll meet you there later. Now leave."

They did as they were told and went straight to the car and left. As Brady turned the car out of the parking lot Michelle said, "Go to the barn, we'll wait there until it's time for the meeting."

* * *

By the end of the school day, Bortz had spread the story throughout the school of how two teachers had gotten into a fist fight in the boy's restroom over some woman, a lover's triangle.

The story he told everyone was that he'd been walking by the restroom and heard shouting. He went in to see what the trouble was all about. He'd found the two beating each other senseless and somehow the dumbasses knocked each other out at the same time.

The best part of the story Bortz came up with, the piece that sealed his story, was that both teachers were still out cold when the nurse, principal and several other teachers were lead there by Bortz. By the time they arrived, the class change bell had rung and they had to move out a dozen or so students who had entered the restroom and were now staring at the two teachers sprawled out on the floor.

The story spread throughout the school.

After the principal heard what had happened, both Jennings and Brooks were immediately suspended from their teaching and counseling jobs and banned from school grounds pending a hearing.

A job well done, Bortz thought to himself after hearing about the suspensions.

Chapter Twenty-Nine

THE GUARDIANS

Father Bob placed chairs inside the church around the blessed Virgin's statue, as instructed to prepare for the four o'clock meeting. It was a quiet alcove, normally only used for prayer and the lighting of candles.

The priest opened the censer, placed the incense on the red-hot coals and closed the lid. It smoked instantly. With a practiced rhythm, he swung it back and forth on its chain releasing the scent of frankincense and myrrh. The incense burned and smoked intensely as the motion increased, filling the church with its sweet-smelling smoke. Father Bob walked slowly through the church purifying it for the event about to take place.

The smoke from the burning incense combined with the glow of the multitude of votive candles to make the statue of the Holy Mother more magnificent than usual.

He sang as he made his way through the sanctuary. While not a great singer, he knew all the words by heart and made up for the quality of voice with strength of volume. He bellowed Ave Maria and it echoed throughout the church.

As people gradually arrived, each one walked over to the priest, shook his hand and made the sign of the cross. Father Bob gave each person a rosary. Brady, Michelle and Brady's brothers were the last to arrive.

Father Bob looked around the room and saw the familiar faces. There was Big John, Officer Hickey, Colonel Hall, Randy, Michelle's dad Charlie, Ed Kline and Mr. Bortz.

All the watchers had been gathered. Michelle and Brady's brothers were also seated and were now a part of this handpicked group of guardians.

These were people of diverse backgrounds, bound to Brady through his miraculous acts of calling the light. They had been selected by Father Bob for this very reason. Their lives were threaded together by events out of their control, yet all linked.

These were the ones who would become witnesses, and eventually *farmers,* who would plant the seeds of faith to revive a church that had lost its belief in miracles and the Blessed Mother.

Brady walked over to the group about the time the sound of the door closing caused all to turn and look at the old man who entered.

No one knew who he was except for Father Bob, Brady and his brothers.

Brady spoke first. "Grandpa, I'm glad you're here."

Giovanni smiled and hugged his grandson. "Of course I am here. I have been waiting for this day since I was younger than you." The brothers hugged their grandfather silently then went back to their seats.

Father Bob cleared his throat. "Everyone, this is Giovanni, Brady's grandfather."

Everyone nodded except Michelle, she simply smiled at Giovanni. Giovanni winked at her and she blushed.

"Please, everyone kneel and let's start our prayers," said Father Bob. Only Father Bob knew they were all going to become part of the Knights of the Light this evening.

Father Bob started the Hail Mary in a loud and haunting voice that echoed throughout the near-empty church. In unison, they all joined in. The prayers filled the church like the smoke spilling out of the smoldering censer hanging from its stand.

While they prayed the Rosary, the sense of faith surrounding him and overwhelmed Father Bob. As they progressed through the stations of the Rosary, with the cadence of prayer echoing throughout the church, he felt as if the ancient ritual comforted everyone. He knew they must be feeling God's presence the same as he did.

Father Bob took the censer off its stand and swung it in large circular movements. With each arch of the orb it released clouds of holy, billowy smoke combined with the sweet fragrance of the incense over the group deep in prayer.

He was both purifying and blessing this group for the great battle that was coming between the light and the darkness.

Once they finished praying the Rosary, Father Bob recited the following prayer:

Holy Michael, defend us in battle. Be our safeguard against the wickedness and snares of the devil. May God rebuke him, we humbly pray; and do you, O Prince of the heavenly host, by the power of God cast into hell Satan and all the evil spirits who wander through the world seeking the ruin of souls.

Amen.

Tears rolled down his cheeks as he stood and looked at the group. "My part is complete for now. I will keep you, the warriors and witnesses of the light, in my prayers as you go on this journey."

He turned to leave and saw the look of questioning on some of the faces.

"Despair not. You each have a journey and a mission that Brady and his grandfather will explain. I will see each of you again, this I truly believe. God bless you all and may the angels keep you safe."

With that, Father Bob left the church.

* * *

Giovanni also sensed the strength of faith among those in the church. Although they had not been told yet, each would have a part to play in this battle if the darkness was to be defeated.

Only Giovanni knew the positive effect of the light caused the spiritual feeling that enveloped them. Having four of the chosen, who served as the sword and the shield of the light in the house of the Lord, multiplied this positive push, the power of the light.

This gathering of the faithful, connected through unrelated events, had been touched by the darkness. Each became true believers in the light through the action of a mere boy. This is what would be required to confront the darkness. Their faith would be tested and they could not falter or all would be lost. In centuries past those who attempted this, did not always succeed and were dragged into the darkness.

Giovanni stood with Brady. "There is much for you to see and many questions you want answered. We will answer all of that now. Do not be afraid for our battle cry is 'Who is like God, I call upon Saint Michael, defend us in battle' against the Beast."

"Please hold my hand," Brady asked Michelle.

One by one, the faithful joined hands, completing the circle with Grandpa holding Brady's other hand. At that moment Brady and his grandfather called the light. In the center of the circle were Hank and Meatball.

Afterwards, Giovanni knew the demons were listening to the Rolling Stones "Sympathy." One of them, Mikey, called it their anthem.

They had no idea the song was written with parallels to the Fátima prophecies. The visions of Fátima were considered by the Vatican as the most prophetic event in the last one-hundred years.

They were just too stupid and filled with hate from the darkness to understand the significance of the lyrics. It was not a tribute to the darkness but a warning to the faithful.

It was Giovanni who met the rocker in 1967 and planted the seeds for the song in his head. It was the voice of the darkness that caused him to write in the first-person narrative. A mere touch in a backstage meeting was all that was needed.

Another item on Giovanni's long list completed.

It was part of the battle plan laid out decades earlier by a simple farm boy. That was his advantage. The darkness viewed him as a simple-minded farm boy. The forces that were gathering would not see it coming.

Chapter Thirty

RAY'S PARTNERS

Ray listened to Jennings on the phone as he attempted to explain what happened with him and Brooks. Ray wondered how he ever thought he could work with these losers.

Sometimes Ray wondered how his father had managed it.

They tried to blame it all on Ray, but if they'd done what he'd told them to do, there wouldn't have been a problem.

Jennings whined. "What'd you goddamn get us involved in? That fucking kid got us fired."

Ray let Jennings rattle on, hearing in detail how he and Brooks had been ambushed and attacked in the restroom. He said they'd forced the kid to take off his shirt and they didn't see any stab wounds.

Ray could tell by the tremble in Jennings' voice he was trying to cover up what had really happened. Ray had told them not to talk with the boy or try to search him. All he'd asked them to do was to find out the student's name and address. Instead, the dumbasses had decided to force the kid to take off his shirt so they could see if he had stab wounds.

"This is fucked up," Jennings screamed. "How the hell are we supposed to get our jobs back? The fucking cops were called, and they think Brooks and I were in a fight with each other over some non-existent woman. This is your fault, you fucking hillbilly."

Jennings paused.

"Hello. Are you still there?" Jennings yelled into the phone. "Hello. You fucking better have some answers to this cluster fuck." He was screaming now, but Ray was holding the phone away from his ear.

Ray knew Jennings was like a dog on the porch barking. Ray needed to let him bark until he wore himself out. Then, maybe Ray could get the information he wanted.

Ray also decided at that very moment that these two were going to get invited to the farm and would never leave.

"Are you listening to me?" Jennings's voice quavered.

"Tell me when you're done screaming and I'll talk," Ray said.

"Fuck you," Jennings said.

Ray waited.

"I'm done," Jennings said softly.

"What is the name of the boy," Ray calmly asked.

"Fuck you. I'm not telling you anything. Didn't you hear what I just said. We got shit canned today."

"I heard you. I'm going to send the boys to meet you at Road Runner Lounge tomorrow night. They will have an advance from me to tide you over for the time being. Now calm down. It's going to be okay. Use some of the money to hire an attorney to get your jobs back. You have tenure, they can't just fire you," Ray said.

Jennings didn't say a word at first. "That's true. Fuck them. We have rights. I didn't think about that."

"That's right, Jennings. Your attorney will call your union steward and get the school to give you your jobs back. You've never had an issue in all the years you've worked there. Right? He'll get you reinstated. It's the law. Just give it some time to blow over."

"Now tell me what you found out about the boy," Ray said forcefully.

"His name is Brady Michael, eighteen years old, a senior who has attended Beavercreek schools since first grade. He lives at 4894 Heller Avenue. That's all I know. There's nothing else in his file."

"You're sure he hadn't been stabbed?" Ray doubted what Jennings had said before. His crew may be stupid, but they'd know if they stuck someone with a hunting knife.

"There's no way that kid had been stabbed," Jennings said, sounding angry. "No way, you hear me?"

"Yes, I do." Ray was confused and decided to work out the problem later.

"Okay, so why did he jump you two in the restroom? Before you answer that, think hard before you fucking lie to me again," Ray said it in a tone that showed he knew a lie when he heard it.

It was like the wind was knocked out of Jennings and he told the real story of what had happened, that is, before he was knocked out.

"There, feel better? That's what I need to hear, Jennings. Never lie to me again. What you told me was very important and you will be well rewarded. The boys will be there at four p.m. tomorrow. Be there with Brooks. We'll take care of you both, so don't be late."

"Hey, thanks man. I'm sorry for yelling. I'm just pissed off about what happened. Your dad always took care of us and I should've known you'd do the same," Jennings said in a voice filled with regret mixed with fear.

"We're all good," Ray said to assure him. "Partners take care of each other. My dad never let you down and neither will I."

"Loose ends," his dad whispered in his ear, "loose ends."

* * *

On their way to the Road Runner Lounge the crew talked about how they would drug the teachers. It was decided that only two would go into the bar. Since Keith had a broken leg, he'd be the one to wait in the van.

The crew would take great pleasure in the task at hand. They had a special hatred for teachers in general and these two in particular. Jennings and Brooks had a better-than-you attitude every time they were around the crew. The teachers viewed them as dumb hicks and they knew it. On the drive back to Beavercreek, they decided the teachers would pay dearly for the way they'd treated the crew.

Ray told them he had questions that were going to require a little more encouragement to get answers out of the two teachers.

The boys were hyped up and excited as if it was the day before Christmas.

They knew exactly what was coming.

Pain!

Chapter Thirty-One

ROAD RUNNER PICKUPS

The crew had driven straight through from West Virginia to Beavercreek, stopping only for gas and cigarettes. They were a sight to behold, all bandaged and in casts. Keith used crutches to hobble around.

Their first stop was the trailer on the farm where they had been living while they were in Beavercreek. It was all part of the disappearing plan Ray had taught them, everything that could be traced to them was to be destroyed.

Keith doused the inside of the trailer with gasoline, laughing with his sore ribs aching. He yelled, "fuck you," as he flicked a lit cigarette into the trailer and with a whoosh it was ablaze. With his crutches, he almost caught himself on fire before he could get away.

"That was goddamn great," Mikey said. "Too bad we can't stay and watch that shit hole burn to the ground."

When they pulled off the dirt road, they could still see the flames rising from the field where the trailer stood. The three of them hooted and laughed.

Mikey turned the van toward Beavercreek and headed for the bar. “Always hated that goddamn trailer.”

It didn’t take long to get to the gravel parking lot where Mikey slowed and pulled the van around to the back of the Road Runner Lounge.

Keith’s laughed out loud. “Hey, looka here. Is that who I think it is?”

“Well, fuck me,” Mikey said. “That’s the fucking ‘Hokey Pokey’ kid from Friday night.”

The men in the van, made a split-second decision that, along with the two teachers, they’d snatch Mr. Hokey Pokey as an added treat for Ray. They were sure he would approve of one more being added to the party.

“I’ll fucking sing that kid our version of “Hokey Pokey” as Ray does his handiwork,” Keith said.

“You put the knife in deep, you peel the skin back tight and you twist it all around, . . .” The crew howled with laughter.

* * *

Matt Beck worked after school at his uncle’s bar mopping floors, cleaning the puke out of the bathrooms and whatever other gross, grunt work his uncle needed done. The job didn’t pay much, but he could buy all the beer he and his friends wanted.

Matt was taking out the trash, but his mind was occupied with thoughts about what a great week he’d had at school so far. With his thoughts elsewhere, he almost ran into the van pulling in near the trash container. “Watch it, shithead,” he said soft enough it probably couldn’t be heard by the occupants of the van.

One reason he'd had a great week was because of all the girls who were talking to him now. A week ago, they had no idea he was alive. Things were looking up for him.

* * *

Mikey, Keith and Mark waited in the van until they saw the two teachers arrive in a brown Plymouth Duster. They watched while the teachers got out of the car, slowly.

Mark laughed. "Looks like those two fat shits got an ass-whipping, too."

Keith sounded pissed. "When we get that kid from Friday, we're going to show him some West Virginia justice. We'll see how it feels to be on the receiving end of the shit stick."

"Calm down," Mikey said. "Let's get these assholes first, then you can show them on the long drive back how pissed you are. Okay?"

"Sure," Keith said. "Sorry, I can't go with you. It's hard to maneuver with these stupid crutches. I can help with the drugging part. Just get 'em out here in one piece."

Mark and Mikey entered the bar and went to the far back booth where the teachers sat.

Jennings and Brooks looked at each other as the two hobbled toward them and sat.

"Christ, did that kid do that to you two?" Brooks asked.

"I was just about to ask the same thing of you?" Mark said.

"Enough with the bullshit." Mikey pulled out a stack of one-hundred-dollar bills wrapped in a rubber band. "That's ten grand. Ray wanted me to tell you there's more where that came from."

"Hot damn, a brick of hundreds," Brooks said.

Jennings smiled and looked at Brooks. "I told you Ray would take care of us."

Mikey pushed the stack of bills toward Jennings. "Put it away and let's drink to fucking up that kid who got you fired."

Brooks went over to the bar and ordered shots and beers for everyone. Over the next hour the teachers drank like sailors on shore leave while Mark and Mikey nursed their drinks.

Ray had learned the teacher's weaknesses from his father and the love of the liquor was just below that of molesting students.

While the teachers were engaged in one of their stories, Mikey laced their drinks with LSD. Before it took full effect, they talked the teachers into going outside to smoke some weed in the van.

After they finished the weed, they were so stoned, they could hardly walk. Keith tied them up with baling wire nice and tight.

"There, how do you pricks like that?" Mark asked as he shoved them into the van.

"Good job," Keith said. "Now it's time to nab that kid."

Mark went inside and said he needed a jump for a dead battery. The barmaid said she'd send out the stock boy to help them is a few minutes.

"That would be great," he'd told her. "My van is at the rear of the parking lot. He can't miss it."

* * *

Matt pulled his uncle's car up to the van and hopped out. "Hello, someone said you need a jump."

No answer.

"Hello." He half yelled, not seeing anyone. As he rounded the side of the van the door slid quickly open and two men jumped out and grabbed him.

"If you say anything or yell out I'll gut you." One man said.

Matt looked down at the buck knife in the man's hand.

"Get in the fucking van now, we just want to talk with you." The other man ordered.

Matt didn't see that he had a choice. He climbed into the van.

When the van door was closed, a third man handed Matt a beer. "Drink this."

"I don't . . . ," was all Matt could get out before he was hit in the side of the head with a nightstick. He slumped down in the van.

* * *

As they pulled away from the Road Runner parking lot, Keith started singing a new version of the "Hokey Pokey". "You put the right fist in, you pull the right fist out, you put the right fist in and you smash him in the mouth." They beat Matt every time the lyrics called for it.

"Holy shit, his fucking eye just popped out," Keith yelled out. "His fucking eye is on the floor." He picked it up and held it in his hand for the others to see. The beating had lasted for almost an hour.

Before they had crossed over the Ohio border into West Virginia all three of their guests were naked and bound with wire.

As instructed, when they crossed into West Virginia and stopped for gas they called Ray. They told him everything except for the surprise.

Ray loved to be surprised, as long as it was the good type of surprise.

* * *

Two guardians had been watching when the van pulled out of the Road Runner Lounge parking lot. Ed Kline and Big John had followed the teachers to the bar and saw them walk to the van with two men. They called in for instructions.

"Strike Eagle, this is the Brick calling. Strike Eagle, this is the Brick."

With a crackle, the answer came back, "Strike Eagle here."

"We're following a white van with West Virginia plates and I believe that the two we were babysitting are in it. BJ says to tell you that the three from Friday are driving the van. What are your instructions? Over?"

"Are you fully fueled, Brick? Over."

"Yes. Sixty gallons. Both tanks topped off, Strike Eagle."

"Follow them, then. We need to know where they're going, Brick," Strike Eagle said.

"Okay, understood. We're on US Route 35 heading east and my best guess is that they're headed to West Virginia, because of the plates. Will call by phone when we can. Brick out."

The CB went silent as Kline and Big John drove into the night following the van. "Aren't you glad I brought you my extra .45?" Big John said as he smiled Kline.

Kline looked at BJ and said, "I fear no evil because we are the baddest SOB's in the valley tonight. Besides we have the light protecting us." With that they both touched the crosses that hung around their necks.

Giovanni and Brady had shown them the evil they were facing and the carnage that lay in its path of destruction. While in the holy circle, Kline and Big John had seen the Beast and heard the words it had spoken in the small house that Giovanni visited before he left Italy.

Giovanni had killed the father and sons but was unable to send the Beast back to the darkness permanently.

They also saw the girls who had been taken here over the years and buried in the basements. The pain inflicted was beyond imagination. They saw the demons that appeared when called by these animals. They saw the girls who were being kept like cattle in the barn for the sick and twisted amusement of this evil.

This fed the darkness with the pain and misery it needed.

They had also seen what had happened to poor Michelle who had been in the wrong place at the wrong time.

Giovanni explained that in all stories of monsters there was a bit of truth. Like with vampires you had to invite them in. While this was just a story it was true with the darkness.

It had to be invited in.

"The darkness needs a doorway to enter a person's life. It needs a legal right to enter your life. When the law of God is broken they have the room to enter. When we violate the laws of God we are outside of His kingdom's protection and the darkness can enter," Giovanni had told them.

"The group we're looking for," Brady had added, "is well beyond this. They've made a bond with the darkness and can call it the way I can call the light."

"We must find them and send them back to the darkness." Brady had told them.

"When we find them, these soldiers of the demonic kingdom will use every deception and struggle to try and turn you to them," Giovanni had added. "When confronted, hold the cross around your neck and say the blessing to our most Holy Mother whom they fear more than anything. She will protect you. This is a fight for only me and Brady."

Giovanni had continued. "That means, once we find them, you are not to get involved no matter what happens. You must stay out of the fight. Do not break the holy circle that is your protection."

Giovanni had made each one swear an oath to the Blessed Mother and kiss the Cross of the Lord around their necks to seal their oath. "You are to be our witnesses to this battle with the Beast, spreading the word of what you have seen to the faithful. She has chosen each of you to spread what you witnessed from this day to your last. It will be a hard path to follow with many hardships," he'd told them.

"No matter who demands it from you, you must never speak my name or Brady's to anyone."

There were questions for what seemed like hours and everything asked was answered. Kline remembered how the hardest questions were asked by Brady's brothers. They were not happy that all of this had been happening and that they never knew. It only added to their frustration that their grandfather was part of the secret.

Giovanni had given each in the group a task to do and as they left the church, each set about to follow what was instructed.

They would find these demons of the darkness, it was just a matter of time.

The hunters would become the hunted.

Chapter Thirty-Two

TIME FOR BATTLE

As the rest of the guardians prepared to leave for West Virginia, Mrs. Hall had the same gut feeling of fearing the unknown she got when Colonel Hall went to war. She looked into his eyes. "Be careful." Her voice cracked.

He understood her fear. "We'll be fine," he said as he kissed her goodbye.

Mrs. Hall waved to the cars as they pulled out. With a rosary in her hand, she started her novena. Not knowing was always the worst part of waiting.

They left Beavercreek early in the morning in two cars and headed east on US Route 35 until they got to the West Virginia border. They would wait there for updates from Mrs. Hall who was acting as base commander and was in contact with Ed Kline and Big John as they followed the white van.

The message they'd been waiting for came in early the next morning. Big John called to say they'd followed the van through the mountains to a farm near a small town called Hico. At first light, they're going to hike into the area and find out all they can before the rest arrive. Then they'll wait for the others at Babcock State Park.

Mrs. Hall thanked Big John and told him to be safe. She gave Colonel Hall the information Big John had given her.

* * *

In Michelle's station wagon, Brady sat next to her, Grandpa and Liam were in the middle seats and his other two brothers were in the back seat.

"There're some blankets in back if anyone wants to take a nap," Michelle said.

"Be careful, though," Brady said. "I put a statue of the Blessed Virgin on the blankets."

She picked up the mic for the new CB radio Colonel Hall had put in her car. "Strike Eagle, this is Annie Oakley."

"I hear you loud and clear, Annie Oakley. Strike Eagle out."

The brothers laughed out loud.

"How about some music?" Michelle said as she pulled out of the parking lot. She put in Aerosmith and was surprised when Brady's grandpa asked her to turn it up.

"Love that band," Giovanni said to no one in particular.

During the drive, Giovanni told the younger boys how evil could choose whatever form would help it in the battle. "Do not talk with them. Do not make contact with them in any way. And most importantly, do not help Brady or me. No matter what happens."

He looked directly at his three grandsons. "Do you understand boys? Do nothing. Even if it looks like all hope has been lost. Do nothing. Your very souls depend on this. Promise me."

Each of the brothers agreed.

"It will be the hardest thing you'll ever have to do," Giovanni added. "To do nothing when two people you love battle for their lives against something too unimaginable to think about. It will test you to your limits."

"This is bullshit, Grandpa," Caleb said, a tear streaked down his face.

"Boys, do not despair, for we are the sword and the shield of the light. We will not be alone in the battle. When all looks blackest and you feel that defeat is at hand, you must chant out loud our war cry of old 'Who is as God'. Hold out your crosses as shields and cry out your faith. It is your faith that will bring aid to the battle."

With that Giovanni hugged Liam then leaned over his seat to hug each of the boys in back.

Michelle's hand slide over to Brady's. She clasped his hand tightly. She leaned over and whispered in his ear, "I will never leave your side. I am not afraid."

Brady could see the look on her face and knew she was ready for this fight. He whispered back, "You must do as agreed also, okay?"

She squeezed his hand again and said nothing more.

Only Brady's grandfather knew there was someone at the farm calling out for Brady's help. The push was calling out to him. It was the bound promise he had made to a boy and now he was being called. They needed to hurry!

* * *

In Bortz's van, were Colonel Hall, his son, Randy, along with Charlie Wolfe and Officer Hickey. The men in the van were all business. There were no jokes or music playing. The atmosphere was tense. They were going into battle.

After a time, Colonel Hall broke the silence. "Before every battle I told my men what Chief Tecumseh said to his warriors before a battle: 'When your time comes to die, be not like those whose hearts are filled with the fear of death, so that when their time comes they weep and pray for a little more time to live their lives over again in a different way. Sing your death song and die like a hero going home'."

No one responded, but Hall felt the tension lessening. "Now let's go over the plan one more time."

Bortz, Hickey, Randy and Colonel Hall were going to the barn as per Brady's instructions. Once there, they were to see if there were any girls being held. If so, they were to free them and bring them back to the van.

Colonel Hall's and Randy's special duties were to render medical aid if anyone was injured during the battle.

Bortz and Hickey would be armed with 9mm Beretta pistols that Hickey had provided courtesy of the Beavercreek Police Department.

"Don't shoot your foot off," Officer Hickey said to Bortz.

Bortz's eyebrows lifted. "Son, let me tell you something about me and guns. I killed more men in Korea up close with a .45 than I want to remember. So, don't you go and worry yourself about my ability to handle a gun."

"Hey, I'm so sorry. I forgot. Just trying to lighten the mood."

Bortz's voice said he was ready to kill whatever came their way.

Colonel Hall nodded and looked around at the men. They were ready.

Brady had warned them there might be a caretaker. If so, he would be armed and wouldn't let them in without a fight. He'd be hiding in ambush in the barn or maybe a tree stand. They might have to lure him out.

Wolfe was to meet up with Big John and Kline. Their job was to get Brady, Giovanni, the brothers and Michelle onto the farm.

* * *

As they drove along the highway in the early morning the CB chatter between the two cars was about gas, food, restroom needs, and the pending fight.

This would be a battle between the light and the darkness. The Angel of Darkness had been cast out of the light and to the earth, with his trusted fallen angels. They didn't know what form the fallen demons would take. Since the demons were intelligent and powerful beings, anything was possible.

Brady had seen everything about the barn and what horror had happened there over the years. He couldn't tell them if they would find any girls or not. But he did tell them that there would be injuries. He told them he'd explain later. The men were instructed to set fire to the barn and burn it to the ground after they got any survivors out.

"Find what looks like a wound in the earth on the side of the mountain," Brady said. "It must be filled in before we leave. It's the pathway to darkness and it must be closed."

"I don't understand," Randy said.

Brady felt a sense of urgency surrounding him. "There's no time to explain now. I promise to tell you about the pathway after the battle has been won. We have to get moving, *now.*"

Brady had assured them they would be met by the men from the Friday night fight once they were in the field. "I know this because I am going to call the light in the center of the field near the house," he explained. "The darkness will not be able to resist being called to it. It would be like a moth is drawn to a flame. The Beast has been looking for Grandpa for decades and now the serpent would surely show himself."

Giovanni took the CB mic. "But there are risks in doing this. I don't believe the darkness has been able to tell that it was Brady calling the light and not me. Their surprise will be that there are two of us to do battle with the darkness.

"If one can kill the person while the soul is possessed, the demon would be cast out permanently. The demons are not above the laws of God and can't survive if slayed with the sword of destiny. The darkness will have no idea that it was there until it was too late. The sword will strike fear in them.

"The important part," Giovanni said. "is that the demon has to be possessing the soul and not separated from the person being possessed. If the demon is separated and manifests its true form, we can only cast it back to the darkness.

"This is what happened back in Sicily on the night I battled the darkness. The demon swore then he would find me and drag me into the darkness before he was sent back into the black abyss.

"The darkness is not eternal like God. The darkness is a created being. The darkness knows there is but one God. They can walk to and fro on Earth. They know that their time is short. They recognize who the saved are. They know the serpent himself is subject to God. They have been seen by man in their natural form and are frightening to behold."

Brady took the mic from Giovanni. "I've seen the Beast. They'll not appear as they are but rather as a deception, always wearing a mask to hide themselves when we confront them at the farm. I'm sure that all the men from Friday night's fight were with the darkness and the same with the teachers. The darkness tried to hide its presence, but the push betrayed them.

"I'm sure the darkness knows that something is wrong and different about me. It must have felt the reverse effect. This confusion is to our advantage."

Brady handed the mic to Giovanni and he continued. "Don't be fooled by the Beast. You are here to be witnesses to this battle. Do not be tricked, they will try to pull you in with their lies. They will find your weaknesses and use them to break your faith. They will know all your secrets, so don't be shocked. The serpent of the darkness was thrown down to earth with his fallen angels. This is the darkness you are going to see in all its ugliness. Be not afraid. When all seems lost and you are at the edge of your faith, chant the war cry of the light".

Chapter Thirty-Three

GATHERING INFORMATION

Kline and Big John watched as two vehicles pulled into the gravel parking lot near the entrance to the Babcock State Park. When they recognized who it was, they flashed their headlights to let their friends know they'd been spotted.

"Finally." Kline wished he hadn't sounded quite so anxious, but he was ready to get started.

Big John raised his eyebrows without comment.

Everyone got out, and greeted one another. It was a solemn meeting. Big John offered them coffee and donuts he and Kline had gotten from the diner in town. Everyone seemed to agree food and hot coffee was just what was needed after the long drive.

Kline motioned toward a picnic table. "Please gather around and we'll fill you in on what we've learned."

Big John spoke first. "The older lady who works the night shift at the diner, Mrs. Cooper, was a wealth of information about the farm and the weird goings on there."

"Fact is, there were times when we couldn't get her to stop talking long enough to ask her questions," Kline said.

Big John sipped his coffee. "She told us the farm was sold under strange circumstances back in the 1950s. Rumors were, it had been in the spinster Miller's family for more than 150 years. Mrs. Cooper heard that Miller sold the farm for cash to a man named Earl Johnson.

"After doing so, as per the story, Miller moved out west without saying diddly squat to anyone in town. No one at the church where she'd attended for fifty years. No one at the bank, where she still had her money. She just up and disappeared into the night like a fart in the wind, according to Mrs. Cooper.

"Mrs. Cooper said that, over the years, hunters have claimed to have seen an old woman on the farm when they were deer hunting on land next to the farm," Big John said. "Legend has it that it's the Miller's ghost that haunts the property."

Brady looked at Giovanni and nodded.

Big John pushed the box of donuts toward Brady's brothers. "Of course that would make her over 120 years old, if these stories are to be believed."

Big John continued. "No one believed the stories the hunters told, Mrs. Cooper explained to us. Most chalked it up to bad moonshine and just plain bullshit talk trying to keep people off their hunting spots."

"Mrs. Cooper's quite a character," Kline said. "She told us none of the stories ever added up," Kline said. "She said she only had an eighth-grade education, but she knew bullshit when she heard it."

Brady's brothers laughed. Zane wiped powdered sugar off his face with his sleeve.

"Yeah," Big John added. "She said this guy who bought the place, Earl Johnson, had shown up a year before and rented a small house just down the road from the diner where he showed up occasionally. He claimed to be a basement digger. That caused Mrs. Cooper to wonder why he moved to her small, do-nothing, town with its poor folks who couldn't even afford basements."

"And," Kline said, "she told us that once he moved to the farm, no one hardly saw him around town again. That's just not how a small town works. She said, in a small town you know your neighbor's business, it's just how it is. He'd come into town occasionally for supplies, but he never fit in."

"So," Big John said, "this digger from who knows where, buys a farm from Miller for cash, after she had refused all offers to sell for seventy years. Mrs. Cooper thinks most people in town feel like the old woman is dead and buried on the farm. They believe Earl killed her. That would explain all the ghost stories of an old lady on the mountain."

Kline continued the tale. "She heard the deed was signed and notarized all proper like, when he took it to the court house to register it, but Mrs. Cooper doesn't believe it. And to make things stranger, Mr. Earl Johnson shows up with a boy he says is his son. No one in town ever saw a wife, just the boy. The boy never went to school according to Mrs. Cooper and I believe she'd know. Must have been home schooled.

"Mrs. Cooper said they always paid in cash in town. Rumors were, they went to Ohio and bought some fancy trucks and digging equipment, and they always paid in cash. There was something not right about that, she added. She thought they might be into drugs or something. They flashed cash around here like they were big shots."

"Did she mention anyone else living on the farm?" Brady asked.

Big John nodded. "Yes. She mentioned some creeps who lived and worked at the farm who weren't like the others who used to live up there. Those other men kept to themselves, were real quiet and hardly ever came to town. Then one day they're all gone. No one ever saw them again after that car crash that killed the boy's father."

Kline picked up where Big John left off. "She said that was when the *new* boys showed up."

"Mrs. Cooper said there are three of them and they are the village idiots from the worst families, always in trouble. Calling them creeps would have been talking nice about them. Not to mention the stories that some of the local girls have told about them and what they'd done to them."

"She went on to say, they're just bad seeds. They go around town like they're better than everyone. The white trash of the white trash, she called them. She's sure they're up to something bad like drugs, liquor or gun running. That ain't digging money that they been making. She said she didn't know why the sheriff hadn't been up there to see what was going on."

"She talked for over an hour about the weird happenings at that farm," Kline said. "She said that locals feel the mountain farm is evil or haunted. It's clear, everyone is scared shitless of these men and that farm."

Big John picked up his cup and took a sip. "We learned there is only one dirt road into the property and that the farm house itself is back in the hollow near the center of the farm acreage. There are also three mobile home trailers on the property and a large barn.

"Cooper told us the farm is over three-hundred acres, and there is a fire road that runs through part of the property that most people don't know about. She advised us that the local hunters are afraid to go near the farm since the stories of missing hunters started a few years ago.

"She said those stories could have been started by the boys, to keep people off their farm but she didn't think so."

"Here's something to add to the list of odd things going on that farm," Kline said. "Mrs. Cooper said that according to the hunters who came into the dinner, there was no game on that side of the mountain. She felt it was odd that no deer ever went there anymore.

"Not even the ginseng hunters would go near there, she said, pointing out that it was a cash crop that everyone took part in to earn a little extra money. Ginseng was worth more per ounce than gold. But no one would dare go on the farm's land anymore because of all the rumors of locals who went ginseng hunting and never returned."

"Mrs. Cooper didn't seem the type to tell tall tales. She was genuinely scared when she told us the stories," Big John said. "I think she wanted our help. She said she wouldn't ask what we were up to, but we should be ready for whatever traps they have laid out for trespassers. It's what we do to trespassers in West Virginia.

"And, she said she'd appreciate it if we go back there for donuts afterwards. She'd like to know if we had a successful trip. If we don't stop by to see her later, she said she'll know we're buried up on that mountain somewhere with the old woman. She said she liked us and she'd sure like to hear what happened on the mountain when we came back. Said she'd have free donuts and coffee for us."

Kline unfolded a piece of paper. "She gave us this map, and on it she'd drawn the directions of where we can find everything. She marked the buildings with stars," said Kline.

Big John said, "At first we didn't know whether to believe her or not. But the more she talked the more I thought one of those ginseng hunters she said disappeared may have been one of her family members or a close friend. She wants revenge and somehow figured we were the ones who could give it to her."

"Okay," said Giovanni, "thank you for the information. It's time to go over the plan and decide if there is any advantage to go now or wait until later. Brady, it's your call."

"There's something I haven't told you all yet," Brady said to the group. He went on to explain about the push calling out and that there was a student who had been grabbed with the two teachers and he was in grave danger.

The brothers looked at each other.

"We need to go *now*," Brady said.

Chapter Thirty-Four

FALLEN ANGELS

All three cars followed the winding road through the mountain and turned right on the dirt road. They drove on the dirt road for almost a mile and then stopped.

This was the place.

Everyone got out of the cars and closed the doors gently, with barely a sound.

They gathered at the back of Michelle's car and Giovanni spoke. "If you cannot do as asked to keep the faith, now is the time to let me know. There is no shame, and no one will think less of you if you want to stay here at the cars."

He looked each person in the eyes and they all nodded, making the sign of the cross, indicating they were going. "Good. I knew that would be your answers." Giovanni smiled.

Bortz, Hickey, Wolfe, Randy and Colonel Hall were to leave first. They had to hike up the side of the mountain through the woods to get to the fire road and reach the barn undetected. They couldn't show themselves until they discovered where the caretaker might be hiding in ambush.

Before Colonel Hall's team departed, Brady told them not to do anything until he'd called the light. He assured them that they would know when it happened.

"The light will make everyone on the farm come to it," he said. "It will awaken the darkness. Only then will the caretaker show himself. After you disable him, go straight to the barn."

Disable. That was a word Colonel Hall knew all too well. Its meaning was clear to all who were going to the barn.

Colonel Hall turned to Brady. "I will be there to stand as witness, you will not be alone."

Brady nodded.

Colonel Hall turned and disappeared into the trees with the rest of his team.

* * *

Caleb, Zane, Liam were standing near Michelle making small talk. "You know we won't let anything happen to Brady, so don't you worry," Liam said.

"I'm not worried," Michelle replied.

"Yes you are, and that's okay," Zane added. "We all know how you feel about him. We see how you look at him."

Michelle turned red. All she could say was, "Thank you."

"That's enough of that," Giovanni said. "The four of you need to follow what we have told you. Stay focused on the task at hand. Do not get provoked and do not enter the fight. You have promised, remember, you have taken a holy oath."

The brothers looked at each other, surprised. "That was a holy oath we cannot break? Caleb asked. "How's that fair?"

"Enough, that's just how it is, and you must accept that fact, all of you, or wait here."

Big John and Kline led the next group. Each had an M16 Colonel Hall had given to them, weapons he'd borrowed from the base.

"If this turns into a gun fight, you will not be out gunned," Colonel Hall had told them when he gave them the M16's.

Brady assured them that once he called the light, the darkness wouldn't bring guns. They'd show up with weapons far more dangerous. They would bring the darkness and all the ugliness that comes with it.

The Beast would be coming.

"All you need to do is get us into the meadow near the house and Grandpa and I will take it from there."

* * *

According to the map the waitress had given them, it was a half-mile hike to the meadow. The farm was beautiful, but this wasn't the time to enjoy the sights. Brady could feel the push so strong now he felt ill. He could tell it was affecting everyone. There was a feeling of gloom falling over them.

Giovanni felt it, too. "Do not let this feeling over take you. Touch your cross and pray to the Blessed Mother. We are almost there. It is now that it starts. It is now that you are to witness what is good and what is evil on earth. It is now that your faith will be tested."

Everyone clutched their crosses and prayed to the Holy Mother. The feeling of gloom slowly passed and Brady could see each one must have felt a renewed strength as they continued.

After what seemed like hours, Kline stopped. "There's the farm house, and I can see the barn." As he stood there pointing, everyone gathered around him.

The barn was huge and seemed like something out of a painting. It was red and in pristine condition. They saw three large backhoes and a bulldozer parked under a large lean-to next to the barn.

The house was just down from the barn, a two-story building made of stone and timber. It was beautiful, not something one would expect to find in the backwoods of West Virginia.

Brady stopped and took a breath. Something was not right. There was an odor, the smell of rotten eggs. Sulfur-like, but different. He knew what it was. The smell of death.

"Smell that?" said Big John. "The last time I smelled that odor was in the jungle in Vietnam after a battle. That's the stench of death."

"Steady, Big John," Giovanni said. "It is going to get much worse. Be strong."

Just as Giovanni cautioned Big John to be strong, Brady heard Zane throw up.

"I shouldn't have eaten all those damn donuts," was all Zane said.

Liam put his arm around Zane's neck. "It's okay, buddy."

Giovanni gathered everyone around him. "We have made it here undetected, but the surprise of what is to take place will be our advantage for only a short while. No matter what, do not break your prayers or the circle.

"Anything can happen. Day may turn to night. The Beast will speak in tongues and languages of old. Only Brady and I will understand and be able to respond. Say nothing. Do not look the

Beast in the eyes. Do not lose your faith. That is what protects you. No contact of any kind.

"You may see the true form of the fallen angels. Do not run. Do not scream. Do not show fear. The Demon wants you to be afraid. They will prey upon your fear.

"Close your eyes if you must. They cannot touch you unless you allow it by inviting them in. You cannot speak to the Beasts.

"Brady and I are the sword and the shield of the light. This is what we have been chosen for, it is our destiny. We will protect you with our lives.

"Gather now in the half circle as we practiced."

A dog sat at each end of the half circle. They lined up in the following order, Hank, Caleb, Liam, Zane, Michelle, Big John, Kline and then Meatball. If all went according to plan the circle would be closed by Bortz, Wolfe, Hickey, Randy and Colonel Hall.

"It's time," said Brady.

Brady walked into the center of the arc and knelt, arms stretched out with palms raised. He called the light. As he rose from the ground, sounds of breaking glass and guttural screaming came from the house.

It was a terrifying sound shattering the quiet of the meadow.

It was the voice of the Beast and it was coming toward them.

Chapter Thirty-Five

COLONEL HALL'S TEAM

Bortz, Hickey, Wolfe, Randy and Colonel Hall hid in the woods, up near the barn. As soon as they'd settled in, they heard the sound.

"Is that what I think it is?" Randy asked.

"Yes son," Colonel Hall said. "That is the sound of darkness, our signal that the battle has begun."

Wolfe pointed over near the barn. "Look."

They saw an old woman in work clothes exiting what looked like a small shed. The image of this old woman, coming out from hiding, was a shock to the group. They'd heard there could be a caretaker on the property, but they didn't expect it to be an old woman.

Hickey scratched his head. "What the hell? Is that who we're looking out for? By the look of her, she couldn't harm anyone, let alone the five of us. There must be someone else." He looked around for someone to agree with him.

Colonel Hall pointed. "Look at her now." The old lady ran downhill toward the house like a world class sprinter.

"What the fuck?" Randy blurted out loud.

"That is who or what Brady had warned us about," Colonel Hall said. "Let's get moving, we have to get into the barn before anyone comes back."

The group moved out from their cover and ran toward the barn.

When they reached the barn, Bortz stopped and pleaded with the others. "We must go to the meadow now. Just listen to those terrible sounds. They need our help."

With one fluid movement, Colonel Hall grabbed Bortz by the arm of his jacket and pulled him hard into the barn door. "No, that's what we were warned might happen. We have to get moving and do what we were ordered to do."

Bortz looked in the direction of the sounds, then nodded and followed the team into the barn.

The barn was huge, with double doors on rollers that opened easily with a slight pull. As the door opened, what was inside wasn't what they had expected.

It was beyond frightening. It was pure evil the likes of which Colonel Hall had ever seen.

In the center of the barn were two bodies, hanging from large steel meat hooks. These hooks were hanging by ropes strung to pulleys attached to large oak beams running across the barn.

It took a few seconds for the group to realize what they were seeing. These bodies had been gutted and skinned like you would a deer.

There was a large green tarp spread out over the floor to catch the splatter from the slaughter that had taken place. Below the two bodies were large galvanized tubs that held the fluids and internal body parts. In the center of one tub was a skull with the eyes still in it.

Off to the side, plywood boards stood with what appeared to be body flesh stretched out like hides on skinner boards to dry. Next to that, was a wire line hung with strips of human flesh drying like beef jerky.

The smell was nauseating.

"What the fuck?" Hickey blurted out, choking back the bile that was trying to escape his mouth. He wiped the sick from his mouth. "Are these the two teachers? For the love of God, what twisted assholes would do this?" He reached into his shirt and held on to the cross around his neck for strength.

Charlie Wolfe doubled over and threw up.

"This is the darkness Brady warned us about," Randy said. "This is the evil they tried to prepare us for."

Even Colonel Hall was visibly shaken by the sight. His voice quivered as he spoke. "We cannot do anything for the teachers. Do your job. Find the girls, if there are any here."

Colonel Hall sent out a silent prayer. "Please don't let us find any more like this."

The men spread out over the vast barn looking any living person or for anything that might be out of place and possibly lead them to someone needing help.

After about five minutes, Wolfe called out, "Over here. I've found something."

In one of the stalls at the far end of the barn there was a secret door that had somehow not been fully closed. As Wolfe opened it, Colonel Hall could tell it led to a lower level of the barn.

Hickey found a light switch at the top of the stairs and flipped it, turning on the lights. He had his pistol out with the safety off.

At the bottom of the stairs they found a long well-lit hallway with cement walls and eight windowless, steel doors.

"This looks like a prison of some sort," Hickey said.

"Hello, is anyone here?" Randy shouted, causing the others to jump.

Bortz found a set of keys on the wall. "These must go to the doors." He opened the door to the first room. Everyone hesitated for fear of what they would find.

"Nothing," Bortz said.

As the door was opened it was lit up just like the hallway. The room appeared to be about eight by twelve feet. There was a sink, bed, shower and a toilet. No window.

It smelled as if it had been newly painted.

In the center of the room was a chain that was attached to the floor. It appeared to be twelve feet in length and had a leg shackle on the end, with a lock attached.

The group was speechless. What horrors had gone on there? How many girls had been kept there and killed?

The need to hurry set in. They left the first room and all shouted, "HELLO, is anyone down here?"

Each room they opened was an exact copy of the first. They rushed from room to room, dreading what could be behind each door. When they opened the fifth room, they found, what they didn't want to see. Chained to the floor and laying on the bed was a naked teenage boy.

"This could be the student Brady told us to look for," Wolfe said.

This boy was so badly beaten his eyes were swollen shut. His poor body had been beaten black and blue. He'd been sliced open from his foot to his upper thigh on both legs. Deep enough to cause severe pain but not deep enough to cause him to bleed out.

"For the love of God," Colonel Hall said, "get that chain off his leg. The key's probably on the key ring with the rest of the keys."

Bortz hurriedly fumbled with the key ring, trying one after another until he found the key that unlocked the leg shackle.

While Bortz and Colonel Hall took off the shackle, Randy removed his clothes. "Here, put my shirt and underwear on him. We can't take him out of here naked."

Randy wore his pants without a shirt.

Colonel Hall saw the tears running down Randy's face.

"Randy, keep your shit together. We are not done, son. Do you hear me? We have not yet joined the fight." He used his father voice, not his colonel one.

"I think it's Matt." Randy said. "He's so beaten up, it's hard to tell for sure."

"I know," was all Colonel Hall managed to say.

Colonel Hall turned to the others. "There could be more prisoners here. Let's get moving and check the other rooms."

To the relief of everyone, the rest of the rooms were empty.

Colonel Hall attended to Matt the best he could. He bandaged the wounds and gave Matt a shot of morphine for the pain. It was battlefield triage, simple and fast, until you could deal with it later in a secure place.

Wolfe found a wheelbarrow next to the barn and brought it to them after the others had carried Matt up to the top of the stairs. "Put him in here," he said. They laid Matt gently into the wheelbarrow to move him down to the field.

"Do we burn the barn now?" Hickey asked.

"No," Colonel Hall said, "it would be too noticeable. We need to prepare to enter the fight now. We must get to the meadow quickly. The Battle is starting."

As they headed down the hill, they saw a sight beyond words. In the meadow, with its long grass, the day had turned into night and what looked like a storm was gathering above it.

In the center of the meadow, they could see a bright white light that was sparking like an overloaded electric transformer, sending flashes of light in all directions.

It was Brady. He'd called the light.

There appeared to be four or five people walking slowly into the meadow toward the opening of the circle of witnesses, directly toward Brady.

The voices and sounds were not of this earth.

"We have to close the circle before they reach Brady," Colonel Hall yelled. "MEN, RUN NOW, RUN AND JOIN THE FIGHT." He screamed out as his battle cry.

"RUN!"

Chapter Thirty-Six

THE EARTH SHOOK

Giovanni watched as four figures emerged from the house and slowly walked across to the meadow. Their movements were awkward and erratic as if their limbs were pulsating as they moved, not how normal people moved.

The earth shook at their approach.

Giovanni moved in behind Brady, shielding himself from view.

As the four men drew closer to the meadow, the light of the day was eliminated, and darkness appeared, turning day into night; the storm was almost upon them. The sky was an ugly, black color with hints of green and yellow in the clouds. The strong wind that blew down was cold and strong from the surrounding storm clouds.

The meadow grass burned as they walked through it.

There was a stillness in the air, just like before a tornado hits.

The sweet smell of grass in the meadow was replaced with the putrid odor of death that filled the air.

There was no rush. The four figures didn't run, they walked with a purpose. The demons were coming and the evil of the darkness was with them.

Smoke was rising all around them as they approached.

Brady knelt in the center of the meadow, hands out and palms upward, and began levitating. The energy surrounding him caused an electrical popping in the air. The light surrounding him was so bright you couldn't look directly at him. Soon, the light was all that lit the meadow and it enveloped the darkness.

Brady was the bait that lured them in.

When the four men reached the opening of the arch they stopped abruptly. They seemed reluctant to enter the circle.

One of the men shouted something at them in a language that no one in the circle understood.

* * *

Michelle looked at them and recognized three of them instantly as her attackers and from the fight. But they were walking as if they had no injuries. How was that?

Just as she looked toward Zane, he reached down and took her left hand. As she looked over, she saw the brothers were holding hands. It made her brave, she'd felt the darkness before and this time she would not be afraid.

* * *

Ray was in the center of the men speaking in the ancient language of Arabic. His voice boomed, sounding as if it came from a loud speaker.

"I have been looking for you all these years," he raged in almost a scream.

"You will regret coming here with these fools. I will drag all of you into the depths of darkness. The pain that I will inflict on you will be never ending. You cannot destroy me; my power is beyond what you can ever defend against. I will peel your skin off your bodies while you are alive."

Giovanni stepped out from behind Brady.

The sounds of voices talking in tongues filled the air.

Giovanni responded in the ancient language. "Don't try using the languages of old. I know them all. You are the soldiers of the Beast. In the name of the blessed Virgin who you fear above all others, I demand that you speak your name."

When they got closer, it was clear that there were four men and a woman who stayed at the rear of the men. There were five of them.

"You are a not a man," Giovanni said to Mikey. "Leave that body and show your true self. I command you in the name of the Queen of the Holy Rosary, demon."

Mikey laughed. "Fuck you old man, you have no power over me. Fuck that whore you pray to!"

Giovanni replied. "The power I command is not mine. It is the light that you most fear."

Keith taunted Big John, trying to get him to *open a door* the demon could enter. In the voice of a child the demon said, "Save me brother, save me. I'm on fire, it burns, it burns, I'm on fire, the train, help me big brother." Keith laughed wildly in Big John's sister's voice. "You're so big and yet you couldn't help your little sister and her friends. You let us all die."

The darkness had found an old wound from Big John's past and was picking at it like a dry scab. Now in Keith's voice. "You were supposed to drive them that day, all those girl scouts were crushed and burned alive by the train because you were too busy, too busy to be bothered." Keith laughed.

"I have them in the darkness. Do you want to see them burning? They are my playthings." Keith laughed wildly.

Big John didn't reply. He stood silent with his hand holding the cross on his neck. He would not break the bond. His faith was strong.

Giovanni spoke. "Demon, I know your name, Enlil, leave that body and face me."

Mikey, Keith and Mark all turned toward Giovanni. "I know your names, Abigor and Abandon." Giovanni stood defiantly in front of them. Drawing their wrath away from Big John.

At the sound of their true names, the ground shook and lightning cracked.

Hail started to fall.

"I sent you back to the darkness so very long ago, or have you forgotten?" Lightning flashed again, with the crashing sound of hail falling outside the circle.

"A mere boy defeated three of the Prince's angels." Giovanni taunted them. "You cried out like cowards as I slit your throats before you could even cry out for your master. It is your images that I left burned into the wall, for all to see; the demons being defeated by the sword and shield of the light.

"Show your true selves for all the ugliness that you are in this world. Do not deceive us with this form you have taken, I command you, the Queen of the most high, commands you!"

Giovanni had been buying time until the others could close the circle. As he looked over, he saw Colonel Hall and the others standing at the far end of the circle. Randy pushed a wheelbarrow with what looked like a body in it.

Keith walked over to Michelle, speaking in her very own voice, mocking her, "no, no Daddy, help me. It hurts, it hurts, you screamed as I shoved my hand into you. Oh, did you like it? Oh, how I love a virgin. How did it feel as I slid the blade into your chest, over and over again?"

The demon was just feet from her face but couldn't approach closer. He couldn't touch her as he reached out. He cried out in the language of old. "What is this?"

"That's right," Giovanni said. "You cannot touch her. You cannot touch any of them. I have protected all of them from your wickedness."

The bodies of the four men were taking on strange twisting movements as the taunting by Giovanni continued.

"And you," Giovanni pointed at Ray, "you're an abomination of the darkness, son of the Beast. You do not fool this old man. You are the hideous cambion, the child demon that was foretold. Your illusion does not work here. I know what you are, and we will send you back to the fire."

The rumbling grew deafening, the lightning clapped overhead, "We will drag you to the darkness old man. You cannot fight all four of us," Ray shouted spitting in his anger.

"You are right, I can't. I'm an old man now. I am too young to die and too old for a fight. It is not I, demon, who will send you back to the Beast."

Brady stepped up and positioned himself next to his grandfather.

He was glowing with the light; his energy was electrical. He walked up and touched Caleb. With that touch, a light went person to person in the circle. As the light reached each person, the crosses around their necks glowed white hot, painlessly burning permanent crosses into their chests as a sign of the Holy Spirit's protection.

This holy tattoo was a protection the demons couldn't enter or touch.

The light formed a complete circle from each witness to the other, glowing and popping with energy, trapping the darkness.

"The demon says, it will kill me," Brady exclaimed, "I am not my grandfather and I will send you forever back from which you have come.

"You will not leave the holy circle," he said in Arabic. "For it is the law of God. The one and only God that you know is the true King of heaven and earth."

With that Giovanni moved next to his grandson in the circle.

In the center stood the four men and Brady.

In an instant, it started.

Keith, Mikey and Mark rushed Brady with hunting knives in their hands slashing and stabbing at Brady. His movements were at a speed that was a blur. It was fluid like water.

The point of his lance pierced the heart of each as they fell screaming in the voices of the demons that possessed them. In just a moment it was over. Three bodies heaped in a lump in the field.

"WHAT HAVE YOU DONE?" Ray screamed, and the earth shook again.

Brady turned and faced the demon holding his weapon above his head. "You know what this is, for it is the lance that pierced the side of our Lord.

"Your fallen angels will never go back to the darkness. Their spirits have forever ended as they are not eternal as our Lord.

"It is the law.

"You have failed your master, demon.

"For I am the sword and the shield of the light."

Ray moved toward Brady with a speed that matched Brady's. Ray's blade slashed toward Brady's body, but had no effect because of the armoring in the jacket.

Ray stopped, in mid motion, staring at Brady. He looked down at the lance sticking out of his chest. It had entered under the ribs and up into his heart.

Brady was faster and better trained.

Ray crumpled to the ground, and hail fell all around. Lightning flashed. A voice boomed from the front of the circle next to Colonel Hall. The ground shook as the old woman walked to the fallen body of the demon child.

When she reached the body, the darkness spoke from the mouth of the old woman. "I will take all of you with me for what you have done here. Your God cannot protect you from me, you fools. You will die a thousand deaths."

"You have no power here. Show yourself, Beelzebub, prince of the demons, I know it is you," Giovanni said. "You cannot trick me. The old lady opened the pathway and called you long ago. Your soldiers lead me here, oh great prince of darkness. You are the fool." Giovanni egged the Beast on.

At that moment, the old woman fell dead to the ground as "the wicked one" took form and grew to his full height.

Brady knew that he couldn't defeat the Lord of darkness on his own since it had shed his human form.

He started chanting "Who is as God?"

Everyone in the circle joined in. "Who is as God?"

Over and over again they called out in unison, sending sparks out into the darkness overhead.

There appeared two additional, bright white lights that entered the circle and took human form. The guardian Angels had left the bodies of Hank and Meatball. They stood next to Brady and his grandfather.

The Beast was silenced, stopping at the sight of two guardian angels appearing.

They spoke together as one, in voices that were all languages as one. "Serpent of the darkness, accuser of the brethren, we command you back to the fire. The Holy Mother commands you. She is what you most fear, deceiver of truth. She commands you to leave this place. For She is coming."

The guardians continued to chant. The sweet smell of roses replaced the odor of death. Hope replaced the darkness and despair that had been felt by everyone before.

"You have no power over me, guardians. It is I who has power over you, I will take you as payment for my lost angels," the Beast boasted. "Every one of you will be with me. Your Blessed Mother is not here to save you. She has abandoned you fools." The Beast laughed.

The chanting grew ever louder and started to drown out the ugly voice of *the destroyer* from the darkness.

She appeared at that moment.

The Guardian Angels, Brady and Giovanni bent to one knee and bowed their heads.

Between Brady and the Beast, She stood in all Her glory.

"Behold Demon, before you are the sword and the shield of my Son's kingdom. They have been chosen to do my work. They will seek out and destroy all your creatures and lost souls of the darkness. The words they speak and command of you are mine. From the darkness, they will bring your evil into the light for all to lay witness.

"I command you to go back to your kingdom of darkness that my Son gave you for your disobedience.

"Fallen Angel, I command you to go back to the fires of pain and agony.

"You will obey my word."

The light pulsed and exploded, pushing the darkness and its storm from the meadow.

In an instant, the demon was gone.

The light was gone.

She was gone.

The battle was won.

Chapter Thirty-Seven

THE PRAYER OF VENGEANCE

The day was won.

The sun reappeared and everyone realized they had been victorious in battle. The witnesses hugged each other in celebration.

Brady felt an arm on his shoulder, and saw it was Matt.

"I knew you'd come," was all he could get out before he gave Brady a bear hug, lifting him off his feet. Matt was overcome with emotion, tears streamed down his face.

"I don't understand what happened," Matt said. "Tell me what's going on. I am so confused. These assholes beat the shit out of me and said they were going to skin me alive. What day is it? I've lost track of time."

Brady placed his hand on Matt's shoulder. "There is a lot of explaining that needs to happen, but now is not the time, Matt. I will have everything explained to you on the way home, I promise."

All of Matt's injuries had been healed when the Holy Mother appeared.

"I don't know how it happened," Matt said. "I heard a woman's voice telling me to get up and walk, that I had been healed. I did as she asked, I could walk and I didn't hurt any more. Who was she? Was she an angel? She looked like one."

Matt cried and started to shake. "She healed me, Brady. Look." He ran his hands over his body from head to toe.

"I know." Brady hugged him again. "I promised you I would come if called. It's all going to be okay now." He whispered in Matt's ear. "They will explain everything on the way home."

Colonel Hall checked Matt over from head to toe declaring, "Son, you have been healed by the holy hand of the Mother of God." He made the sign of the cross.

Matt looked confused, but he didn't ask what Colonel Hall meant.

The miracle they witnessed between good and evil in a meadow in West Virginia would change all their lives forever. They had seen the Blessed Mother with their own eyes and heard Her speak.

They had seen the Beast and the fallen angels in their ugliness.

When all had seemed lost, the Angels came when called.

It was now up to each one to spread the word, in their own way, of this divine struggle between the light and the darkness.

"Our story," Brady said, "will have us criticized by the very church we all love. You must be strong in your faith against forces within the church that will launch the most vicious attacks against us.

"No matter what, you must never tell of the names of the man and the boy who could call the light. It's the secret you've sworn to keep until your dying day."

Brady noticed his brother, Liam, kneeling in the meadow. He walked over to him and saw Liam had Meatball's head in his lap. The big dog was motionless.

Liam looked up at Brady with tears coming down his cheeks. "He's gone. Bring him back Brady, bring him back." He pleaded. "Bring him back now, Brady. Call the light and bring Meatball back, please."

Zane and Caleb joined them and were also pleading with their brother to bring the dog back.

Their grandfather joined them. "He cannot. Neither Brady nor I can bring him back. He was over half a century old. When the guardian left his body, the very life of him left also. It was the guardian that kept Meatball alive all these years. Don't be sad, he's had a long and good life. He is now with the guardian in the light.

"He was always Guardian Raphael's dog. He is where he should be. I will miss them both but I will see them again. Rejoice in what you have seen here, my grandsons. We will bring him home and bury him in my rose garden in a place of honor."

"What about Hank?" Liam looked around for Brady's dog.

"He is fine, boys. Hank is not as old as Meatball; the guardian could leave and re-enter without him passing."

Hank appeared and walked over to lick Liam's face.

"Boys, go to the station wagon and get some sheets and blankets to wrap our friend, Meatball, in for the journey home," their grandfather asked.

Zane and Caleb slowly got up. "We'll go."

Colonel Hall broke the sadness of the moment. "It's time, men. We must finish what Giovanni told us to do. Our job is not finished here until we burn that house and barn of evil to ashes."

He turned to Big John. "You and Kline can go get that dozer and backhoe moved from the two next to the barn before we burn that sickness to the ground. While you're up there, cut down those bodies, and put the mess in the barn into the front loader. Then bring it down here to the meadow so we can load the rest of this evil in it."

Colonel Hall brought up a subject no one had talked about. The bodies of the five people in the meadow. The bodies of these five had become pure evil.

"Bortz, Hickey, and Wolfe, burn that house to the ground," Colonel Hall said.

"It'll be our pleasure," Wolfe said.

"And burn all three of those mobile homes marked on the map on the farm," Colonel Hall added.

Caleb and Zane returned with blankets and sheets from Michelle's car to wrap their fallen friend. With care and sadness, they wrapped the old dog.

"There," Liam said, "now we can take him home." The three brothers carried Meatball over to a large walnut tree and placed him in the shade. "We'll be back soon old buddy," Liam added, choking on his words as they headed back to the meadow.

Giovanni took Brady, Zane, Liam, Caleb, Randy and Michelle with him to find the entrance to the darkness on the mountain.

It had to be closed.

"The pathway," Giovanni said, "has been opened on this mountain for almost one-hundred years. I have been looking for this for a very long time. It was the old woman who had caused the tear in the fabric between this world and the darkness."

"How're we going to find it?" Randy asked.

"Follow your nose," Brady said. "Follow that smell of death. Do you smell it?"

"Yes," they all said as they were making their way up the side of the hollow.

After about a twenty-minute hike it was Michelle who saw it first. "Look," she pointed. Up on the side of a rock wall was what appeared to be a cave.

"Shit," said Zane. "Look at all the dead birds."

There were dead birds and small animals scattered all over the front entrance of the cave.

"That's close enough," Giovanni said. "The vapor coming out of this wound in the earth is poisonous to anything that breathes its noxious odor. Randy, go down and tell Big John we found the opening and to bring the equipment up here."

Randy turned and ran back down the way they'd come as fast as his football injury allowed.

"What is this place?" Michelle asked.

Giovanni looked at the opening. "This is the spot where the evil came from. It is a gateway used for decades, a portal that allowed these demons to come into this world. We will throw the bodies of these lost souls into its depths and close its entrance forever. It is the same thing that the church did back in my village, at the farm where I first did battle with the darkness. The church will buy this land and select a group of faithful monks to live in a monastery here.

"They will forever make sure that this doorway is never re-opened," Giovanni said.

"There are places like this, all over the world, places that once had such entrances. There are also some that need to be closed. I have closed many over the years. This was not my first, nor will it be Brady's last."

"In my travels as a diamond and gem dealer, this is what I have been doing all these years my grandsons. I was chosen by the light, just like your brother. It is our life's work to stop this evil. It is not an easy road to follow and Brady will need your help in the coming years, if you so choose.

"Brady will need you also, Michelle. You must always remember while you are hunting them, they will be hunting you. All of you. It is a battle where you can never let your guard down.

"I'm in," said Liam without hesitation.

"Me, too," said Caleb, followed quickly by Zane.

They turned and looked at Michelle and she said with a look that showed her true feelings, "I will never leave Brady's side. He will never fight this alone. I will be with him until the end."

Brady was humbled at this show of unwavering support.

Giovanni smiled at Brady. "I told you this is what they would say. You will not bear this task alone. I will not worry with them by your side now."

Brady pointed. "Here they come."

The dozer and backhoe could be seen coming in the distance. The arm of one of the bodies dangled over the lip of the bucket of the loader, bouncing to and fro in rhythm to the sound of the engines. Brady thought how odd it looked, something beyond odd. Something so terrible reduced to nothing.

While the bodies were dumped into the emptiness of the opening, Brady said a prayer of forgiveness for the damned in Latin, making the sign of the cross as he finished.

"Fill it in," Brady said.

Big John and Wolfe proceeded to fill the opening, first with large rocks and then finally with mounds of earth. When they finished, it was as if the opening never existed.

Brady stood before the mound and got everyone's attention. "Please bow your heads." His voice boomed with new confidence as he said the prayer of vengeance.

"Oh, Queen of the Blessed Rosary, I beseech thee to grant me the vengeance for which I seek, to send the evil before me back into the darkness, from which it has come. For I am the sword and the shield, with my voice, I speak the authority that which you have bestowed upon me. For the serpent fears you above all others. Generation to generation we have served you, honoring a promise made on the hill at Calvary. I honor my forefathers' pledge to seek out the darkness. Make my hands fast and accurate. When I call out to you, I beg of you to heal those who have suffered at the hands of this evil. I freely accept the pain and will endure the suffering of the innocent, as my honor to you. Being one of the righteous, I rejoice when vengeance is done, for it is my reward."

When Brady had finished, he placed the statue of the Blessed Virgin they had brought with them in front of the mound of dirt. He turned and looked at everyone who had gathered there.

With his arms raised above his head and toward the heavens he spoke. "From this day until the end of time, this place will be forever Holy Ground."

"Amen," everyone said in unison.

While the others headed to the cars, the brothers went to the tree where the body of the old dog they all loved rested in the shade of the tree. Each brother gently picked up an end of the blanket Meatball was wrapped in and carried him to the vehicles. There, they placed him gently in the back of the wagon for his final trip home.

While they drove slowly down the dirt road, Brady looked back and watched the fires burning with thick clouds of black smoke filling the sky. *It was a fitting end for this place of evil,* he thought.

"How about some music?" Michelle suggested as she popped in an eight-track tape. The Rolling Stones came on playing, "Sympathy for the Devil".

"Turn that up, please," Giovanni said. "You have to love this warning I had Mick write."

Caleb looked at Zane, Zane looked at Liam and Liam looked at Brady, eyebrows raised.

"It's true," was all Brady said.

During the long drive back, their grandfather told many stories of events from the last fifty-plus years that led up to the battle in the meadow.

Giovanni explained everything and left no detail out. He told them of the three secrets of Fátima that the church acknowledged but also of the ten additional secrets foretold to him and only shared with each Pope, when it was time.

For in these small details, would be what would keep them safe from the evil that waited for them in their travels.

Chapter Thirty-Eight

MRS. COOPER

The pickup truck carrying Big John and Kline parked in the lot adjacent to the diner just as the sun was starting to fade in the foothills of West Virginia.

When they walked into the diner, Mrs. Cooper was standing behind the counter with a box full of sweets, two hot coffees and a smile a mile wide.

"I knew you boys would be back," she said matter of factually. "I could tell by the determination on your faces that you were men on a mission. Scary really, to tell you the truth. Around here, we call it the *don't fuck with me* face, if you know what I'm saying."

The cigarette that had dangled from her lips came alive as she took a long drag and then blew a perfect smoke ring that grew larger as it flew across the room. Her pause gave them a chance to talk, but they waited, knowing she had more to get off her chest.

"Saw the smoke up there. You must a tore someone a new asshole, is what I'm thinking." She eyeballed them, not waiting for a response. "It's not like those bastards didn't deserve it. They had it coming for years, I'd say. Tell me honestly, is the evil on that damn mountain gone?"

Kline answered. "Yes, and it's never coming back. We burned those sons-a-bitches to the ground, you might say. They'll never be doing what they'd been doing, not ever again."

"And what was that they were doing?" She looked directly at Kline.

Kline said nothing.

"That's what I thought," she said. "Better not talked about, huh? That's what we say around here. Good. I hope they burn in hell's eternal fire."

She has no idea how true her wish was, Kline thought as he looked at Big John.

"I have something to tell you, Mrs. Cooper," Big John said. "Please sit down."

She paused as she sat, trembling slightly, and snuffed out her cigarette.

"Your boy wasn't up on the farm, never was. He's alive."

"But how did you…?" She gasped as her hands went to her mouth.

"Our Lady, Mrs. Cooper, She told me to tell you he's down south. Call your cousin Maggie in Nashville, tell her you know about the baby and it's all okay. Your son wasn't killed on the mountain."

"What?" She pleaded, looking in his face for answers. "How did you know about my son? My cousin?"

"Mrs. Cooper, please listen and remember what I'm about to tell you. This is a special message for you. She said your church singing was beautiful, she heard it all. Your faith was without question."

"How can you know all this?" Mrs. Cooper stammered shaking her head. "It's not possible. Who is this *she* you keep talking about?

How can you know any of this?" A tear ran down her face, but she wiped it away with her apron.

She looked at Kline and then Big John. "When you two left here, I called the preacher, told him what y'all were set to do about that evil on the mountain. That farm plagued this town for generations. I knew in my heart that you'd need our help. Preacher Donnie called the congregation together for an emergency revival that lasted all day. In fact, I just got to work.

"The church seemed to shake as we sang and prayed for you." Her voice was a whisper.

Kline nodded. "Yes. She told us to tell you, 'you held the serpents and drank from the jar'. Your faith was unwavering and she heard your prayers for our safety. She sent the message about your son to ease your pain."

Kline reached out and hugged her. In that brief moment of contact, the light went from Kline to Mrs. Cooper. A gift to her that showed all they'd seen and experienced on the mountain, telling her to spread the word of the miracle to her fellow faithful.

Once Mrs. Cooper got her breath back, she wasted no time in dialing the first person on the church daisy chain, the word of the emergency meeting was sent.

Kline and Big John pulled out of the lot in the pickup truck, heading back to Beavercreek. They saw a group of people entering the diner. They knew the crowd had to be members of the First Pentecostal Church arriving to hear and bear witness to the miracle on the mountain as it had been told to Mrs. Cooper.

Chapter Thirty-Nine

THE DRIVE HOME

As Michelle drove the car back to Ohio along the back roads of US Route 35, Giovanni spoke. "It's time for all of you boys, and Michelle, to fully understand why Brady and I were chosen by the light to battle the darkness. From your grandfather farthest removed, on my side of your family tree, from across the sea, a promise was made on that hill at Calvary to a crying mother. A promise of a mere boy who vowed to stop the evil that had killed her son.

"I will never let this happen again, the boy said with tears in his eyes as he looked at the woman's son hanging on the cross. The woman touched his face with her hand and said, *and so it shall be.*

"The Roman boy then looked around the crowd that had gathered. He saw what appeared to be a strange man in robes, but upon looking closer, he could see through its deception. In its true form, it was the Beast. It had come to watch the fall of the *Son of God.*

"The boy looked at the Beast and gave it the sign of death, one that a Roman soldier gives to his enemy in battle. The Beast nodded its head in acknowledgement and with a flourish of its hand accepted the challenge from the boy.

"Every generation since that moment on the hill, one child of his lineage was chosen by the light. In my family, it was me and in yours, it was Brady. Why we were chosen, I am not sure and may never know.

"This is why I have always tried to do so much with you boys. I was not sure who or if any one of you would be chosen. Your mother and dad never had any idea about me or Brady. We need to keep it that way. Do you understand what I am saying?" He looked at each one.

"They work so much that all they can worry about is paying bills and putting food on the table. They were more than glad to have me help with you boys. It eased their guilt that they were not able to spend time with you. Since I couldn't always be there, I gave Hank to Brady the way my Grandfather gave me Meatball to be a guardian.

"From the time I was a small boy of five, the light appeared to me. It has been the same for your brother. Brady was not allowed to tell anyone but me, what was going on, what the light was teaching him. He wanted to tell all of you, believe me as I had to remind him constantly that you couldn't know. He couldn't put you in harm's way.

"Until this week. It was time for all of you to know the truth.

"The Holy mark on each of your chests, will be the protection that you never had before. You are always to keep it hidden and never show it. There are those in the church who know what it means to be the bearer of the marks. Always remember that the darkness cannot touch you unless you let it in. Brady will explain the rules in greater detail over the next few months.

"Never forget the rules."

On the long drive home through the winding roads he told them more about his diamond and gem buying trips around the world and what he had really been doing.

While he was hunting the darkness, it was hunting him, he told them.

"I am the prize that the Beast most desires. That is what you saw in the meadow. It raged at the sight of me. I have sent many of the serpent's fallen souls back to a place where they cannot return. He will now be looking for the both of us. Brady has something that they fear above all others, for it has the blood of our Lord on it.

"The darkness will now also be looking for all of you.

"Your brother and I are the sword and the shield of the light. We have been called to rid the world of this darkness that you have witnessed. I am sorry to say I am getting too old to do this and it is time for your brother to take over for me.

"Boys, I know what your answer will be before I ask this of you but I have to ask anyway. I need you to help Brady."

"Grandpa, we are already helping and will always help," Caleb said with Zane and Liam agreeing.

"Just tell us what we need to do," Liam said.

"That is for your brother to decide. He will help get you prepared for what is ahead and what to expect. You must heed everything he asks of you, for it is not as a brother he asks but as the sword and the shield of the light. Do you understand?

"When he speaks to the darkness, it is with the words and the voice of the light. These battles are life and death, not games, for you could be dragged down to the darkness. There is nothing Brady can do to bring you back if that happens." He looked at each of them in the car.

The brothers and Michelle said nothing for miles after that and Giovani knew his words had terrified them. They had all seen the Beast and knew they could be dragged into the darkness. But, he also knew that would help Brady.

No one said a word until "American Pie" finished playing on the eight-track. That was when Michelle broke the silence. "At the next exit, we'll stop for gas. How about something to eat?"

"It's about time," Zane said. "I was going to pee myself if you didn't stop soon."

Everyone laughed. Giovani caught Brady's eye and they both nodded.

Brady spoke. "Grandpa and I have decided we need to go to Austria to visit a man who did business with those teachers. Grandpa feels that it may lead us to someone he's been trying to find for almost forty years.

"I was thinking spring break would be a good time to go. How do you guys feel about going with me? That includes you, Michelle."

"Where's Austria?" Caleb asked.

"Europe," Michelle said.

Without a moment's hesitation, "Europe? Oh hell, yeah," was Caleb's response.

All agreed.

In the back of the station wagon Hank had his head out the window as he sat next to his fallen friend.

Chapter Fourty

HOME

Father Bob greeted the men as they entered the church with a firm hand shake and a hug. He was so relieved to see their faces again. When they'd left the church to go to West Virginia, he had no idea who would be coming back. He was so unsure of their success, he'd made funeral plans just in case.

Their faces reminded him of those he'd seen who'd returned from war, solemn and tired looking. Yet, a sense of elation and hope radiated from each of them. Even the young members of the team had matured.

He clicked them off by name. Hickey, Big John, Kline, Wolfe, Bortz, Colonel Hall, and Randy were all there. Plus, a boy he didn't know. Father Bob looked around. Had he been premature in his elation? "Where are the rest?"

Colonel Hall stepped forward. "Don't worry, Father. They're not coming, but all are fine. I have been instructed to tell you everything that happened on our trip. I am not to leave out any detail of what was heard, said or what we saw. We each have different parts to tell you and it will take a while. I am to tell you that you need to remember everything, for you will need to tell this story again."

"Of course," said the priest. "Let's go to the rectory where we'll be a little more comfortable. On the way over there I have something to show all of you first."

The men looked at one another with raised eyebrows, as if a little uncertain at what the priest was about to show them.

"Okay," Colonel Hall said.

"Please follow me." Father Bob motioned to them. They all followed him out of the church and down into the grotto where he stopped.

"When Big John called me from the diner in West Virginia, he asked me to pray for all of you. I came out here to do so. From sun up until sun down, I prayed the Rosary, pleading for your success and salvation. The Ladies of the Rosary were so concerned when they found me, they stayed and prayed also not knowing and not asking why.

"Something strange and wonderful happened while we prayed. The grotto became dark and filled with a circle of bright white light. The sound of static popping was deafening. You could feel the energy in the air.

"I knew the battle had started and all of you were in danger." Father Bob could feel the tears gathering in the corners of his eyes. He brushed them away.

"Look." He pointed.

In the center of the Grotto were ten burned spots forming a circular pattern on the grass, with four more burned spots in the center of the circle. The men nodded at each other indicating they knew the spots showed where each had stood in the meadow. There was also one spot outside of the circle.

"Father," Colonel Hall said, "I'm sure you have many questions and I have been instructed to answer all of them."

"Yes, please, I need to hear it all," was all Father Bob said.

"Father, before we get started, I have one question for you," Charlie Wolfe said. "How are the Ladies of the Rosary doing?"

"Simply amazing! They prayed all night and sang songs of glory. I'm sure they'll feel forever blessed. I finally had to make them leave at five-thirty this morning. That's how they are doing. It has been the answer to what they have always prayed for. They witnessed a true miracle."

For more than three hours the men filled in every detail and answered every question that was asked of them by the priest. They also introduced Matt and told Father Bob why he was with them.

Father Bob gave Matt a long hug.

As the men prepared to depart, Colonel Hall stopped and turned to Father Bob. "One last thing, Father. I have been told by Brady that you are to say nothing about the events that have unfolded here."

Father Bob frowned. "Never? To no one?"

"He said that you will know when it is time."

"How will I know?"

Colonel Hall smiled. "He said you would ask that and he said to tell you, 'you will know it is time, when it is time'."

The two men shook hands and Colonel Hall left with Matt.

Chapter Forty-One

BACK TO SCHOOL

Before they left West Virginia, the students in the group decided no one would go back to school until Friday. Everyone needed time to recover from the trip and a couple of days off would work wonders.

Matt had driven back with Randy and the men in the van. They had done their best to explain to him what had happened, but were somewhat limited in all that they could tell him. He had no clear memory of what had happened in the meadow and that was probably best. Matt couldn't distinguish between what was a dream and what was reality. They told him the men from the Friday night fight had grabbed him and that everyone had come to rescue him. How they found him or why he'd been taken, he simply didn't want to know; the thought of it was too much to tolerate.

There was no need to say more.

Matt's only concern now was what to tell his parents.

"Don't worry, Matt," Colonel Hall said. "I'll explain everything to them. I am sure they've been panicked since you disappeared and will be relieved to see you. Pissed, maybe, but still relieved to see your smiling face. Just let me do all the talking. Trust me, it won't be any worse than when you got arrested at the football game."

Matt just nodded in agreement. Matt, however, had a secret only Brady knew.

When they got to his house, the driveway was filled with cars.

"Well," Colonel Hall said, "looks like this may be a bit harder than I thought. Still, let me do all the talking, okay?"

Matt reached for the door handle, but the door was opened and the yelling started.

Matt's mother was beside herself. "Where have you been? Why no phone call?" The questions were non-stop.

It was then Matt's mother noticed Colonel Hall. "Who the hell is this?" She yelled at Matt as she pointed at Colonel Hall.

"Mom, please listen, please Mom, you have to listen to what Colonel Hall has to tell you. He will explain everything."

Colonel Hall then started to talk in a firm tone. Everyone in the room, Matt's father, aunts and uncles all grew quiet. He told the story in detail, leaving out nothing. When he finished, everyone just looked at Colonel Hall and Matt in utter disbelief.

Colonel Hall had left out names, but had told the story as he was instructed.

"Bullshit," his mother said breaking the silence. "I'm calling the police."

"Mom, please Mom, look at me." Matt walked toward her. "Look into my eyes and you will see the truth."

Matt's mother grew suddenly quiet as she walked over to where her son was standing and stared at his eyes.

"Mom, I can see now. My eye was brought back. The lady in the meadow gave me my eye back. I can see, Mom. Look for yourself."

His mother looked again and knew it was true. She dropped to her knees and cried.

Matt had lost his right eye in an accident when he was eight and had worn a glass eye ever since.

"It's all true." Matt said, as he looked at each member of his family. "Everything Colonel Hall has told you is the truth."

* * *

At school on Friday morning, it was as if nothing had changed.

Brady and his brothers walked from the parking lot to the rear of the building. Standing there were Randy and Michelle waiting for them. The brother's girl friends were there, too.

Brady smiled. "Why did I know all of you would be waiting for us?"

"Get used to it," Michelle said.

Everyone laughed as they walked into the building together.

When they got to Weasels' Corner, they saw the whole paint-the-bridge team sitting at a nearby table.

Only Linda got up and walked over to Brady's group. "Where the heck have you guys been? The rumors have been flying all over the school about you since last Friday night."

Michelle turned toward Linda. "Whatever you've heard is all true. How's that? And you tell your *secret* boyfriend that if he ever gets near Brady again, I will personally whip his ass."

Caleb and Liam started to laugh but put their hands over their mouths to hold it down. It was like a fart in church, there wasn't going to be any holding it in.

"You don't have to be so sore about it," Linda said in her usual snotty attitude. "It's not like it's anyone's fault, you know."

Michelle had both hands on her hips facing Linda. "Screw you, Linda. It is someone's fault. It's all Greg's fault and we all know it, so take your fat ass and waddle back to the rest of those cowards, tell them I said to piss off. You don't scare me, trust me I've seen scary and it's not you."

Zane couldn't hold back. "You go girl." He doubled over laughing.

All through the day the students gave Brady and his tagalongs wide berth in the halls. At third period class change, as they rounded the corner on the second floor where the sophomores hung out, chanting of "Brady, Brady, Brady" boomed in the hallway.

Standing in the middle of the group of about thirty-five students was Matt. As Brady approached, Matt was patting his hand over his heart and then pointing at Brady.

Brady looked directly at Matt and returned the gesture.

Michelle and the boys were all moved by the show of thanks and stood back to let Brady receive Matt's rousing thank you to him.

While the chanting continued, Dean walked up clutching a Bible and joined the chanting. As he did so he also patted his heart and pointed at Brady in the way Matt had.

Dean never spoke to Brady again, after their meeting in the hallway. The boys would see him carrying his large black Bible as a shield wherever he went. Some of them knew he'd felt the darkness that night on the tracks and knew why he feared it would return.

With time, everything got back to normal for the most part. No one talked openly about what had happened. Everyone had fallen into their regular routines. That is, except for the planning and training for spring break, that was anything but normal. It was a very exciting time for all in the group.

Brady was less than excited as the fate of everyone he loved rested on his shoulders. Part of him wished his brothers and

Michelle hadn't been so eager and had declined to join him. Yet deep inside, when they all said yes, they would help, he was so proud of them for their courage. He would not be going alone.

For he was the sword and the shield and, like his grandfather before him, he would hunt the darkness.

Chapter Forty-Two

OLD FRIENDS

The old priest carefully stepped down from the train car and looked around. He moved a little more briskly when he saw the familiar face, the way older people do when they know some-one important to them is watching.

"Father Anthony, it is so nice to see your smiling face." Giovanni gave the priest a warm hand shake and hug. "Did you have any trouble getting here?"

"It was quite the trip for this old and tired body." Father Anthony found a bench and fell into it. "Could you not have picked some beautiful beach somewhere, one with a warm breeze and palm trees?" he smiled. "I have never been to Yugoslavia, let alone visited this village, Medjugorje. It was not easy getting here. At least the June weather is lovely."

Father Anthony paused. "But I made it and I am ready for whatever you have planned."

Giovanni nodded silently.

Father Anthony continued. "It is a lot harder to get around since I have been sick. I am just assuming you already know this, so I hope wherever it is you're taking me, it is not far.

"Yes, I am sad to say I do know about you being sick." Giovanni's eyes softened.

Father Anthony waved a hand in the air. "Do not get me wrong. I was happy to get out of my room at the Vatican. I hate having everyone fussing over me. Doctors and nurses, they mean well, but I am just tired, if you know what I mean. They are going to panic when they realize I am not there. When your letter came, I did what I always do, packed this old traveling bag and left without saying a word to anyone." This made him laugh softly.

Giovanni sat next to Father Anthony. "I understand how you feel. I am sad to tell you, I am as sick also. Like you, this old body of mine is worn out."

Giovanni leaned back on the bench and relaxed. "I promised you five years ago, when we last met that we would meet again. So here we are. I arranged for us to stay at a farmhouse here tonight so that we may rest before we head out in the morning. There will be hot food and something warm to drink waiting for us at the farmhouse. I have also brought some fine Cuban cigars you love so much so that we can smoke and talk into the night."

Father Anthony smiled and nodded, with a gleam in his eye. "Cuban cigars? You outdid yourself, I see. I am impressed."

"We will take a scenic ride thru the country side in a taxi that is waiting for us and then we will be there," Giovanni explained. "I have arranged to have a chef, all the way from Paris, here to prepare a fine meal for us for this evening."

"You flew a chef all the way here from France? Well now, I am impressed. You are full of surprises today, aren't you?"

"Yes, of course. Only the best will do for my oldest and dearest friend."

After a forty-minute ride, the taxi stopped at the end of the dirt road. Two men with large rut sacks awaited them.

"Perfect timing," Giovanni said for Father Anthony and added "Popolno cas," in Slovenian for the taxi driver.

Giovanni got out of the taxi and greeted the men as friends, shaking their hands and kissing them on both cheeks. Speaking in French the three men talked briefly.

He turned to Father Anthony. "These are the chiefs from France," Giovanni said. "And, I might add, my very dear friends. This is Chef Louis and his apprentice Yanis. They are the best Chefs in Paris in my humble opinion of course" Giovanni smiled.

Both men shook the priest's hand and kissed him on the cheeks. Speaking in Italian, as a sign of respect, Chef Louis said, "It is a pleasure to meet a friend of Giovanni's. I hope the meal is to your liking. We have followed the recipes exactly."

"Oh, I am sure it will be amazing. Thank you for traveling so far to cook this fine dinner for us," Father Anthony replied.

"You should go. Dinner is ready, and you should head to the house before anything gets cold," the robust Chief advised them.

Speaking in French, Giovanni bid the men good bye and waved as the taxi left back down the dirt road.

Giovanni pointed toward an old farmhouse in the distant foot-hills with mountains behind it. "There is our palace for the night." The small wooden house had a sod roof. Smoke wafted lazily from the stone chimney and an oil lamp in the front window invited them in.

"Beautiful," Father Anthony exclaimed.

Giovanni gestured toward the door. "I hope you are hungry. We are having an amazing French stew with homemade French bread and local fresh butter. And, if we are lucky, there will be an array of French pastries and cakes for desert."

"Please tell me it is the famous French stew I have heard so much about," Father Anthony asked.

Giovanni smiled. "It is."

As they opened the door to the farm house, the smell of freshly brewed Brazilian coffee, baked bread and French stew filled their senses. In the center of the room was a large wooden table with fresh cut flowers on the table, set with the finest china and crystal. On the side table was an array of freshly baked French beads, pastries and two cakes.

"Oh, my." Father Anthony exclaimed. "This looks like we are in a French restaurant."

"Exactly," Giovanni said grinning.

The two old friends ate and talked through the night of all the adventures and troubles that they had seen and helped right over the course of their long friendship. They toasted to lost friends and to new friends that had been made. Their energy had been renewed being together and neither felt sick any longer. Sleeping was the last thing on their minds as they smoked the fine Cuban cigars and drank the French wine that had been stocked in the kitchen. The hours passed quickly as each filled the other in on the latest events that had been happening and what had been set into motion and had yet to happen.

* * *

In the morning at sunrise the two old friends left the farm house. It was a slow and steady walk up the hill along the rocky terrain.

"What is this place called?" Father Anthony asked.

"The locals call this hill we are climbing Crnica Hill in the Bijakovići hamlet," Giovanni said.

When they reached the top of the hill, Giovanni motioned for Father Anthony to stop. "We are here."

"Thank goodness," Father Anthony said, stretching his sore back. "I have gone about as far as these old legs are going to take me."

Giovanni reached out his hands and clasped Father Anthony hands tightly. "I have a gift for you, my old friend. One I wanted to share with you." Giovanni looked into Father Anthony's eyes. "For all the years you have done as you have been asked and never once questioned why. You have kept it all confidential for so long and never given in, no matter the pressure from those that demanded the secret from you. I want you to know you have helped change the world. I could not have done it without you. And I could not have asked for a better friend."

Giovanni looked into Father Anthony's eyes and paused. "So, this is our gift to you."

At that moment Giovanni called the light. A bright and blinding white hot light glowed on the hilltop. It was the Holy Mother, there in all Her glory.

* * *

"My sons, I have come to take you home." She reached out to both men embracing them in Her loving arms.

"This is as I dreamed it would be," Father Anthony said to Giovanni.

She carried their souls with Her, and the light vanished from the hilltop. The bodies of the two men lay on the small grassy patch, holding hands as if they had fallen asleep.

On a hill, not far away, two young girls witnessed the miracle of the appearance of the Holy Mother. Giovanni had made sure the girls would be nearby. The event would be the start of a renewing of the faith, in a part of the world that all within the church, had deemed lost.

It was all part of Her plan.

Chapter Forty-Three

THE LETTER

Father Bob heard a knock, knock, then a pounding sound at the rectory door. "Really? Can I not get a minute to myself?" He left the kitchen table and headed toward the door.

"Coming, I'm coming." He shouted. "Quit pounding on the door for the love of the Lord."

The knocking grew louder until he finally opened the door.

"Where's the fire? Or are your pants on fire? Couldn't you hear me shouting that I was coming?" He held the door open wide.

Standing in the doorway was a young priest with bulging eyes. "Sorry, Father, sorry. Please forgive me for the urgency, but I am under orders from the Vatican."

Father Bob remembered the last time a Vatican emissary had knocked on his door. What an adventure that had turned in to.

The young priest held out an envelope with the Holy seal on it. "I am Father Joseph and I have a letter for Father Bob from the Pope himself. Are you Father Bob?"

"Yes, yes, of course I am. A letter from the Pope, you say?"

Father Bob held the door open wide. "Sorry, sorry, I had no idea, please, please come in. Yes, come in please." Father Bob was stuttering. "Didn't mean to be cross, sorry, please forgive me for my rudeness. Do come in."

Once inside, the young priest handed the envelope to Father Bob.

On the front, it read in black calligraphy, "He who believes in miracles."

Father Bob's knees almost buckled.

"Father, there is more. I have instructions to take you back to the Vatican. The Pope's jet is waiting at Wright-Patterson Air Force Base. Please pack a small bag and the rest of your things will be sent to Rome later."

Father Bob couldn't believe his ears. "Rome? I can't go to Rome. What will happen to my parish here?"

A second priest walked in, his timing such it was as if he'd been waiting for Father Bob to ask that question.

"Hello Father Bob, I am Father Jacob." He took Father Bob's hand and shook it vigorously. I will be taking over for you here. I will help you get your things packed. I understand they're expecting you at the Vatican as soon as possible."

Father Bob felt light headed and put his hand on the wall to steady himself.

"I am also to tell you that Giovanni and Father Anthony have entered the light," Father Joseph said.

"What? Oh." That was all Father Bob could manage to say, shaking his head. His knees buckled, making him unsteady.

Father Joseph continued. "This is a direct message from His Holiness. He said that you would understand its meaning. You do understand?"

"Father Bob, Father Bob, are you all right? Father Bob, are you going to pass out, I was told you might."

"Yes, yes, I understand, and no, I'm not passing out," But, he wasn't sure. This was all happening way too fast.

Father Joseph broke open smelling salts and placed it under Father Bob's nose. "There, that's better, right? Hold on to my arm."

Father Bob reached out to push the smell away. "Get that out of my face. I'm okay, I just need more time…"

"There is no time," Father Joseph said. "We must go now."

"But, but…"

"We are under orders to not delay getting you to Rome. We must hurry. You are to meet with the Pope in his residence first thing after we land. Please, I will try to answer all your questions on the flight to Rome."

* * *

With the jet in the air, Father Bob was filled with questions that could only be answered by a boy who wasn't on this plane. Part of him wondered if he was just dreaming and he was still in his warm comfortable bed asleep. But, it wasn't a dream. He'd been part of something that wasn't yet finished.

It was then he noticed the large tan envelope with a Vatican seal in the seat next to him. Father Bob picked up the envelope and saw his name across the front of it. His hand shook as he broke the wax seal on the envelope and took out a bundle of letters with a red ribbon around them. Each had been sealed with wax, bearing a name and a date on each of the letters. There was a folded letter in the group that wasn't in an envelope and it was addressed to him.

Father Bob,

You have been chosen to carry on the work I can no longer accomplish. The letters, as you can see, are addressed with a date and a name of each individual they are to be delivered to.

The seals are only to be broken by the person named on the envelope. You are not to share or make anyone aware of these names or dates. Your first letter is to be delivered to an Albanian-born nun in Calcutta. You are to give her this "Miraculous medal" that is attached to this letter. This is the original medal that Sister Catherine Labouré wore that she designed at the direction of our Holy Mother.

You are going to have an amazing journey and will endure many hardships along the way. You will see the light and the darkness in your travels. Always remember that you are never alone and in times of trouble, you only need to call out and your prayers will be answered.

You have seen things that others pray to see.

I have stocked my old apartment with your favorite wine and my favorite cigars that I am sure you will grow to enjoy.

The boy will contact you when he needs your help.

Do not trust anyone in the church hierarchy, for the darkness is within its gates. There will be more letters as time goes on. You have big shoes to fill and I believe you can fill them.

Father Anthony

Father Bob looked out the window of the jet as it climbed into the clouds, "You two have taken care of everything," he said softly to himself.

THE LIGHT AND DARKNESS

If you believe in angels, you must believe in demons. *"When Saint Dominic was preaching the Rosary near Carcassone, an Albigensian was brought to him who was possessed by the devil. Saint Dominic exorcised him in the presence of a great crowd of people; it appears that over twelve thousand had come to hear him preach.*

"During the exorcism, the demon was forced to speak the following about devotion to the Mother of God: "Listen well, you Christians: The Mother of Jesus Christ is all-powerful, and She can save Her servants from falling into hell. She is the Sun which destroys the darkness of our wiles. It is She who uncovers our hidden plots, breaks our snares, and makes our temptations useless and ineffectual.

"We have to say, however reluctantly, that not a single soul who has really persevered in Her service has ever been damned with us; one single sigh that She offers to the Blessed Trinity is worth far more than all the prayers, desires, and aspirations of all the saints.

"We fear Her more than all the other saints in Heaven together, and we have no success with Her faithful servants. Many Christians who call upon Her when they are in the hour of death, and who really

ought to be damned according to our ordinary standards, are saved by Her intercession.

"Oh, if only that Mary (it is thus in their fury that they called Her) had not pitted Her strength against ours and had not upset our plans, we should have conquered the Church and should have destroyed it long before this, and we would have seen to it that all of the Orders in the Church fell into error and disorder.

"Now that we are forced to speak, we must also tell you this: nobody who perseveres in saying the Rosary will be damned, because She obtains for Her servants the grace of true contrition for their sins, and by means of this they obtain God's forgiveness and mercy."

—St. Louis de Montfort,
"The Secret of the Rosary" (d. 1716)

And so it is written.

Coming Soon

SWORD OF VENGEANCE

Continue reading for a sneak preview...

Chapter One

BERTIOGA

The small fishing boat, the *Santa Maria*, made its way up the shoreline slowly as it did most every morning. With only Sundays as a day of rest, the old diesel engine beat out a rhythmic sound and belched out a thick black cloud into the morning breeze that blew into shore. The boat traveled parallel with the coastline, with freshly baited hooks on its lines. The catch would be sold in the market that day.

On the beach, Felipe Navarro opened his family-owned café, the Praia, for breakfast. It served the tourists who stayed at the small beach houses up and down the sleepy little beach town of Bertioga. It was a small outdoor bar and grill with wooden tables and chairs. Handwoven hammocks lined the beach, hung from wooden posts driven into the sand.

To encourage tourists to eat and drink at the Praia, Navarro provided the only free open-air showers on the beach for the sunbathers to use to freshen up after swimming in the ocean and laying in the sun before eating the locally famous home cooking of the owner's wife, Mirella.

Native music played during the day on loud speakers, casting the local sounds of Brazil across the breeze of the beach. It was a lovely place to have a drink and eat the amazing foods of Brazil's local cuisine. Fresh fish, meats and breads were available along with fruit pastries served with the finest coffee brewed fresh for each customer.

Felipe was running late opening and he knew that his first customer, an old man named Wolfgang Gerhard, would be there soon to swim and then eat his breakfast. Felipe dreaded having to start each day serving the old man. Gerhard was a demanding and rude customer.

It had been the same routine for more than three years. The old man would swim down and then back up the coast every morning, wearing only goggles and a swimsuit that was much too small for a man in his late sixties. No matter the weather, he would swim. He arrived in an old green colored four-door Range Rover with one or two armed men. The men who came with him would stand on the shore and watch Gerhard swim, not bothering to hide the black leather shoulder holsters they wore. Their hair was cut short on the side and cropped on the top. These were men who had seen war.

The men who guarded Gerhard never ate or had coffee with the old man. Instead, they watched his every moment and did not allow any other beach goers near him while he was eating. Constantly on vigil, they had never spoken to Felipe or his charming wife.

While Gerhard swam his guards used binoculars to keep an eye on him. He swam father out than any tourist dared go, a good quarter mile perhaps, where the water was fifty to seventy-five feet deep.

Mirella would laugh and say to Felipe, "Where are the sharks when you need one?"

Felipe shook his head, hoping the guards couldn't hear his wife.

Mirella lit the wood oven. "There's something strange about that old man and those dangerous men with him. I ask you, why would an old man like that need guards? Old and fat guards, not the young, local ones the celebrities used. Answer me that. Who is he really? That's what I want to know."

Felipe had heard it before and didn't respond.

She shook her head as she poured flour into a large ceramic mixing bowl to start making bread for the day. "I wish they'd stop coming here. They scare away the other tourists."

The café's main guests were Europeans who were visiting family and friends who had moved to the little beach town, especially over the last forty years due to the wars in Europe.

Spaniards, Italians, Japanese, Ukrainians, Polish and Germans all settled in Brazil over the last hundred years, with each keeping their own traditions and languages. They had no desire to be absorbed into the local communities where they lived.

When the American students arrived, it was quite a welcome change for the locals. They found the young people to be polite and quiet. They tipped everyone who waited on them.

The students rented the small house from Felipe and paid in full for the month in Cruzeiro Novo bank notes, never wanting change back.

When the students first came into the café, the boy who was in charge, spoke fluent Portuguese with no accent. Felipe was impressed, to say the least. He thought that he would test the boy and spoke to him in the Nheengatu language, thinking the boy would never have heard the language. To his confusion and surprise the boy answered him in Nheengatu and asked if he wanted to speak in Apalai, Bororo or any of the other of the local dialects as he was fluent in all.

"*Señor* Navarro, if you want, I can speak Italian, French, Galician or German. You tell me which you prefer. My name is Brady," he said as he reached out his hand to shake the startled owner's hand. Brady held Felipe's hand longer than he expected.

The physical contact with Brady had a mesmerizing and intoxicating effect on the café owner.

Caleb looked at Liam and said, "I love it when he does that."

Michelle and Zane both looked at each other and winked.

* * *

It was the gift of tongues that gave Brady the ability to speak, read and write any language new or old. It was one of the gifts of the light.

The trip to this lazy beach town had been in the making since their spring break trip to Austria during Brady's senior year in high school in 1976, three years prior. Two years of preparation had gone into the planning and logistics by a multitude of people before they stepped foot on this sandy beach.

Favors had been asked from friends, "new and old". The call had been sent and all had answered, Father Anthony had told Brady.

The encounter with the teachers in that restroom back then led them to Austria and Wolfgang Gerhard. This Nazi had information on a person that Brady's grandpa had been seeking for thirty years.

From that unpleasant meeting with Wolfgang in Austria, information, which he gave up unknowably, lead them to this very beach.

Brady knew this was quite different from how the café owner was used to being treated by the regular tourists. The Europeans tended to be demanding, rude and never tipped for services rendered. They were inherently racist toward the mixed culture in the community.

Bertioga was a melting pot of races and the Europeans despised the locals for it.

Brady had booked Felipe's house on the south end of the beach, at the furthest point of the bay, because the owner had said it was quiet there and no one would bother them.

The house offered the best view of the bay and was nestled into the lush jungle cover that surrounded the town. Wild fruit trees were all around the house: mango, lemon, lime and banana trees.

"Whatever you need, please just ask," Felipe said when the young people agreed to lease the house.

Brady had told Felipe he would not be coming to breakfast in the mornings. It would only be his friends. Felipe didn't ask why. Michelle and the boys went to breakfast every morning. They always arrived with a note from Brady listing what each wanted for breakfast written in Portuguese. Felipe seemed amazed by the clarity as Zane read the note.

"When you're at breakfast, don't let the old man or his guards shake your hand or touch you," Brady told them when they first arrived. "If you do, they will feel the push of your Holy Mark."

"Don't worry," Michelle said, "I'm not going to touch any of those creeps."

"Since you're Americans, they'll be interested in everything you do on the beach. Even if they don't appear to be looking, they are. So, don't do anything they might find suspicious. Act like students, don't pay any attention to what they are doing."

The plan was for the three boys to play soccer in the sand and swim. Michelle would lay in the sand, working on her tan while the old man swam. When he finished swimming, and came in for breakfast, Michelle would shower in her swimsuit, slowly, to get the attention of the guards and the old man. All eyes were to be on her as she rinsed the sand and shampoo out of her hair. She had a body that they could only remember from their youth. Their wives, if they had any, would have lost this youthful look long ago.

"Michelle, are you sure you're okay with this?" Brady had asked when they discussed the plan.

"Of course," she said. "All the running and swimming you had us do the last year has given me an amazing body." She smiled. "Wouldn't you agree?"

Brady felt his face heating up and said nothing.

On the second day of their stay, Mirella brought a homemade ointment to the café for Liam to apply to his skin so as not to burn. She'd said the day before she felt sorry for the pale-skinned one. When she approached Liam, all she could do was motion with her hands for him to put it on his body.

He accepted the gift with a smile. "Thank you very much," he said.

Mirella nodded and smiled back. She knew a little English but seemed reluctant to use it.

"Maybe now you won't look like the lobster boy," Caleb said. Zane gave him two thumbs up, laughing.

After five days, they had the old man's routine down to the minute and were ready to make their move.

In that same time the guards and the old man had grown fond of watching the young muscular girl shower.

As usual, Brady was on the *Santa Maria* as it made its path down the coastline. On this day Brady slipped over the side of the boat into the seventy-three-degree ocean water wearing a speedo, goggles and three-foot long fins. Strapped on his back was what appeared to the boat crew to be a fishing spear of some kind.

The captain had tried to talk Brady out of going in the water alone. But, only briefly. Brady had paid him in fifteen one-ounce gold ingots, far more than the day's catch would ever fetch.

"Good luck my friend," the old fisherman shouted at Brady as he swam towards the beach. The captain then turned the *Santa Maria* and headed back to the dock.

It was the swim that Brady had trained for all those years. There was a mild chop in the ocean as he started toward the shore. It was an easy swim, but his timing had to be perfect.

* * *

Michelle, Caleb, Liam and Zane arrived well before the old man and his guards and set everything in place for the morning's task. The towels and beach bags were laid out as usual and Michelle lay near the showers, so the guards would have an unrestricted view of her sunbathing. She took off her jean shorts and top.

"Damn," Caleb said, when he saw the swim suit that Michelle was wearing. "Their eyes are going to fall out of their fat heads," he said, wondering if Brady would approve of her new swimsuit.

Zane and Liam had noticed, too. They both wolf whistled at her.

Michelle gave them her best stink eye look, which only made them laugh.

"Does Brady know you're wearing that string swim suit?" Caleb said half laughing. "If not, he's missing quite the show."

The boys all laughed out loud. Michelle gave all of them the one-fingered salute. "Of course, he's seen it. He's the one who picked it out."

That shut the brothers up.

Felipe and Mirella arrived and waved at them as he went about opening the café. Mirella smiled and waved at Liam who was sitting in a beach chair applying the ointment she had given him.

It was a beautiful morning, not a cloud in the sky. The high for the day was expected to be eighty degrees. A perfect day for a swim.

At exactly eight A.M., the old man arrived as expected in the Range Rover with his two guards. What was not expected was the second Range Rover with four more guards. The group headed down to the café where the old man stripped off his clothes in the open on the beach and put on his swim suit and goggles.

"That's disgusting," Michelle said quietly to Caleb. "I think I threw up in my mouth watching that."

"Shit balls," Caleb said to Michelle. "What's with the four extra guards. That's not part of the plan. What're we going to do?"

Zane kicked the ball over close to where Caleb and Michelle stood, then used it as an excuse for Liam and him to join them for a talk.

Michelle whispered. "We do exactly as we planned. Brady is already in the water, headed this way and there's no way to stop him. This is happening no matter what transpires on this beach. Do not panic. We have trained for this. Remember, we are the sword and the shield. Be not afraid."

"I'm not panicked or afraid," Liam said. "Hell, I live for this."

"Hell, yeah," Zane added.

"That's why I love all of you boys," she said with a wink and a smile.

"We must keep their attention away from the water and the old man's swim. Follow my lead and be ready. Don't forget, Brady said we will know when it's happening and that's when we will need to act."

The old man headed into the water after talking with the men for about ten minutes, way longer than usual and what was planned for.

"He should've already been in the water swimming by now," Caleb said.

When the old man finally started to swim out away from the shoreline, the guards took out binoculars and watched his progress in the water. Their interest had to be changed to something else.

"Fuck," Zane said to Caleb, "this is going to go bad fast."

At that moment, Michelle walked over to the shower with her beach bag and turned the ice-cold water on.

Standing next to the shower, she slowly removed her swimsuit bottoms and top and dropped them on the sand. She stepped into the streaming water and started to shampoo her hair. The contrast between her darkly-tanned skin and the white non-tanned portions of her body were spellbinding and quickly attracted the full attention of all the guards.

Turning, as if in slow motion, Michelle washed her hair and her body. The shampoo suds cascaded down her body. She timed her movements to the music belting out the slow rhythm of the Brazilian love song. This slow-motion ballet in the morning sun was doing what was needed.

No one was watching the old man swim; the men were mesmerized by the show being put on before them.

The brothers were not watching Michelle. They were watching the guards and preparing for the shit storm that was coming.

* * *

Brady swam toward the path taken by the old man each morning and was surprised that it was far easier than expected. As soon as he could see the old man making his way down the coastline, Brady knew that all the years of planning were at hand. He took one last look at the distance and direction between them and dove underwater, swimming as hard as he could toward the old man.

He surfaced to check his bearings, saw that old man was about twenty-five yards away. Brady adjusted his angle slightly and dove under again, aiming to come up behind the swimmer.

When Brady broke the surface next, he was a mere ten feet behind his target and started to close the distance. The old man continued to swim, apparently unaware of Brady's approach. Brady knew the push would betray him soon. It was time to move quickly.

Brady went underwater and closed the final ten feet and came up from below, like a white shark attacking a fur seal.

The old man choked on ocean water apparently from the sudden and unexpected appearance of a swimmer. Brady put a left arm lock across his neck, and with his right hand he drew the Holy Lance.

Brady called out, "Oh, Angel of Death, you can hide no longer."

As he slid the lance under the old man's rib cage and into his heart, a scream from the Demon finally came out of the man's mouth. The sound echoed as if from a loud speaker as it screamed.

"Demon you know what has pierced your body, for it is the Holy Lance of our Lord."

The sea started to boil, and the body of the old man rose out of the water as the sky suddenly darkened over them. Dead fish rose to the surface of the bubbling water. Thunder clapped as lightning danced overhead.

"Demon, I command you to be forever banished from this world and of yours. For I am the sword and the shield of the light.

It is the law and you have failed your master. These words and commands come from the Holy Mother whom you fear most."

* * *

Michelle noticed the gaze of the guard nearest her lock onto the linked gold chain around her neck near the Holy Mark on her chest. He turned in a panic, most likely about to sound the alarm when the first sound of the screaming Demon hit the beach.

In one fluid motion, Michelle spun around and reached into the beach bag next to her and pulled out her suppressed Browning m1911. Her first shot hit the guard in the middle of the forehead killing him before his body hit the sand. Blood splattered the guards closest to him.

The only sound was the ear-splitting screams coming from the Demon in the water. The guards seemed to be staring at the darkening spot in the boiling ocean where the old man was last seen. Even though these men were battle-hardened, it was as if they were frozen in a state of confusion. Instead of shooting back, those closest to their fallen comrade wiped the blood and brain from their faces. They failed in their training and at that exact moment, the brothers had the advantage.

The brothers pulled out suppressed Uzi machine-guns that had been hidden under the towels on the beach. They dropped the remaining guards, with full auto firing before the guards could pull their Luger pistols out of their shoulder holsters.

Blood splattered the area around the guards, turning the sand a crimson red.

* * *

It was all so quiet and quick; Felipe and Mirella looked out toward the ocean at the strange sights and noises coming from where the old man had been swimming. Only when the screaming stopped had they looked around and noticed the carnage on the beach near them.

Mirella was shocked at seeing the six men laying in clumps on the beach. She walked over to the bodies and spit on them. "Fucking Germans," she said in broken English.

Michelle, with her bathing suit back on, walked over to Felipe and handed him a bag containing one-hundred-thousand in US dollars and said, "You must leave."

"I know." Felipe replied. "Brady explained it to us."

"Go to the Italian embassy," Michelle said. "Vatican passports are waiting for you to take with you to America. Use our car, you cannot stay here. Go now!"

"Hurry," Liam said, "the others will come looking for those who did this."

The brothers left the machine guns in the sand next to the bodies as a message to those who would come later that day.

Felipe and Mirella waited only long enough to watch the students swim away in their fins and goggles.

* * *

At about one-half mile out they met up with Brady. "Everyone okay?" he asked.

All replied with a yes.

The body of the old man floated face down in the water and there was a blood stain in the water around it. As they treaded water, holding hands, Brady spoke in a booming voice as he said the prayer of vengeance.

"Oh, Queen of the Blessed Rosary, I beseech thee to grant me the vengeance for which I seek, to send the evil before me back into the darkness, from which it has come. For I am the sword and the shield, with my voice, I speak the authority that which you have bestowed upon me. For the Serpent fears you above all others. Generation to generation we have served you, honoring a promise made on the hill at Calvary. I honor my forefathers' pledge to seek out the darkness. Make my hands fast and accurate. When I call out to you, I beg of you to heal those who have suffered at the hands of this evil. I freely accept the pain and will endure the suffering of the innocent, as my honor to you. Being one of the righteous, I rejoice when vengeance is done, for it is my reward."

When Brady finished, he looked at everyone and said, "Let's go. We have a two-mile swim to meet the boat."

* * *

After what seemed like forever, they stopped. Brady turned his back to Caleb. "Reach in my bag and pull out a flare."

Minutes after firing the flare, an unmarked gun-metal grey colored Dabur gunboat appeared on the horizon speeding to where they were treading water waiting to be picked up. As the boat pulled alongside them, the captain looked over the side, focusing on one and then another as if counting. "I cannot express how glad I am to see all of you here."

Once on board they were given bags with clothes in each person's exact size. "Father Anthony sends his regards," said the man standing before him. "My name is General Beigel and my crew has been selected by me personally. All your secrets are safe with us as has been your Grandfather's. Was your mission successful?"

"The Angel of Death is dead," Brady said.

The general gasped. "Please tell me this is true."

טיוט זיא טיוט ןופ דאלמ

Brady spoke Hebrew to him as a sign of respect and truth in this moment.

"After your Mossad grabbed Eichmann in 1960, as you know, every Nazi in South America went into hiding. The Doctor disappeared like smoke in the wind.

"The doctor successfully went underground, buying the identification of a Nazi officer who was returning to Germany. He has been living under the name of Wolfgang Gerhard.

"Gerhard had given Mengele his identification to live under when he left Brazil in '71. For that, he was given a fortune in rough diamonds as payment. Finding Gerhard's location was a mere accident of coincidence. We then traveled to Austria and talked with the real Gerhard. We discovered where Josef Mengele was living since he stayed in contact with Gerhard in Germany to get messages to his family."

"No wonder we could never find him," the general said.

"Tell your Grandfather that the Mighty Men of King David will always be there when called upon. If not for his letters to Dayan in '67 and '73 all might have been lost. For this, we will never forget." The general told Brady with tears in his eyes. "I look forward to the day when I can shake his hand."

The general looked into Brady's eyes. "As it was with your Grandfather, it will be with you. We will be forever at your service."

Brady nodded.

The general looked at the rest of the Americans. "All of you, please get comfortable down below. We have food and warm drinks ready for you. We have equipped this gunboat with extra fuel tanks and will refuel at the 700-mile position. So please get some rest and let us take it from here," the general said with a smile.

"We have a twenty-two- to twenty-five-hour journey until we stop and transfer you to the sailing ship which will take you to Jerusalem for your meeting at the Church of the Holy Sepulcher."

He looked at the group of five. "I was just thinking, you are about the same ages as my children, and, yet, you have brought about the revenge of a nation on one of its most wanted. Thank you."

Brady saw the tears return to the general's eyes.

The general handed Brady a handwritten note:

.לארשי ןופ טאַטש יד ןבעל גנאַל טיוט זיא טיוט ןופ ךאלמ רעד

Brady translated for the others. "The Angel of Death is Dead, long live the state of Israel."

"Yes," said the general. "I will send it as an encrypted message to headquarters in Israel."

When the gunboat reached international waters, the crew raised the flag of Israel with its Star of David blowing proudly in the wind as the Israeli national anthem "Hatikvah" played on the ship's loud speakers.

THE CALL OF VENGEANCE SERIES

THE PRAYER OF VENGEANCE

THE SWORD OF VENGEANCE

THE SONG OF VENGEANCE

AUTHOR ACKNOWLEDGMENTS

This book would not have been possible without the guidance and wisdom of author and publisher, Mark Gilroy. He freely gave me his time and industry expertise as to what I needed to do but, most importantly, what I needed not to do, to see the book published.

I also want to thank Sid Frost who gave invaluable help in editing *Prayer of Vengeance.*

And finally, I want to thank my family for listening to my many bonfire stories and encouraging me to finally commit one of them to book form.

ABOUT THE AUTHOR

John Stafford, Sr., is a widely-recognized, highly successful, and innovative businessman in the jewelry industry. His debut novel is a mix of good and evil that reflects his profound spirituality and observations of the world.

You can contact John at: john@callofvengeance.com

Connect with John @ Facebook.com/callofvengeance